TO TWIST A WITCH

The Jinx Hamilton Series - Book 15

JULIETTE HARPER

Skye House Publishing, LLC

Chapter One

The scene in the lair stopped Kelly Hamilton in her tracks. Festus stood whisker-to-whisker with an overweight Persian. Locked in a staring contest with fur standing on end, the werecat ignored the calico kitten playing with his furiously lashing tail.

A few feet away, Rube watched the interaction with avid interest, one black paw shoveling popcorn into his mouth out of a red-striped bucket.

In a voice dripping with faux cordiality, Festus said, "Miss Myerscough, we got off on the wrong paw. Let's start over. Thank you for bringing my granddaughter to Briar Hollow. You must be exhausted."

Turning to the raccoon, he said, "Why don't you show our guest to her room? Make sure she gets a pot of our most special tea."

That ominous suggestion galvanized Kelly into action. "Good evening, everyone," she said, descending the remaining steps at the double quick. "Festus, why don't you introduce me to our guests?"

When he saw her, Festus's whiskers drooped a notch. "Hi,

1

Kelly. The runt playing with my backside is my grandkid, Willow. This is her nanny. Miss Myerscough."

The kitten looked up long enough to say "hi" before going back to swatting Festus's tail. Making a point of ignoring the werecat, Kelly said, "I'm so sorry I wasn't here to greet you, Mrs. Myerscough. You must be so tired. Let me show you to your room so you can rest before supper."

"Thank you," the Persian said. "That would be lovely. I'm sure Mr. McGregor didn't mean to be unpleasant. It seems there's been some confusion about the day and time of my arrival."

Still in full-on diplomatic mode, Kelly said, "These things happen. We're glad to have you here. Come this way."

As she ushered Mrs. Myerscough toward the guest rooms, Kelly looked over her shoulder and made eye contact with Festus. She mouthed, *"Don't. Go. Anywhere."*

The werecat pursed his whiskers, but responded with a curt nod. Minutes later when Kelly returned, she found Willow leaping for a feather toy the fairy mound had dropped from the ceiling. Festus and Rube sat on the hearth, a checkerboard between them.

Kelly planted her hands on her hips and said, "Nice try, you two. We need to talk."

"Sure, Kelly," Festus said. "What would you like to talk about?"

The attempt to be disingenuous fell flat. "Don't you even think about pulling that with me, Festus James McGregor. Both of you knock it off. *Now.*"

Still affecting wide-eyed innocence, Festus asked, "Knock what off?"

"Whatever you had cooked up to do to Mrs. Myerscough. I swear to Bastet, you are the most incorrigible... "

Willow put herself between Kelly and the werecat. "Don't

you talk to my grandpa like that!" she declared with fervent loyalty. "Whatever he was gonna do to Mrs. M., the old hairball deserved it!"

Festus started to laugh, but the expression on Kelly's face stopped him. "Be respectful of your elders," he told the kitten, but the words lacked even a suggestion of conviction.

Willow didn't back down. "But you said Miss Myerscough acts like she has something shoved up..."

"Never mind what I said," Festus interrupted. "You must be hungry. DARBY!"

When the brownie appeared out of nowhere, Willow hissed, arched her back, and retreated with a series of mincing hops.

Festus regarded her with beaming approval. "Nice technique. Curl your lip next time so they can see your fangs. Willow, this is Darby. He's in charge of grub around here. Darby, get the kid whatever she wants."

The kitten's face lit up. "Can I have cream, gran... Festus?"

"Yeah, sure. Darby, whip an egg up in that cream so she doesn't get the runs."

Darby blinked in confusion. "To where would she be running, Master Festus?"

"Just do it, Short Stuff," Festus growled. "You ask too many questions."

Kelly waited until Darby and Willow were out of earshot. "Honestly, Festus, you're either going to be the most wonderful grandfather in the world or a totally corrupting influence."

It was the werecat's turn to look confused. "Aren't those two things the same?"

Rube, who had done an exemplary job of keeping his mouth shut, snickered.

"And *you*," Kelly said, wheeling on him. "You do not have to do everything Festus tells you to do. It wouldn't hurt you to try to rein him in from time to time."

Alarm filled the raccoon's furry features. "Uh, yeah, Kells, I kinda do have to do what he tells me, 'cause he's my boss. Far as I can see the only people holding his reins is you and Jilly."

The fur on the back of Festus's neck stood up. "Nobody holds my reins."

Kelly reached down, snatched the werecat off his feet, and positioned him at eye level. "Do you want me to call Jilly in from the field and test that theory?"

Dangling in her hands, Festus scowled. "Jilly is on assignment with the ROMO squad and doesn't need to be bothered with child care issues. Now, if you don't mind, put me down."

Bringing the ginger tom closer to her face Kelly said, "Don't make me tell you again. Lay off Miss Myerscough. I do not want Glory coming home from her honeymoon to chaos manufactured by the two of you. Got it?"

"*Bastet's whiskers!* I've *got* it. Now put me down."

When she deposited Festus on the rug, Kelly turned to Rube. "How about you?"

"*Geez!* Okay already," the raccoon said. "The old battleaxe is off limits."

"While we are having this discussion," Festus said, "may I point out that no one consulted me about turning my grandkid over to an old maid who wears her fur too tight?"

"You know as well as I do that Willow needs the supervision of a female werecat for the first year of her life," Kelly replied. "Quit being difficult. Go to the war room and play with your drones or something."

Festus lowered his ears. "The GNATS drones are a sophisticated piece of Fae technology."

Kelly pointed toward the war room. "*Go!* You, too, Rube."

"No can do, doll. It's cribbage night in Procyon. I am outta here, so if anything happens requiring an albino, I got one."

"You're going to think alibi when I get done with you," Festus grumbled, but he did as he was told and stalked off.

~

Glory came through the portal first. Chase followed pushing a hotel cart loaded with shopping bags and luggage. Waving gaily, the new Mrs. McGregor called out, "Hi everybody! We're home!"

Looking up from his work, Beau Longworth said, "Welcome back! Did you enjoy your honeymoon?"

Before she could answer, a bright pink foam ball shot out of the archives. The gyrating sphere bounced across the open space in front of the portal with a calico kitten and Festus in hot pursuit.

The werecat bellowed, "You better run you little hairball! Nobody gave you permission to rifle through my desk."

Then, realizing that he had an audience, Festus skidded to a stop, sat down, and nonchalantly licked his paw. "Well," he drawled, "I see the prodigals are all starting to slink home. Nice of you people to drop in from time to time."

Ignoring her father-in-law, Glory fixed her eyes on the kitten, who had taken refuge under Beau's desk. "Hi, sweetheart," she said. "You must be Willow."

The little cat craned her neck around one leg of the desk and gave Glory the once over. For her part, Glory sank to the floor and said, in a voice filled with love, "Would you like to come over here and meet me?"

Calling on the ability all cats have to play coy, Willow batted the ball between her front paws. "Yeah. But you gotta tell Festus not to smack me 'cause I took his toy."

The werecat's whiskers quivered with outrage. "*That* is not a toy. It's a spherical BEAR-issued dexterity development device."

Chase let out a belly laugh. "A dexterity development device? What's catnip? A performance enhancing drug?"

Festus narrowed his eyes. "For a lightweight like you, yes. For a professional consumer like myself, nip sharpens my reflexes and focuses my mind."

"Right," Chase said. "The next time you stumble home from The Dirty Claw stoned out of your fur, I'll shoot a video so you can see how *focused* you are."

Willow snickered. "Come on gramps," she said, slapping the ball in his direction. "Everybody knows it's a toy. Admit it already."

Extending his claws, Festus skewered the foam. "What did I tell you about stupid grandfather names? Get your furry butt over there and get to know your parents."

The kitten moved forward with tentative steps. She stopped in front of Glory, curled her tail around her body, and said, "Nice to meet you."

Glory started to reach out and then stopped herself. "May I pick you up?"

"Oh, for Bastet's sake," Festus said. "Pick the runt up already."

Scooping the kitten into her arms, Glory cooed, "Hi, Baby Girl."

Willow's rumbling purr echoed in the fairy mound. "Hi," she said, rubbing the top of her head against Glory's chin.

Chase sat down on the floor beside them. "Hello, Willow. I'm your Dad."

Willow cocked her head to the side and sniffed. "You're a mountain lion like Festus."

"Yes, I am."

The kitten cast her eyes down. "My real Dad was a mountain

lion. He was really big and strong. You smell like him."

Chase put out his hand and scratched the kitten behind the ear. "Has grumpy old Festus been taking care of you?"

Willow's eyes went bright. "Yeah! Festus is *so* cool. Mrs. Myerscough hates him."

Chase cut a suspicious, side-long glance at his father. "Is Mrs. Myerscough your nanny?"

"Uh huh. She called Festus a whiskey-soaked flea-bitten alley rebate."

Working hard not to smile, Chase said, "I think you mean 'reprobate.'"

"*That*," Festus said, "will be more than enough character assassination for today. I've got work to do."

Glory's face crumpled. "But we just got home! We have presents for everyone and I thought we could all watch the wedding video."

Festus made a hacking sound. "Pickle, I was *there*. Everybody else watched the damn thing on the livestream. Nobody needs to see that fat Elvis impersonator's backside in gold lamé again."

Willow jumped in. "I'll watch it with you... Mom."

"Suck up," Festus muttered.

Ignoring the werecat, Glory kissed the kitten's head. "Thank you, sweetheart. I appreciate that."

Snuggling closer, Willow asked, "Why did you choose to go with a fat Elvis impersonator? Don't you think Elvis was cuter when he was at Sun Records in Memphis?"

Delighted and stunned, Glory looked to Chase for help. "Are all werekittens this precocious?"

When Chase ducked his head, Festus stomped over and confronted his son. "Look at me, boy."

Chase obeyed, but he wasn't happy about it.

"You didn't tell her, did you?" Festus demanded.

"Tell me what?" Glory asked, a bilious note creeping into her voice that matched the green tinge on her cheeks.

After Chase squirmed and fumbled with a few words, Festus took over. "As usual, I'm the one who has to do the dirty work around here. Brace yourself, Pickle. The first two years of any cat's life are roughly equal to 25 in human terms. The effect is more pronounced in werecats. The runt there may be little, but she has the mind of an exceptionally advanced teenager."

Puffing her chest out, Willow said with undisguised pride, "Mrs. Myerscough says I'm a holy terror and way too big for my britches."

Now completely at a loss, Glory asked in a weak voice, "Where is Mrs. Myerscough?"

"In one of the guest rooms," Willow said. "Before Rube left he took her some tea even though Kelly told him not to. Mrs. M. has been asleep ever since."

Checking his watch, Chase said, "It's 3 o'clock in the afternoon. Dad, what was in that tea?"

"How should I know?" Festus shrugged. "You'd have to ask the striped moron."

"Gladly. Where is he?"

"Cribbage tournament in Procyon. No idea when he'll be back."

Chase put his hand over his eyes. "If you were to hazard a guess, when would you say Mrs. Myerscough would be likely to wake up?" Then, as if the idea had only just occurred to him, he added with a note of fear, "She *will* wake up, right?"

"Of course the old bat will wake up," Festus said with irritation. "I'm sure as hell not doing time in the slammer for offing a fat Persian."

"Good. Now answer my question. How long do you estimate she'll be 'resting?'"

"Let's put it this way," Festus purred. "Darby shouldn't bother setting a place for her at the supper table."

Chapter Two

The retreating sun cast the bookstore in shadow. Behind a glass-fronted cabinet three pink noses poked through a gnawed hole in the baseboard. The mice listened, whiskers twitching.

Then, by silent vote, the trio agreed to venture across the exposed open space to the counter. Scaling the power cord dangling from the computer, the mice headed for the package of cookies resting beside the keyboard.

Working as a team, they gnawed and tore the thin packaging to create an opening. Pulling a cookie free, the mice exchanged high fives and dove into their feast.

An hour later when the streetlights came on, the tiny raiders had switched to leisurely poking through the odds and ends on the counter. Accustomed to quiet Sundays alone, the mice weren't expecting what happened next.

Near the front window a book resting on a top shelf rocked back and forth. As the mice watched, the volume scooted forward, teetered on the edge, and toppled to the floor.

The book landed on its spine, pages splayed open. The lines

of type contorted and bulged outward until the words looked as if they were stretched tight over the skin of a balloon.

The phrases twisted and shattered, blowing a ragged hole in the book. Broken letters rained across the floor. Human fingers grabbed the tattered edges of the opening and a wolf's head jutted upward.

The beast's nostrils flared. Trembling, the mice shrank away in search of invisible, safe places. The wolf's ears flattened and its yellow eyes blazed. The creature grabbed the pages with both hands and pulled itself free, growing in scale and proportion.

As the fetid, dank odor of stagnant water and rotting wood filled the store, the mice fled. The wolf's thick, human-like lips pulled into a feral grin. He stretched, straining the buttons of the incongruous white shirt he wore. The movement revealed a triangle of smooth tanned skin.

The beast threw his head back and howled. Lashing out with inchoate fury, he raked books from their shelves, overturned displays, and shredded magazines.

Grabbing hold of a heavy oak table, the wolf threw the piece hard against the bookshelves and howled again.

A disembodied voice issued a harsh command. *"That is enough, Andre. Come to me."*

The beast danced in place, snarling and clawing at the air.

"Do not defy me, Andre. That will not go well for you. Come!"

Whimpering, the creature waded through the chaos he'd created. At the back door, he grasped the knob and turned, wrenching the door open with such force the hinges bent and came away from the wood.

In the alley a man stood under the glow of a guard light. The harsh illumination accentuated his cadaverous features and raised highlights in the black, wavy hair that fell over his collar.

The wolf shuffled forward, head bowed, and fell to his knees to nuzzle the man's hand.

Long fingers stroked the dark fur. "You must learn to control your impulses, Andre. Do not behave recklessly at our next stop or you will be punished. Do you understand?"

Anxious, fearful eyes met his. The man's hand cupped the wolf's muzzle. "So eager to please. Be a good boy, my pet, and perhaps the day will come when you earn your freedom. You'd like that, wouldn't you?"

The wolf whined and leaned into his master's caress.

"Very well. Now come. Work awaits."

Briar Hollow, 8:00 a.m., Monday

Bertille lifted one hand off the steering wheel to wave at Jeff Hamilton who was sweeping the sidewalk in front of the sporting goods store. She made a mental note to walk over later and give him a rare 1781 copy of *The Art of Angling* by Richard Brookes she bought for pennies at at estate sale.

She could make a huge profit on the book if she chose to list it for sale online, but over the past weeks Bertille had grown fond of Jinx's father and his merry band of fishing dogs.

Her own father had been a commercial fisherman in Louisiana, but in his free time he crafted elegant lures in his small, cluttered workshop. Jeff's enthusiasm for the sport gave Bertille a sentimental feeling.

She'd placed the book in the store safe to keep it away from the resident mice. Although she'd forged a détente with the rodents, they hadn't completely overcome the urge to chew at the soft corners of old books.

During her first week in Briar Hollow, Bertille used her basic understanding of Common Rodent to explain to the mice that she had no desire to hurt them. In exchange for free food, she asked only that they improve their manners in regard to her inventory. They were working on it.

Turning down the alley that ran behind the buildings on her side of the square, Bertille pulled under the covered parking spot reserved for her use. Before she could cut the engine, a warning frisson ran up her spine.

The building's back entrance stood open, the door hanging at an awkward angle on damaged hinges.

A movement under the water meter caught her eye. The three store mice cowered in the weeds beckoning with frantic getstures. Bertille got out of the car and went to them, going down on her knees so as not to tower over the frightened creatures.

"What happened?"

All three began to chatter at once. Bertille frowned as she deciphered broken phrases from their squeaks. "Some kind of monster came out of a book and wrecked the store?"

Three heads bobbed up and down.

"You spent the night out here because you're too afraid to go back inside?"

More nodding. Closing her eyes and summoning her powers, Bertille probed the interior of the building. Whoever or whatever the mice saw was no longer there.

"He's gone, my little friends. You can go home. I won't let anything hurt you."

She didn't have to make the suggestion twice. The three mice made a mad dash for a crack in the brick by the back door. The last mouse, however, stopped and looked back at Bertille.

"What is it?"

Concern furrowed the mouse's brow as he answered with a stream of anxious chatter.

"You're worried about me? Don't be. Go on with your friends. We'll talk later."

Bertille started to reach for the doorknob, but stopped. If the damage inside was as bad as the mice suggested, she'd have to report a break in to the police in order to file an insurance claim.

That meant preserving any potential evidence like fingerprints. Using her shoulder for leverage, she pushed the door open only to step back when a familiar odor hit her full in the face.

Damp earth. Stagnant swamp water. Sulfur. The scent of the deep bayou.

Advancing with cautious steps, Bertille's heart sank at the chaotic scene. Shelves raked clean of books. Overturned cases. Broken glass. Ripped periodicals.

The mice said the monster flew into a rage for no reason. If he took anything with him when he left the store, identifying the item wouldn't be easy.

Returning to the alley, Bertille got into the driver's seat of her car and found her cell phone. She dialed the sheriff's office. "Yes, hello. This is Bertille Bergeron. I own the new bookstore on the square. My building was burglarized overnight. Would you please send someone over?"

She listened to the dispatcher's instructions and then replied. "Yes, I understand. I won't touch anything. I'll be waiting in my car in the alley. You can send the deputies back here. I only stepped inside to look around. The front door is still locked."

Ending the call, Bertille tossed her phone onto the passenger seat. Leaning her head against the wheel, she tried to drive away the fear that crawled through her system.

The mix up with Stella Mae Crump and the grimoire hadn't been a fluke or a random inventory accident. An intruder had been biding his time in one of her books all along.

The grimoire had come with her from New Orleans, but she had no idea which book had harbored the creature the mice saw. Was it linked to her former life in Louisiana or something acquired since she'd moved to Briar Hollow?

Bertille couldn't say for certain, but she feared the inescapable conclusion that some dark aspect of her former life had followed her to North Carolina.

Chapter Three

SHEVINGTON, JINX

The moments before bad events crash into our lives often stand out with odd perfection. That morning when we awakened in Aunt Fiona's guest room, I wasn't thinking about anything going awry in Briar Hollow. My focus was on memorizing every moment with my daughter before Lucas and I were forced to leave her in the Valley.

Addie's eyes popped open with the rising sun. Trundling over the crib rail, she scrambled into bed between me and Lucas. Tugging at her father's ear, she announced, "Go fly a kite."

No, my daughter didn't tell her dad to buzz off. Although her pronunciation and syntax seemed to improve by the hour, Addie still possessed a child's literal mind. She said exactly what she meant.

Addie wanted Lucas to get up because we'd promised her a day of flying kites in the big meadow between the city and Shevington University.

Forcing one of his eyes to half mast, Lucas mumbled, "Addie, it's too early to get up."

"Not too early," she insisted, giving his ear an energetic yank. "Sun up."

Groaning, Lucas said, "Jinx, wake up and do something with your daughter."

Burying my face in the pillow, I said, "Why is she *my* daughter when she does stuff like this?"

Addie turned her attention in my direction. "Stan and the bunnies come too."

We'd brought our child to Shevington to surround her with security measures that would keep her safe from Morgan le Fay. You'd think an eight-foot Sasquatch would fulfill the scary body-guard role nicely, but Stan showed up in Aunt Fiona's garden within five minutes of our arrival with his arms full of baby bunnies.

Addie fell in love with Stan on sight, giggling with wild excitement when he lifted her to his shoulders and took her on a tour of the neighborhood.

The bodyguard who shadowed their movements wasn't eight feet tall. Lauren Frazier trends more toward lethal force than bunny rabbit cuteness, but she pulls off her deadly streak with style.

The dark-haired Gwragedd Annwn noblewoman's vaguely elvish features colored with pleasure when she met Addie for the first time. Going down on one knee to put herself on the little girl's level, Lauren said, "Hi Addie. I'm you're new friend Lauren."

Addie fixated on Lauren's lapel pin, a diamond the size of a marble surrounded by golden waves. The words "LF Security" had been embossed into the precious metal.

"Pretty!" Addie said in an awestruck voice.

Lauren undid the piece of jewelry, which was held in place with a magnetic catch, and affixed it to the collar of Addie's dress. When I protested that something might happen to the impressive bling, Lauren gave me an odd look. "So what? It's just a diamond."

Put that on the list of thoroughly Fae answers.

As the head of an elite stable of bodyguards, Lauren has contracts to protect High Sídhe nobles living in the human realm cities of New York, Las Vegas, and Los Angeles.

She only goes into the field for the most important clients. For the moment, she has one focus—my daughter.

That morning I admitted defeat, threw off the covers and sat on the edge of the bed blinking to clear the sleep from my eyes. When a polite knock sounded at the door, I said, "Yeah, come in."

The rapping repeated itself. Addie flopped down beside me and announced, "Cups don't have fingers." With that, she extended her arm, mimed grabbing the knob, and pulled.

The door edged open and two cups of coffee floated into the room. One circled the bed and went into a patient hovering mode while Lucas dragged himself upright; the other glided into my hand with serene accuracy.

A bubble appeared above the cup framing Aunt Fiona's smiling face. "Good morning, honey. I'll have pancakes ready when you all get down here. I talked to Barnaby and he's whipping up a perfect kite breeze over the big meadow. Stan made the cutest dragon kite for Addie I've ever seen."

Addie's face lit up. "Dragon!"

I looked down at my child and couldn't stop myself from ruffling her soft, golden hair. "What happened to 'draggy-on?'"

She offered me a dazzling smile. "I'm learning."

"*That*," I said, "is what scares me."

From the bubble, Aunt Fiona said, "We've been working on her pronunciation while you and Lucas are off tending to business. She's very smart, Jinx. Much smarter than you were at that age."

Staring blearily at my oblivious aunt, I said, "Thanks. I figured that part out already."

Behind me Lucas chuckled as he pulled on his robe. "I think it's the job of kids to show up their parents. Let's go downstairs. I'm hungry."

"You two go ahead," I said. "I'm not awake yet. I'll be there in a few minutes."

Lucas scooped our giggling daughter into his arms and the pair disappeared through the door leaving me to sip my coffee in peace. I got up and wandered over to the window, pleased to find a phalanx of GNATS drones on station around the cottage.

Major Aspid "Ironweed" Istra himself had explained the drones to Addie the afternoon we arrived in Shevington. I quietly snapped a picture of the adorable scene; a fairy in combat fatigues and a purple beret suspended inches from my child's face talking to her about surveillance protocols.

Addie listened with a delighted expression and instantly christened the drones, "Magic bugs."

Ironweed chewed on his cigar to keep himself from laughing. "Close enough. Your magic bug friends are going to be with you all the time to make sure you're safe."

He gestured to one of the tiny craft suspended above Aunt Fiona's sofa. The pilot glided over and assumed a position off the commander's left shoulder. "Addie, this is GNATS 32. The pilot's name is Sgt. Poppy Periwinkle. She's in charge of your security detail."

Staring at the drone, Addie asked, "How does she fit in there?"

"She doesn't," Ironweed said. "The pilots work from a flight control center at the fairy barracks, but if you want to meet Poppy in person, she'll come over after her duty shift today."

Addie nodded happily. "I like fairies!"

Clamping down on his cigar, Ironweed said, "Doesn't everybody?"

He tried to sound gruff, but Addie saw the good-natured humor in his eyes. When she winked at him, Ironweed couldn't control himself any longer. They both burst out laughing.

Two or three hours later I answered the door to find Sgt. Periwinkle waiting for me. Her iridescent wings flashed in the light.

"Good evening, Witch of the Oak," she said, whipping off her beret. "Major Istra said your daughter wanted to meet me."

Stepping aside to let the fairy fly through, I said, "Relax, Sergeant. We don't stand on ceremony around here."

"Affirmative, ma'am. In that case, please call me Poppy."

"And I'm Jinx."

Aunt Fiona came bustling out of the kitchen wiping her hands with a dish towel. "Hello, Poppy, dear. Are you all out of oatmeal cookies at the barracks?"

"No, ma'am. I've been assigned to head the aerial protection detail for your grand-niece."

"Then you have to stay for supper," Fiona declared. "Hang your beret on the hook by the door."

We watched as the diminutive soldier threw her beret like a Frisbee. The purple headgear hit the center hook, spun three times, and came to a wobbling stop. Lucas let out a whistle.

After he introduced himself, my husband said with enthusiasm, "That was a stellar throw! I can do the same thing with my fedora. How do you get that kind of accuracy with such light-weight headgear?"

Before we lost the two of them to a technical discussion about hat flinging, I carried Addie into the room and introduced her to Poppy.

The fairy sergeant answered all my daughter's questions ending with, "If you ever want to talk to me, Addie, crook your finger like this and I'll fly to you. I'll be able to hear what you say and I can talk to you over the drone's speakers."

Remembering that conversation now, I picked GNATS 32 out of the formation and gave the designated signal. The craft broke ranks and flew to the window.

"Poppy? Is that you in there?"

"Affirmative, Witch of the Oak. Good morning."

"Good morning, and it's Jinx, remember?"

"Yes, ma'am."

Since the woman was on duty, I let it go. "You'll be with us in the big meadow this morning?"

"Roger that. We'll be with you wherever you go." There was a pause as the craft edged closer. "We've got her back, Jinx. We'll keep your little girl safe."

The kindness and determination in the words eased the ache in my heart some, but not much. From the moment we'd arrived in Shevington, I had become increasingly convinced I was the worst mother in the world.

"Thank you," I told Poppy. "That means a lot. Sorry to have bothered you."

"No bother," the fairy said. "Any time." The drone pivoted and resumed its position.

I needed to vent, but my choices for an audience were limited. I didn't want to put more of a burden on Lucas's shoulders. Tori was at Drake Abbey with Connor. Aunt Fiona would only cluck and tell me everything would be fine. My mother was running things back in Briar Hollow.

As I mentally ran down the list of potential sounding boards, the voice of the Mother Oak rose in my thoughts. *Come sit with me, my child. We will talk.*

It's been a long time since I've wised off to the Mother Oak, but I couldn't stop myself. "Great. One more thing to take me away from my child."

I felt more than heard the Oak sigh. *"I do not seek to take you away from Addie. I wish to ensure that when you are with her you are fully present. You are far too preoccupied with the erroneous presumption that you are a bad mother because you must attend to multiple responsibilities."*

That shut me up. I hadn't stopped to consider that I really am a working mother; granted the work might be unique, but the guilt wasn't.

"You're telling me I'm wasting the hours I have thinking about the ones I don't."

"Yes, but there is more I have to say. You are overwhelmed with good reason. Come sit beneath the shelter of my limbs. Your family will understand. I promise I will not keep you from them for long."

The Oak was right. When you're in service to one of the Great Trees, no one questions that arboreal business comes first —not even Addie, who greeted the news of my errand with, "Say hi, Big Tree!"

I kissed her, then Lucas, using the gesture to whisper in his ear, "I'll join you in the big meadow."

His eyes searched mine. My husband knew I was troubled, but as a career DGI agent Lucas doesn't question the private business between a Tree Witch and her boss.

When I stepped beyond the confines of Fiona's tidy yard, I found Shevington's streets buzzing with early morning energy. Over the past few years I've come to have at least a speaking acquaintance with almost everyone in the city. Merchants doffed their caps to me and some of the women dropped a curtsy.

Though still not comfortable with the etiquette of my position, I've finally accepted that to the people of Shevington I'm not just any tree witch. I'm *their* tree witch.

I sat on the stone bench at the base of the tree's trunk and breathed a sigh of relief as the privacy shield descended. A fresh cup of coffee and a plate of bacon and eggs appeared beside me.

"You cook?" I asked, picking up the napkin.

"My talents are many and varied. You must be more mindful of your well being, Jinx. You will have need of your strength in the days ahead."

Taking a bite of perfect, crisp bacon, I said, "Have I ever mentioned you're not good with opening lines?"

"On multiple occasions."

"Okay," I said, reaching for the coffee. "Hit me. What's coming at us this time?"

Chapter Four

DRAKE ABBEY, THE MIDDLE REALM

The yellow drake raked his front claws against the paving stones. Smoke and sparks curled from his nostrils. Refusing to give ground, Blair McBride crossed her arms and stepped closer. Locking eyes, dragon and rider exchanged silent glares.

Cradling a coffee mug in both hands, Tori Andrews watched from the shelter of the Drake Abbey cloisters. "What's that all about?" she asked Maeve who was tending the campfire.

The flames guttered and highlighted the woman's honey-brown features. Following Tori's gaze, she studied the confrontation in the courtyard. "They're arguing."

"I got that part," Tori said, "but I need the subtitles."

The dragonrider frowned. "Sub what?"

Connor Hamilton jumped into the conversation. "Subtitles. Humans use a form of storytelling that relies on moving pictures. If the performers and audience don't share a common language, words appear at the bottom of the screen to replicate the dialog."

Beside him Davin, who was mending his flying leathers,

said, "What powerful sorcerer created this enchantment of pictures that move?"

"One of the most creative humans ever to have been born," Connor said. "Thomas Alva Edison. He also invented the light bulb."

Davin frowned. "A bulb of light?"

As Connor launched into an enthusiastic recitation of Edison's catalog of inventions, Tori continued to watch the living tableau in the courtyard.

Whatever Blair was telegraphing to Giallo made the dragon lash out with his tail, which came within inches of knocking over Brick Deaver's worktable.

The burly construction foreman from Shevington would vent his own anger if he arrived for work the next day and found his blueprints for the Abbey restoration scattered to the winds.

Maeve left the fire and came to stand beside Tori. "They don't do this often," she said in a low voice, "but they both possess strong wills and hot tempers when provoked."

"Giallo could take a wall down with that tail."

"Be more worried about him flaming the construction supplies."

"Any idea what got this started?"

"I suspect Giallo is displeased with Blair because she has not shifted since we arrived in the Middle Realm."

Before Tori could ask why that mattered, the drake planted his forefoot with such force bricks cascaded down an adjacent wall.

Squaring her shoulders, Maeve said, "That's enough. Both of you."

Giallo's voice blasted through Tori's thoughts. *"I am cursed with a stubborn rider."*

"And I," Blair said, punching the dragon in the chest, "am cursed by your meddlesome interference."

The drake's head reared, steam jetting from his nostrils. *"Husband! Stop."*

Giallo's mate, Eingana lumbered out of the cloisters, her pearlescent scales glowing in the last rays of the setting sun.

"I will not abide another restless night because of this petulant child," Giallo growled.

"You would endure the fires of hell and more for Blair McBride and many years have passed since she was a child," Eingana replied. *"You impress no one with your bold words and hot breath."*

"Child or not, she persists in denying her nature."

"She," Blair said through clenched teeth, "is standing right here. If I'm keeping you up at night, sleep somewhere else."

Before Tori could register the movement, Giallo unfurled his wings and sprang into the sky. *"The only wise words you have spoken this day,"* he said, surging away from the Abbey with powerful strokes.

Eingana turned to Maeve. *"You will look after my daughter?"*

"Nysa will be fine," Maeve replied. "Go on. Calm him down."

Lifting off the stones, Eingana followed her mate toward the Sea of Ages.

Throwing up her hands, Blair wheeled and stalked into the deepening shadows beyond the courtyard.

Maeve started to go after her friend, but Tori caught hold of the dragonrider's arm. "Let me do it. Sometimes a neutral party stands a better chance of being heard."

Tori caught up with Blair in the Abbey's labyrinth, an overgrown serpentine garden of inlaid stones the workers uncovered cutting brush on the grounds.

The dragonrider paced down a long, straight section of the

path with angry strides. When she turned to retrace her steps, Blair saw Tori and stopped.

Making an effort at composure, Blair shoved her hands in the pockets of her leathers and said, "I'm sorry you saw that. Give me a few moments to calm down and I'll return to the cloisters."

"I've seen worse," Tori assured her, sitting on a stone bench. "Come on. Take a load off."

Blair blinked, processing the strange phrase. "I'm not sure I'm in a mood to sit still."

"Are you in a mood to take a drink?" Tori asked, removing a silver flask from the pocket of her jacket.

When surprise registered on the dragonrider's face, Tori said, "Festus gave me the flask for Christmas. He considers whisky to be essential equipment for any operation. Come on. It'll do you good."

"I've always said Giallo would drive me to drink," Blair grumbled, closing the distance between them and accepting the flask.

She took a swallow, grimaced, and coughed. "By the gods, what is this?"

"Whisky made in Scotland. It's called Laphroaig—115 proof. That means it's strong."

"An unnecessary explanation," Blair said, handing the flask back to Tori, who took a drink herself.

After passing the whisky between them a few times, Tori said, "Let me go out on a limb here. You're refusing to shift because you're feeling the pressure of leadership and spending a night roaming around as a weretiger seems self-indulgent."

Blair let out a bemused snort. "Are you always so direct or only when you drink?"

"Pretty much always," Tori said, "plus I have a best friend

who forgets to take care of herself because she's the Witch of the Oak."

The dragonrider took another swallow of Scotch. "I did not ask to be a leader."

"Didn't you? You're the one who stood up to Master Kian and refused to allow Giallo and Eingana's daughter to be reared under repressive conditions."

Fixing her gaze on the Sea of Ages, Blair said, "I didn't ask anyone to follow me."

"Leaders who fight on the side of right don't have to ask. If you want to take care of them and this place—and I know you do—you're going to have to take care of yourself first."

"Has anyone ever told you that you can be annoying?"

"Frequently. I'm the sidekick. It's my job."

"I don't know what that means."

Stretching out her legs, Tori said, "Jinksy is the hero of the story. I'm supposed to be the wise voice that whispers in her ear, gets her to think about stuff, and occasionally to lighten the hell up."

"You are her second in command."

Tori tipped the flask again. "Am I? Most of the time I don't feel like I'm in command of anything."

After several beats, Blair asked, "Did you know my parents were born here at Drake Abbey?"

"No, I didn't."

"My parents and Giallo."

"What happened to your parents?"

"They were killed in the Spica jungle trying to protect Master Jaxon. They all died along with their dragons. Our wing suffered a terrible loss that day."

"Don't you mean *you* suffered a terrible loss?"

Swallowing hard, Blair said, "In those days the wing and my family were indivisible. I do not know how to separate the grief."

"Was that when Kian assumed command of the Citadel?"

"Yes. In the beginning Kian tried sincerely to follow in Master Jaxon's footsteps, but the two men were cut from different cloth. Kian couldn't lead and many of us couldn't follow."

"You were still loyal to Master Jaxon?"

"My loyalty to Jaxon will never fade," Blair said. "He and my father were best friends. I thought of the Master as a beloved uncle. My father was, as you have described yourself, the sidekick."

Tori blew out a long breath. "It's not a bad job until somebody gets killed."

"You speak as if you understand loss."

Draining the last of the whisky, Tori said, "My father died about a year ago. He ran a lumberyard—not an adventurous bone in his body. He wasn't a leader and he didn't care enough about anyone to sacrifice himself on their behalf. My mother was the strong one in that relationship."

"How do you honor your father's memory?"

A bitter laugh escaped Tori's lips. "I don't. I'm not sure he deserves to be honored. You don't have that problem, Blair. Use the legacy you received from Jaxon and your father. Lead in their memory."

In the dim light the dragonrider studied Tori's profile. "How did your father die?"

"Foolishly," Tori replied, pushing herself upright. "He was a weak man who couldn't control his impulses. He paid the price for his flaws. Now, I'm going back to the campfire and you're going to shift. Don't argue with me."

"I won't argue. If you ever wish to speak again of your father, I will listen."

"Thank you, but I try not to waste any more breath on that man than I have to."

As Blair watched Tori walk away, she felt the tiger in her soul pad closer to the surface. The big cat pressed against her consciousness, eager to be released from the cage of her thoughts. Once she shifted, they both could roam free in the night. Without fully comprehending why, Blair wished she could give that gift to Tori Andrews.

Chapter Five

A light struck the books piled on the corner of Beau's desk. The beam glanced off *New Voyages to Carolina: Reinterpreting North Carolina History* and hit the desk calendar highlighting a date.

"Yes, yes," Beau said, taking out his pocket watch. "I know the volumes must be returned, but that is not until..."

He stared at the timepiece, then slapped the gold case against the palm of his hand to ensure the mechanism was running. "Did I work all night?"

The fairy mound materialized a candle burning at both ends.

"As I am already deceased, an extended stretch of labor will scarcely harm me, but it was not my intention to remain at my post through the dark hours of the night."

The candle dropped lower, illuminating a work schedule.

"I know," the colonel sighed. "We are quite behind with the labor of cataloging the collection. The arrival of Miss Addie coupled with an impromptu wedding and the Stella Mae Crump fiasco were not conducive to productive endeavor. I am most grateful that Miss Glory and Chase have returned from their honeymoon. I do hope that she will be better able to focus on tasks at hand today."

A vintage cabinet television replaced the candle. On the black and white screen, Festus, in human form, walked Glory down the aisle of a Las Vegas wedding chapel.

"Please spare me an additional viewing of that video," Beau said. "When Miss Glory said she wished to watch her wedding, I did not anticipate we would be expected to sit through the ceremony four times."

A picture of Glory wearing a sparkling tiara appeared in the center of the screen. "I am aware that all brides feel as if they are queens on the day of their wedding, but may I point out that only a single coronation is required to elevate a monarch to power?"

The fairy mound produced a montage showing Glory at work on her column, jitterbugging with Darby, reading to children at the library, and packing baskets of canned goods for the local food pantry.

"She is a good soul," Beau said, a note of fondness in the words, "I merely require some time to recover."

The antique TV disappeared only to be replaced with a flashing red arrow emblazoned with an image of Linda Albert, the local librarian.

"There is no need to nag. Miss Linda will not open the library for another few minutes. I cannot allow her to see me in such a disheveled condition. I must retire to my chamber and seek fresh attire."

The fairy mound chimed in agreement, but made a shushing sound when Beau pushed his chair away from the desk. The arrow sprouted whiskers and a tail pivoting in the direction of the hearth.

"Ah," the colonel said, lowering his voice, "I forgot they were there. I will be quiet as I pass."

On the hearth Willow lay curled against Festus, head tucked under her grandfather's chin and one tiny paw wrapped around his foreleg.

The night before Festus made it through two viewings of the wedding, primarily because Darby laid out a steady supply of snacks. When Glory started the video for the third time, the werecat decamped to the hearth and fell asleep.

Although Willow tried to stay awake out of loyalty to her new mother, she joined Festus on the hearth early in the fourth viewing. At the end of the evening Chase and Glory had decided to leave her there for the night. For all his gruff sarcasm, Festus would protect the kitten with his life.

Looking at the irascible shifter cuddling the kitten, Beau wished he could share the story of Willow's arrival with Miss Linda. There was so much about life in the lair that his friend would find both delightful and comical, but alas, those details were off limits to human ears.

Beau tidied his papers and picked up the books. He climbed the stairs to the first floor and entered his micro apartment. As a corporeal ghost he didn't need rest or a razor, but sartorial standards mattered.

The colonel put on fresh charcoal trousers and a white shirt, which he tucked into the waist of the pants. Flipping through the collection of vests in the armoire, he selected a maroon watered silk with a matching cravat.

He arranged the folds and secured the neckwear with a gold Masonic pin. Tori teased him about his "man scarves," but the arrangement disguised the lump under his shirt created by the Amulet of the Phoenix.

The colonel smoothed his hair and sat on the sofa to pull on his riding boots. Then, donning a lightweight summer jacket, he plucked a white panama hat off the wardrobe shelf.

Satisfied that his appearance met the 19th-century gentlemanly standards to which he held himself, Beau stepped into the deserted store and let himself out the back door.

Kelly held responsibility for The Witch's Brew that day, but Gemma was on call if she needed help. Jinx and Lucas were still in Shevington getting Addie settled. Tori and Connor had chosen to spend a few days at Drake Abbey.

Although it was early, Beau knew he would find Linda at the library. She loved to be alone in the building with her beloved books, but out of consideration for her working patrons opened the door at 7 a.m.

Beau walked to the end of the alley and turned toward the square. At the corner he spotted Jeff Hamilton unpacking a shipment of fishing rods in the sporting goods store and waved good morning.

As Beau crossed the street, a movement in one of the courthouse windows caught his attention. The ghost of former Briar Hollow mayor Howard McAlpin waved from one of the second story windows.

Since the streets were deserted, Beau returned the gesture, marveling at the improvement in McAlpin's afterlife disposition. Now the official courthouse haunt, Howie staged regular and tasteful ectoplasmic appearances, and had even consulted with Beau on varying the content of his performances.

With the sun climbing in the sky, and the morning air still cool, Beau's spirits soared. The need for Addie to live in Shevington had cast a pall over the lair, but the old soldier breathed a private sigh of relief over the blessed quiet.

Before he stepped off the curb to cross the street to the library, Beau noticed the building's front door ajar. Linda maintained the adamant position that the air conditioning system was not to be squandered on the great outdoors. Perhaps an early patron had been careless?

A strange foreboding washed over the colonel when he entered the lobby. "Hello? Miss Linda?"

No answer.

Beau approached the desk. A cup of coffee sat beside the computer keyboard. Tendrils of steam rose off the dark liquid. A warning alarm sounded in his mind. Putting the books he carried on the counter, Beau called again, "Miss Linda?"

At the back of the building, a door opened and closed.

"Miss Linda? Is that you?"

Out of habit, the colonel's hand reached for the hilt of the sword he no longer wore. He looked around for a potential weapon, but saw nothing. It would not be the first time he'd gone into battle with insufficient armaments.

"Show yourself," Beau commanded. "If you do not reveal your identity immediately, I will summon the authorities."

He took a step past the desk only to gasp under the force of a frigid wind. Beau interacted with the human realm as a solid being, but his true nature made him acutely aware of environmental energy.

Dark foreboding tugged at the colonel's heart. The departing soul of another had just passed through him—a soul he recognized.

He saw her hand first—the curled fingers outstretched and beckoning. The gesture took him back to the battlefields of the Civil War. He'd seen many young men wordlessly reaching across the mortal void in that same manner.

Linda lay on her back between two rows of shelves. Her open eyes stared at the ceiling, the terror of her last moments frozen in that lifeless gaze. A single bite mark had punctured her carotid artery,

Beau recoiled at the thick, metallic scent of the blood

pooling under her head and shoulders. Though he knew there was no hope, he knelt beside the body and put his fingers against the undamaged side of the woman's neck. The skin was warm to the touch, but his probing fingers felt no pulse.

"Oh, Miss Linda," he said, the words leaden with grief and regret. He knew she had died within seconds of receiving the wound, but the thought of what she had endured first bowed his head.

Only then did he notice the book wedged in the dead woman's left hand—*Le Loup Garou* by Alfred Marchard. Beau translated the French; *The Wolf Man*.

A folded piece of sheet music protruded from the pages. The title delivered the killer's message with precision. *Sweet Adeline.*

Fumbling for his phone, Beau started to call the sheriff, but then stopped. Once the wheels of human justice began to turn, their own investigative efforts would be hampered.

Reaching for the reliable, methodical part of his character, Beau used the phone to photograph Linda's body and the surrounding area.

He returned to the lobby and took pictures of the front door and desk, then retraced his steps, venturing into the rear of the library to document the back entrance he'd heard open and close.

The killer had still been in the building when Beau arrived. The fiend must have left some trace of himself. Returning to the body, Beau knelt on the tightly woven, carpet.

At first, he found nothing, but then, mere inches from Linda's throat three dark hairs protruded from the rug's fibers. Removing a notebook from the pocket of his coat, Beau tore out a page.

He carefully plucked one of the hairs free, placed it on the paper, and folded the sheet into a tight square. Only then did he dial the sheriff's office.

"Good morning. This is Beau Longworth. I am at the public library. Something terrible has happened to Miss Albert. Please send someone immediately."

John Johnson and Beau watched as two attendants from Jenkins Mortuary wheeled Linda's body out to a waiting hearse. The Sheriff saw the stricken expression on Beau's face.

"You all were friends?" Johnson asked.

"We were. Miss Linda and I shared a great love of history. Our work on the historical commission brought us into frequent contact. Where are they taking her?"

"To the funeral home until the coroner can get here from Cotterville and examine the body. Let's me and you sit down and have a talk."

Beau followed the sheriff to the reading room where they each took a chair. "Anything more between you and Linda than friendship?" Johnson asked, flipping open his notebook.

"I am a widower," the colonel replied. "Although I held Miss Linda in the highest regard and would have been honored to keep company with her, my loyalty to my late wife prevented me from doing so."

The sheriff studied him. "You're Jinx Hamilton's uncle?"

"In truth a distant cousin, but given the difference in our ages, Jinx began referring to me as her uncle when she was a child and has continued to do so."

Johnson made a note. "You don't sound like you're from around these parts."

"I am a native son of Tennessee, but as I found myself alone in the world, I moved to Briar Hollow to be near Jinx and her family. As you may know I have a unique connection to the community. The ancestor for whom I am named is buried in the local cemetery."

"Yeah, I remember the newspaper article about that. You look like the guy. So you came over here this morning to return some books?"

"Yes, I have long been aware of Miss Linda's habit of opening early for the convenience of her patrons. I often avail myself of the quiet morning hour to enjoy a uninterrupted historical conversation with Miss Linda."

"Tell me what you saw when you came in."

As the colonel described the empty foyer and still steaming coffee cup, Johnson continued to scribble. "I fear the brigand was still on the premises," Beau said. "When I called out for Miss Linda a second time, I heard a door open and close at the rear of the building."

Johnson looked up. "Did you touch the door knob?"

"I did not."

"Good. We'll check it for prints. What about the bod... what about Linda? Did you touch her?"

Beau lowered his head. "I knew her spirit had left this world, but I could not stop myself from probing for a pulse. Her body was warm to the touch, but without any sign of life."

"You know anything about that book she was holding?"

"*Le Loup Garou* by Alfred Marchard. The volume is rare, but it is the popular basis for the legend of the werewolf. The title translates to *The Wolf Man*. I am frankly surprised Miss Linda had a copy in the collection. I cannot think there was a demand for the volume. Perhaps it was acquired for someone on interlibrary loan."

"Huh," Johnson said. "That's an interesting suggestion. We'll look into that. Anything else?"

"I do not believe so."

The sheriff snapped the notebook closed and tucked his pen under the flap of his uniform shirt. "Okay, you can go, but I may need to talk to you later."

"Of course. I am at your disposal, Sheriff Johnson."

Chapter Six

The eyes of the townspeople followed Beau as he crossed the courthouse lawn. Howie, standing in a corner window, mouthed the words, *"I'm sorry, Beauregard."*

The colonel swallowed against the lump in his throat and forged ahead. Kelly met him at the door of The Witch's Brew, a knot of regulars standing behind her.

"Is it true?" she asked without preamble.

"I fear so. An intruder accosted Miss Linda in the library early this morning and took her life."

A storm of questions erupted.

"Did you see anyone?"

"How was she killed?"

"Does Sheriff Johnson think he knows who did it?"

"Do we have a killer loose in town?"

"My God. Do you think the person who killed Fish Pike has come back?"

Kelly took command of the situation. "All right, everyone. Beau has had a terrible shock. Let's give him some room. I'm sure if we're in any danger Sheriff Johnson will put out a community bulletin. Go on now. Go back to your coffee. Help yourself to the pastries on the counter. On the house."

The offer of free food directed attention away from Beau, but the relief didn't last.

"Look!" a man's voice cried. "The deputies are going over to that new book store. Something's happened over there, too!"

As everyone rushed back toward the front windows, Beau laid his hand on Kelly's arm. "May we have a private word in my quarters?"

Nodding, Kelly followed. Before she could close the door, Rodney dashed over the threshold and vaulted onto the back of the sofa.

Beau sank onto the cushions as if all the energy had drained from his body. The rat stepped onto his shoulder, raised a pink paw, and stroked the colonel's sideburn.

"You are kind my little friend," Beau said. "How did you learn of Miss Linda's death?"

Rodney pointed down.

"The fairy mound alerted you?"

He nodded, spreading his arms wide.

Frowning, Beau said, "I don't understand."

Glancing out the door, which she'd left open a crack to keep an eye on the customers, Kelly said, "He's saying the fairy mound knows most of what happens on the square. Are you all right, Beau?"

"I have seen far worse deaths on the battlefield, but I am unaccustomed to finding a woman the victim of such egregious violence."

Kelly hesitated. "Was it... was she... in bad shape?"

Beau answered by handing her his phone. "I photographed the scene."

"That must have been hard for you," Kelly said, "but it was good thinking." She thumbed open the photos and flicked through the images, her expression darkening. "That wound on her neck is a bite."

"Yes," the colonel agreed, "and the volume placed in her hand would suggest the killer was a werewolf."

"That's unlikely. The Registry regulates the American werewolf community. There hasn't been an incident in more than a hundred years. Besides, werewolves don't attack with precision. Once they taste blood, they can't stop themselves. This killer had enormous control and..."

She stopped, frowned at the image on the screen. "Beau, did you notice the publisher on this piece of music?"

"I took note of the title. I assume the presence of the music is meant as a threat to Miss Addie."

"I agree, and I know who delivered the threat. Morgan le Fay."

"A logical conclusion, but how can you be certain?"

Turning the phone around, Kelly pinched the image until four words filled the screen. "Because the publisher is listed as *La déesse des corbeaux*. The Goddess of the Crows."

Sheriff Johnson stood at the front window and watched Beau Longworth. When the man disappeared into *The Witch's Brew*, Johnson spoke to his deputies.

"You boys go on outside. I want to check this place out for myself. I better not catch either one of you talking to the lookie loos. There's gonna be enough rumors going all over town without you idiots helping."

The two men mumbled "yes, sirs" and exited the building. As soon as the door closed, Johnson took the toothpick out of the corner of his mouth and popped a breath mint.

Nobody in Briar Hollow, with the exception of his wife,

understood the elaborate hoax John Johnson lived. Long ago he perfected the ruse of being the genial and somewhat dull small town sheriff.

He pretended not to notice the strange things that happened right under his nose. He hired deputies bright enough to do the job and dim enough to believe what he told them to believe. But Johnson saw it all and said nothing.

The Sheriff didn't think Beau Longworth had any involvement with Linda Albert's death, but the man sure as hell was not Jinx Hamilton's Tennessee cousin uncle.

Johnson's gut told him Linda's killer wanted to send a message through Longworth and straight into whatever went on behind the scenes at Jinx Hamilton's store.

But how did the pieces of that message fit together? A French book about werewolves, the piano music to *Sweet Adeline,* and a single, fatal bite to the jugular.

The sheriff scrubbed at this jaw. "Okay, Linda. How did this thing go down?"

Everyone in town knew the librarian walked to work. She preferred to enter the building through the front door. Johnson could imagine her standing outside, keys in hand.

If the killer was already in the library, they would have heard the lock. The deputies found Linda's purse on the desk in her office, so she probably went there first.

Johnson crossed the lobby, pausing at the opening to the stacks, which afforded him a clear view of the rear entrance. He doubted the killer would have stood in the open, but Linda probably never even glanced that way. People familiar with and comfortable in their surroundings don't practice vigilance.

The Sheriff guessed she probably flipped on the lights, put her bag on the desk, and went back to the lobby for that steaming cup of coffee Beau Longworth found at the front counter.

The coffee maker, a complimentary amenity for patrons, sat on a table to the right of the front door. Johnson opened the machine and found a dark roast pod in the compartment.

Taking a rubber glove out of his shirt pocket, the sheriff extracted the plastic cup and noted a thin film of moisture on the bottom side. Linda must have waited while her cup filled.

The killer wouldn't have risked jumping her there. Even at that early hour, someone on the square might have seen something or heard Linda if she called out.

Johnson dropped the coffee pod into an evidence bag, which he sealed and labeled. "Okay, Linda," he said to the empty room. "So you've got your coffee and you go to the main desk. Why?"

The sheriff clucked his tongue against the roof of his mouth while he considered the question. "Maybe you started the computer system."

He went behind the counter, using his flashlight to check under the desk and scan the carpet before he pulled back the rolling chair.

Still using the crumpled glove in his hand, Johnson edged the mouse a fraction to bring the screen to life. The general library email account filled the screen.

Scanning the subject lines Johnson stopped on a message dated from the night before that had been opened a few minutes after 7 a.m. The *"Unusual Request"* referenced the book that had been found in the dead woman's hand.

Dear Ms. Albert,

I have been searching regional North Carolina libraries for a copy of Le Loup Garou *by Alfred Marchard in the original French. To my surprise and pleasure, I have discovered that your facility recently came into possession of the volume.*

Would it be an imposition to ask that you scan the first chapter and email the file to me? I believe there to be errors in the translated edition in my possession. I will, of course, pay for your time and trouble.

Best regards,
J. Jones

Johnson let out a dismissive snort. "J. Jones. Right. Fake name, generic email address." Switching windows, the Sheriff found the digital card catalog open to the book's record in the library's collection.

"You took the bait, Linda. This email got you to go looking for the book and that's where the killer waited for you."

Standing, the sheriff took out his phone, opened the clock app and started the stopwatch. He retraced the librarian's likely path. She'd known where to find the volume, so the Sheriff walked briskly to the blood stain in the stacks. Adding a brief amount of time to scan the shelves, the trip took between 20 and 30 seconds.

The outline on the carpet described the position of the body. A picture of the killing formed in his mind. Linda heard something, turned, and the attacker struck. Fifteen seconds to bleed out—but no blood spray. *How had the murderer managed that?*

"Because he contained the flow while he eased you to the floor," the sheriff said, almost gagging. "He swallowed your blood."

Once Linda was down, the killer arranged the body and started for the back door, but then Beau Longworth entered the lobby. Even when he was in danger of being caught, the killer just opened the back door and strolled out cool as you please.

"Have you done this before, you bastard?"

The sheriff used his glove to open the back door. He stepped into the empty alley. The deputies hadn't found tire tracks, only the marks of a man's shoes that disappeared at the sidewalk.

As he studied the area, the sun moved from behind the clouds. The burst of light glinted on something gold lying in the gravel. Bending, Johnson found himself studying a cufflink engraved with a fleur-de-lis.

"Well, well, well," he drawled. "You weren't so careful after all."

From the front of the building one of the deputies yelled, "Sheriff? We've got another crime scene over at that new book store."

Johnson used his pen to scoot the cufflink into an evidence bag. The day was getting more complicated by the minute, but at least Larry Anderson from *The Briar Hollow Banner* wasn't breathing down his neck for a scoop—yet. It wasn't much, but the Sheriff decided to take his luck where he could get it.

Chapter Seven

Lawrence Anderson willed his breathing to slow. The gag triggered an attack of claustrophobia. Panic coursed through his system. Every nerve screamed for him to fight the restraints that bound him to the chair, but the movement would attract too much attention.

He wanted the beast to stay crouched in the corner. The thing studied the bound man with interested yellow eyes, occasionally lifting its snout to sniff the air. The tips of ivory fangs showed above black lips that glistened under the fluorescent lights.

At the window of *The Briar Hollow Banner* office a thin, sallow man watched the flurry of activity on the town square. Two sheriff's deputies unrolled a length of yellow crime scene tape in front of the library. They used the flimsy barrier to hold back a growing crowd of onlookers.

When the creature in the corner whined, the man didn't bother turning his head. "Quiet. You've had your fun. Be a good boy and wait for your next meal."

Beads of sweat covered Anderson's forehead and rolled down his face. He blinked as the salty liquid stung his eyes.

"It's unpleasant, isn't it, Mr. Anderson?" the man said. "Being deprived of the liberty of movement. Through the centuries I, myself, have endured long periods of confinement. At least you are afforded the light of day and a view of your surroundings. I wish to have a civil conversation with you. If I remove the gag, will you be cooperative?"

The newspaper editor bobbed his head, realizing that his captor could see him and the interior of the office reflected in the glass.

"Excellent," the man said, leaving his outpost and dragging a chair opposite the captive. He undid Anderson's gag and tossed it on the editor's desk.

Coughing, Anderson said, "May I have a drink of water, please?"

"I do appreciate good manners. Where might I find a cup?"

"There are bottles of water in the refrigerator in the back room."

"Andre, fetch."

The beast stood on two legs and loped toward the small kitchen.

Flicking a speck of dust off the knee of his trousers, the man asked, "What do your associates call you, Mr. Anderson?"

"Larry."

"I am Jean-Baptiste Dampierre. If we are to negotiate with one another, is it not more cordial to do so as friends?"

Anderson's eyes darted back and forth. "Uh, sure," he said, casting his gaze downward at the sound of shuffling steps on the hardwood.

In his peripheral vision, he saw human fingers wrapped around a plastic bottle—and dark fur protruding from an incongruous white shirt cuff.

Dampierre caught the stolen glance. "Does Andre make you uncomfortable, Larry?"

With a convulsive gulp, Anderson said, "He terrifies me. What is he?"

"Once he was a mere human not unlike yourself."

Jerking his head up, Anderson asked, "Is that what you're going to do to me?"

Chuckling, Dampierre unscrewed the cap and held the bottle to Anderson's mouth. The editor gulped the cool liquid.

When half the bottle was gone, Dampierre said, "Better?"

"Yes. Thank you."

"You have quite the active imagination, Larry. I would have thought a journalist would have a greater capacity for dispassion."

"No one could be dispassionate about something that looks like that," Anderson said, nodding to Andre who had returned to his corner. "What is he?"

"My business with you does not involve dissecting Andre's pedigree."

"If it's money you want, there's nothing on the premises."

Dampierre sniffed. "Money? How crass and human of you. No, I don't want money. I want information about one of your employees."

Anderson's expression grew wary. "Who?"

"Glory Green."

Lunging against his restraints, the editor cried, "Don't you hurt her!"

Dampierre's fist shot out. The blow drove the editor's teeth against his bottom lip, splitting the skin, and sending a thin line of blood down his chin.

Using the same hand that had delivered the vicious blow, Dampierre ran a finger across the stream and brought the red stain to his mouth. "Ah, B-negative. Not my favored vintage."

He removed a handkerchief from his pocket and wiped his

hands. "Let us begin again. Do not presume to give me orders and there will be no need for me to redirect your attention."

Licking his lip, which had begun to swell, Anderson rasped, "Why are you doing this?"

"Does the name T.E. Lawrence mean anything to you?"

Confused, Anderson said, "The British guy from the movie? Lawrence of Arabia?"

"A prosaic response, but accurate. Lawrence described the printing press as the greatest weapon at the disposal of any modern commander. You, Larry, are in control of a weapon I need."

"But *The Banner* isn't printed here," he protested. "We email the files to Cotterville. I don't own a printing press."

Dampierre passed a hand over his eyes before regarding Anderson with a pained expression. "I'm sorry, Larry, but I cannot endure slogging through the tedium of your literal mind. Different methods are required to make this a productive exchange."

"I'm trying to answer your questions," Anderson said, the words shrill with fear. "I'm sorry if I said the wrong thing. Tell me what you want me to say and I'll say it."

Dampierre's voice dropped to a sultry level. "Larry, look at me."

Their gazes locked and Dampierre's pale eyes deepened to an azure glow. "Calm yourself. Would you like for me to remove your restraints?"

The lines on Anderson's face smoothed into a blank mask. "Yes."

Taking an ivory pen knife from his pocket, Dampierre cut the plastic ties. "That is better, isn't it?"

"Yes."

"Now, I want you to tell me everything that you know about

Glory Green and any insights you might have into her character. You may begin."

Speaking in a low monotone, Anderson described his first meeting with the woman who wrote an advice column for his paper. "Glory is quirky. Sometimes she gets so nervous I swear she turns green. She has trouble getting clothes that fit. Her sleeves are either too long or she trips over the hem of her pants."

"Is she a competent writer?"

"She's an earnest one. The readers love her for her honest, caring responses. Sometimes she's funny and I don't even think she means to be."

"Where does she live?"

"When she first moved to town she lived in Jinx Hamilton's store."

"Why would she take up residence there?"

Anderson's brow creased. "I really don't know. I think maybe she did some bookkeeping for them or something. Now she lives above the cobbler shop with Chase McGregor. They're engaged."

Dampierre offered him a thin smile. "I will be certain to offer my congratulations at the earliest opportunity. Would you say that you and the future Mrs. McGregor have cultivated a close friendship?"

"I'm fond of Glory. She's eager to learn the newspaper business. Even if she does come across as ditzy, she's not dumb only insecure."

"Do you have a family, Larry?"

"No. I never married. My parents are dead and I don't have any brothers or sisters."

"My condolences, but that does facilitate what we have to do next. I want you to get up, walk to your desk, take out paper and pen, and write what I dictate."

Anderson complied, moving like a sleepwalker. With his hand poised over a legal pad he said, "What do you want me to write?"

"I think the traditional phrasing will be best. 'I, Lawrence Anderson, being of sound mind and body... '"

Chapter Eight

After years of interacting with the Great Tree, I never expected the Oak to give me a straight answer. But, in true Mother Tree fashion, she fooled me.

"I bear news of a death in Briar Hollow."

I sat up so abruptly I knocked my plate onto the ground. A squirrel rocketed down the Oak's trunk and helped himself to my scrambled eggs.

"What?!" I gasped. "Who?"

"The librarian, Linda Albert."

Pain pierced my heart. Linda was a sweet, even-tempered woman. A thousand images flooded my brain. Linda laughing while she worked a booth at SpookCon. The day she came into the shop after she'd traded her gray bun for a cute pageboy, and how she'd colored with pleasure when Beau complimented her.

Linda had been Aunt Fiona's friend and she'd become mine. I couldn't imagine life in Briar Hollow without her. Everyone loved the way she dedicated her time to making the library a safe, welcoming space. Her talent for pairing readers with the stories they most needed in their lives was the stuff of legends.

My heart clutched at the thought of Beau. He had to be utterly devastated.

"*You are correct,*" the Mother Tree said. "*Colonel Longworth suffers immense grief. He discovered the body.*"

It was too much to hope the Mother Tree would give me both the event and the solution, but I tried anyway. "Who killed her?"

"*In solving that puzzle you will uncover deeper layers of deceit. Not all threats are delivered with the force of a murderer's hand.*"

Great. A chilling non-answer, but one that suggested we could achieve productive closure. If Linda Albert had to die, I intended to ensure her loss meant something.

Standing, I said, "I need to talk to Lucas. We should coordinate with Greer and Festus as soon as possible."

"*Sit.*"

By this time, you may have noticed that brevity is not the Mother Tree's long suit. If she issued that one-word command to get my attention, it worked.

But while my body stopped, my mouth didn't. "How can you expect me to sit here chatting with you when there's been a murder that affects someone I love?"

"*I wish to speak of those you love. You harbor fears of inadequacy in the raising of your child. You share those fears with every woman from whom a new life has come into the world.*"

Careful not to disturb the squirrel who was now eating what should have been my toast, I sank onto the bench. "Telling me I'm not the only woman who thinks she's a bad mother isn't much help."

"*Already you afford Addie a gift that was denied to you. She will not reach maturity ignorant of the Fae world.*"

"What about the things I'm not giving her?" I asked in an anguished voice. "Like play dates and kindergarten, birthday parties with her friends, a yard, and a puppy."

I thought I heard a tsking sound in the leaves overhead. *"As we speak your child plays in the garden of your aunt's cottage with young Naomi Frazier and a kindling of rabbit kittens."*

"And her father and I are probably going to have to leave her even sooner than we expected to solve a murder I already suspect is tied to Morgan le Fay."

"I would counsel against an early departure. Spend the day as you planned with your daughter and return to Briar Hollow this evening. There is nothing you can do in the moment to alter that which has already occurred. You will solve Linda's murder with reasonable speed, but dealing with Morgan le Fay will require more time. Pace yourself for what will be a long race, my child."

Rather than accept good advice graciously offered, I chose to behave like a petulant child. "If this is the part where I'm supposed to feel comforted that I have your permission to spend the day with my daughter, it's not happening."

The air stilled. Not one leaf on the Great Tree moved. Sensing a change in the tone of the conversation, the squirrel backed away. After a few steps he hesitated, grabbed the last piece of toast and disappeared up the Oak's trunk.

"We have no time to waste with your useless self-recrimination or churlish sarcasm. I had hoped you would learn with time what I am about to tell you, but as you seem bent on a confrontation, I will oblige. You will not have a normal mother-daughter relationship with your child. You were the vessel that brought her into this world, but Addie's tasks in life are her own to fulfill. Accept that, Jinx Hamilton, and move forward."

Something hot rose in my chest, a suffocating blend of anger, hurt, loss, and dread. "What did you say to me?"

"Addie's way lies with the dragons. Do not burden her with the conventions of your limited thinking. Do your job, Jinx Hamilton, and let Addie do hers."

"She's a *baby!*"

"*One who grows in understanding with the passage of each moment while her mother seems to regress. You and your daughter will share much in this life, but that relationship will not be built on the inconsequential things that currently occupy your thoughts.*"

Even though I would be the first one to admit how much I *didn't* know about raising children, I had picked up a few of the more obvious details. "Babies need to bond with their mothers."

"*Addie is not a human child. She is the daughter of a Fae witch and a Gwragedd Annwn. Have you not wondered why she knows all those in her world? Why her vocabulary exceeds her experience?*"

It hurt my pride to say yes, but I did.

"*The bonding of which you speak took place in your womb. You will know your daughter. You will become closer to her than you can imagine, but that will not happen over kindergarten play dates and birthday cakes.*"

Tears filled my eyes. "Are you being intentionally cruel? Did it ever occur to you that *I* will miss those things."

"*I am attempting to expand your mind. You are Fae and yet you persist in reasoning like a human.*"

"Because I thought I *was* human until Aunt Fiona showed up in my kitchen after her fake death to tell me I'd awakened magic I didn't even know existed."

The words came out in a hot rush. That first morning in the apartment over the store seemed a lifetime away in some respects; in others, I was still as shocked by my new life as I'd been that day.

"*It matters not what you thought in the past, only what you now know. In Shevington Addie will be both safe and happy. You must go to Briar Hollow and she must stay here. Do not waste your energies railing against what has already been determined. Go fly a kite.*"

Unlike Addie's literal use of that phrase, I was pretty sure the Mother Tree had just told me to get lost. Or more accurately, to quit whining and get to work.

Normally, the Oak and I at least exchange a polite good-bye, but after her final pronouncement She went silent. Apparently schooling me on my role as a Fae parent didn't include any soft, placating pats on the way out the door.

Fine. As it happened, I did have a date to go fly a kite and I intended to enjoy myself doing it. Or at least to enjoy myself until I broke the news to Lucas that an unsolved murder waited for us back home.

Chapter Nine

BRIAR HOLLOW

Sheriff Johnson stood in the center of Bergeron Books. He shoved his hat high on his head and rotated to survey the riot of destroyed displays and shredded publications.

Sniffing, he said, "Ms. Bergeron, do you know what that stink is?"

"Please, call me Bertille. I have no idea. It smells like something wet and stagnant."

Johnson's brows shot up. "Smells like swamp to me. You keep bottles of bayou water in this place?"

The proprietress regarded him with a serene, neutral expression. "Why on earth would I keep bottled bayou water?"

The Sheriff shifted his toothpick to the other side of his mouth. "I don't know. Maybe some voodoo thing?"

"I'm a Methodist."

Johnson snorted. "Don't be saying that too loud. This is Baptist country."

"Duly noted."

"Anybody mad at you?"

"I haven't been in town long enough to make enemies, Sheriff."

"How about the kind of enemies that travel?"

"Why would you ask me that?"

Johnson reached into his pants pocket and held out a sealed plastic bag. "We found this over at the library."

Taking the bag, Bertille studied the gold cufflink inside while the Sheriff watched.

"Kinda screams Louisiana, don't you think?" he prodded. "Isn't that thing on the state flag."

"This thing," she replied, handing him the bag, "is a fleur d'lis, a symbol with a strong association to France. The Louisiana state flag shows a pelican feeding her young."

Johnson locked eyes with Bertille. "You don't say."

"I do say."

After that exchange, neither spoke. The silence lengthened until Johnson's deputies grew uncomfortable. The younger men shot each other nervous looks that Johnson caught.

"You boys go on out back. Search the alley."

The deputies scrambled for the door leaving Johnson and Bertille alone.

"Does that cufflink mean anything to you, Ms. Bergeron?"

"Sheriff, may I remind you that my store was burglarized last night, which makes me the victim, not the suspect."

"Your store was burglarized last night and Linda Albert was murdered this morning. You can see how that would make a man in my position suspicious."

Bertille froze. "Linda's dead?"

"Yes, ma'am. Didn't you see our cars over at the library?"

"No, I came to work on the side street by the sporting goods store. The courthouse blocks my view of the library at that angle. I waited for your deputies in the alley."

Studying her closely, Johnson said, "Beau Longworth went over to the library this morning to return some books and found her. You don't look so good. Do you need to sit down?"

"No," Bertille said. "I'm just shocked at the news. Linda was a dear woman. She was the first person to welcome me to Briar Hollow."

Softening his attitude, the Sheriff said, "I know. I liked Linda a lot."

"Do you think the killer dropped that cufflink?"

Johnson stared at the evidence bag in his hand. "That's one theory. We don't have a lot of local men wandering around Briar Hollow wearing French cuffs."

In spite of the seriousness of the conversation, Bertille laughed. "That's true, but I also haven't met many small town sheriffs who could identify a French cuff to save their lives."

Johnson glanced toward the open back door, but his deputies were nowhere to be seen. He removed the toothpick from his mouth and dropped it in his shirt pocket.

Lowering his voice, he said, "In order to do my job, Bertille, I find it's better to be what the good citizens of this town expect me to be."

The unspoken implication wasn't lost on her. "But you see more than you let on."

"I do."

"Do you have any reason to think the person who killed Linda was the same person who broke into my store?"

"I guess that depends on whether or not we find the other cufflink in this mess."

Bertille hesitated and then asked, "Did the library smell like swamp water?"

"No."

"You'd have more to go on if it did."

Johnson looked out the front window at the crowd gathered on the courthouse lawn. "We would. Can you tell if anything's missing?"

"I won't know that until I start to clean up."

Retrieving a fresh toothpick from his pocket, the Sheriff said, "We have to go through the motions, but I'll try to get the scene turned back over to you by tomorrow morning. The sooner we know if anything was taken the better. Why don't you go over to The Witch's Brew and get yourself some coffee?"

"I have a coffee maker here."

The Sheriff turned away from the window. "They make a real nice vanilla latte over there and I can recommend the bear claws. Go on. Seeing as how we're working two crime scenes at once, I reckon we'll be here for several hours."

Bertille cocked her head and studied his craggy features. "Sheriff, if I didn't know better, I'd think you wanted me to go to The Witch's Brew for a reason."

A good ole boy grin split Johnson's face. "Sure do, Ms. Bergeron. You look like you could use a cup of coffee."

Every pair of eyes in the coffee shop locked on the front door when Bertille entered the store. Her status as a newcomer in the community saved her from a barrage of questions, but not the curious scrutiny.

She stopped inside the threshold, pinned in place by the force of the patrons' combined stares. Reading the situation, Kelly came out from behind the counter and closed the distance to where Bertille stood.

"Good morning, Bertille," she said in a strong voice every nosy customer could hear. "We saw the Sheriff's cars leave the library and go to your shop. Have you had some trouble?"

Taking her cue from Kelly, Bertille answered with similar volume. "More inconvenience than trouble. At first I thought someone had broken in, but now it's looking like raccoons caused all the damage."

From the vicinity of the chess tables a male voice said, "Damn trash pandas can tear a place all to hell in nothing flat. Look what they did to Fish Pike's house. Sheriff couldn't even search the place for evidence after he turned up dead."

Someone else chimed in. "You make it sound like the raccoons were in on the murder."

"Wouldn't put it past 'em," the man said. "I'm telling you the raccoons around here ain't normal. I still say I saw one wearing a fanny pack."

That touched off a murmur of good-natured ribbing, but Kelly wasn't taking any chances. She kept up the facade with Bertille. "What a mess. Have you called the Vermin Vigilantes?"

"Yes," Bertille said, played along, "but they can't squeeze me in until later in the week. I could really use a cup of coffee. My machine got turned over and destroyed."

"My heavens," Kelly said, putting her arm around Bertille's shoulders and steering her toward the counter. "No one should have to deal with a trashed business without coffee. I'm so relieved that you're okay. You know what happened at the library?"

"The Sheriff told me," Bertille said, watching while Kelly made her drink. "I'm in shock over the news about Linda."

That touched off a fresh round of speculation among the customers that effectively diverted their attention, but the two women stuck to the ruse of casual banter while Kelly whipped up a latte.

"It's on the house," she said, setting the cup on the counter. "You've had quite a morning."

"Thank you. I really appreciate that. Paying you all a visit today was on my list of errands. Is Tori back from her trip to Raleigh?"

"No, but we're not expecting her until tomorrow."

Bertille put on an indecisive face. "Oh. That kinda creates a problem for me. I loaned a couple of books to her from my inventory and now they've sold through my online store. I was hoping to get the packages shipped out today since I can't do anything else until the Sheriff and his deputies finish at my place."

Their eyes locked over the cappucino. Raising her powers, Bertille telegraphed, *"We need to talk. Alone."*

Kelly answered with an imperceptible nod. "Let's go upstairs to Tori's apartment and look for those books. She wouldn't want you to miss out on a sale and I need to water her plants anyway. I'll ask Beau to watch the counter."

When the colonel emerged from his micro apartment, Bertille touched his arm. "Mr. Longworth, I'm so sorry about your friend."

"Thank you, dear lady."

"I'll remember Linda in my prayers."

Wiping a tear from the corner of his eye, Beau said, "You are most kind."

Stepping closer, Kelly lowered her voice. "Are you sure you're up to watching the store for a few minutes? Bertille and I need to talk in private, but I could call Gemma."

"That will not be necessary. I am most grateful for the distraction. Does this conversation concern the morning's events?"

"Yes."

"Then take all the time you require. We must work together to apprehend the culprit so that Miss Linda's soul will be at peace. That is the only thing that matters now."

With that, he turned on his heel and stepped behind the counter, rolling up his sleeves as he went.

Kelly and Bertille made idle chit chat as they climbed the stairs. At the vestibule, Kelly laid a finger against her lips. Bertille nodded and remained silent until they'd gone through the entrance to the apartment and closed the door behind them.

The instant they were alone, Kelly said, "Are you really all right?"

"I'm fine," Bertille said, "but I wouldn't mind sitting down."

Kelly nodded toward the sofa. "Make yourself at home. I'm going to raid Tori's coffee pod stash. I'll be right back."

She disappeared into the kitchen. Bertille heard a cabinet door open and a coffee machine come to life. When Kelly returned she carried a cup emblazoned with the words, *"I don't wake up to drink coffee, I drink coffee to wake up."*

Taking the opposite end of the sofa, Kelly got down to business. "What really happened at your place?"

She listened as Bertille described finding the store vandalized and reeking of fetid swamp water. "Do you think that whoever broke into your shop killed Linda?"

"It's hard to imagine that the two events aren't related, but Sheriff Johnson said there was no discernible odor at the library."

Kelly frowned. "That's odd. What else did he say?"

Bertille sat her cup on the window sill. "He said that he sees more than people realize *and* he pretty much ordered me to come over here."

Arching an eyebrow, Kelly said, "Well, I'll be damned. That's unexpected. If that good ole boy sheriff routine of his is an act, he's got it down pat."

"I suspect that may be to satisfy and control the curiosity of locals. He showed me a cufflink that he found at the library."

Pausing with her coffee halfway to her mouth, Kelly said, "Linda Albert's killer was wearing French cuffs?"

"Not just French cuffs, but gold cufflinks engraved with a fleur-de-lis. The sheriff asked if that meant anything to me."

"Does it?"

"Yes, but I didn't tell Johnson that. I recognized the cufflink because it was one of a pair I bought in an antique shop on Royal in New Orleans. I commissioned the engravings from a local jeweler."

"How can you be sure they're the same cufflinks?"

"The design is a standard fleur-de-lis, but the jeweler etched the two wings in a unique way. It's his trademark. The cufflinks are diamond shaped with fluted edges. He told me they were bespoke pieces cast in the 19th century. Normally I wouldn't alter an antique, but the shop specializes in authentic reproductions, so I commissioned the engraving."

"Who did you give them to?"

Blinking back tears Bertille looked away. "A man I believed I loved. We quarreled. For two weeks, he refused to take my calls. When I went to his apartment to try to work things out, I found the door ajar. The place was deserted, wrecked, and smelled like a swamp."

Chapter Ten

JINX, SHEVINGTON

When I left the Mother Tree I fumed all the way to the big meadow. Have you ever stopped to think about that word—"fume?"

As a noun, it means a vapor that's dangerous to inhale. Judging from the way people made room for me to pass, the stench of my seething anger preceded me.

My footfalls punctuated the drumbeat of my thoughts. *"I've been a mother for two weeks. My baby went from birth to toddler in three days. And now you're describing me as nothing but the* vessel *that brought her into the world?"*

It's not nice to wish root rot on a Mother Tree, but what the hell did the Oak want from me? Telling me that Addie had more growth leaps ahead made me want to stay in Shevington more, *not* go back to Briar Hollow—even to solve an innocent woman's murder.

If I left Addie now, what would I find when I came back? I forced the thought from my mind.

I found Lucas, Addie, Stan, Naomi, and Barnaby in the middle of the meadow. Naomi and my daughter both flew gaily decorated kites; a dragon for Addie and a unicorn for Naomi.

Stan lay sprawled on his back emanating a slow buzz of snores. A cup of tea from Madam Kaveh's floated beside Barnaby who was grading exams. That left Lucas to watch the girls, even though I spotted GNATS 32 and the rest of the squadron hovering on station.

My husband caught sight of me, waved, and then I saw his brow crease. If he could spot my mood at roughly a hundred yards, I needed to dial my emotions down several notches.

Lucas stood and met me half-way. "How did things go with the Mother Tree?"

Trying and failing to moderate my answer, I pinned his ears back with a terse rehash of the Tree's lecture.

Using his bottomless well of patience, Lucas waited until I ran out of steam. "Feel better now?"

"Not really."

He put his arm around me and said something unexpected. "Honey, does it really matter how fast Addie grows?"

I wanted to smack him. "Doesn't it matter to you?"

"What matters to me is that she's safe and that we develop the best, most open relationship with her possible."

What do you do when your husband manages to say the right and wrong thing simultaneously. "What about all the things we'll miss?"

"What about all the unique experiences we'll have because our daughter isn't like anyone else in the Three Realms?"

My mouth opened, but no sound came out. Lucas's acceptance of our circumstances rendered me speechless. I knew his way meant far less emotional suffering and far greater potential for a positive outcome, but I was too mad and too stubborn to say so.

"We're not a human family, Jinx," Lucas said, pulling me closer and kissing my hair. "Our normal isn't going to look like your idea of what normal should be."

My head dropped onto his shoulder. "I haven't told you everything. The Mother Tree said there's been a murder in Briar Hollow. Linda Albert is dead. The Oak described her death as linked to deeper levels of deceit."

Lucas stiffened. "Morgan le Fay is behind this."

Even though I suspected exactly the same thing, in the moment, I couldn't help going to a place of denial. "We don't know that."

"Yes, we do. "

"But why would Morgan kill Linda?"

"To trap us, or maybe test us."

My throat closed so that the next words came out as a croak. "The Oak said we should take today with our daughter and go back home tonight."

"Now see," Lucas said, hugging me tight. "The Mother Oak does care how you feel."

The sound of Addie's laughter drew my attention to the field. She pulled on the string making the kite dive and whirl. "Look at her, Lucas. We just became a family. I know we have to help catch Linda's killer and stop Morgan, but how can we leave our baby?"

"Our biggest job is to protect her. We can't let Morgan find her or Merlin's wand."

I agreed, but the missing pieces in the puzzle of Addie's birth in another timestream nagged at me. "I want to go to the waterfall and talk to Knasgowa. How did she get Merlin's wand and why would she give it to Rodney instead of me?"

"All the more reason to go back to Briar Hollow."

Don't play chess with Lucas. While you're still formulating strategy, he's executing his end game. There was no way I could protest going home now. Elbowing him in the ribs, I said, "Nobody asked you to be logical, bub."

His chest vibrated with laughter. "*Bub?* Did you seriously call me 'bub?'"

"Be glad I went with bub."

"Honey, if the Mother Tree disturbed you this much, what she told you must have been what you needed to hear."

At that, I closed my eyes and buried my face in his shoulder only to look up when I heard a snapping sound. Addie's kite hovered in front of us, still tethered to our daughter's chubby hand several yards away.

The dragon's mouth moved. "Mama, you and Daddy have to go home and find out who hurt the book lady."

Some kids make pretend phones out of tin cans and string. My child animates a paper dragon and has him play messenger.

"How do you know about that, honey?" Lucas asked.

"I heard you and Mama talking."

My husband and I exchanged a meaningful look. Future parental conversations would take place behind a privacy incantation. At any age, it looked like Addie would always keep us on our toes.

"Take your kite back up in the air, Addie," I said. "Your father and I need to speak with Barnaby."

The dragon's paper wings lifted the kite skyward where it executed a series of intricate rolls rejoining Naomi's unicorn.

My grandfather sipped at his tea while I explained the situation in Briar Hollow. "I agree with Lucas," he said when I finished. "A violent death so close to your store and the fairy mound does not feel coincidental. As much as you do not wish to, you must go back and uncover the truth behind this murder."

Looking past him at the sun shining on Addie's golden hair, I said, "I don't want to leave her."

A massive hand came to rest on my shoulder. At some point in my recitation, Stan had awakened.

"Please don't worry, Jinx," the sasquatch said. "Lauren is the best Fae security specialist in the Realms. Fiona, Poppy, and I will shower Addie with love until you get back."

The earnest expression on his furry face made my eyes brim with tears again, but I didn't cry. We had the day to be with Addie and I intended to make the most of every second.

"I know, Stan," I said, "and I love you all for that. Now, where's *my* kite?"

As the sun dipped toward the mountains in the distance, we stood in Aunt Fiona's garden. I'd had a brief mirror call with my mother before supper to tell her we'd be back soon.

Bending down, I scooped Addie into my arms. "Are you going to be okay, baby?"

Addie nodded and asked, "You gonna be okay too, Mama?"

Yet again blinking away tears, I said, "Yes, I'll be okay, but I'll miss you something awful. Daddy and I will be back as soon as we can."

My daughter put her hands on my face and looked deep in my eyes. "You have to do what the Big Tree says, Mama. She didn't mean to make you mad. Honest. Don't be mad at her."

Holding my daughter tight, I whispered, "Okay honey, I promise. I won't be mad at the Mother Tree."

My eyes met Aunt Fiona's. "Don't forget what we talked about."

That was code for "only let Addie have her wand when you're there to watch her."

My aunt gave me a bright smile—too bright for comfort. "Of course, honey. You can rely on me."

That was both a true and utterly terrifying assurance.

I shifted my gaze to Barnaby. On the way back from the big meadow we had discussed contacting Connor and Tori. If

Morgan was making some kind of move, Nysa had to be brought to the Valley as soon as possible.

"You'll send Connor and Tori to Briar Hollow?" I asked.

"The instant our work has been completed."

With that, I couldn't delay our departure any longer. Walking away from Aunt Fiona's cottage that evening was the hardest thing I'd ever done. When we were out of sight of the house, I released the sobs I'd fought to hold inside all day. Lucas wrapped me in his arms and let me cry for a long minute.

Then he held me away from his body and said, "I don't want to leave her either, but if we don't do our jobs, Morgan will win."

"The hell she will," I said, scrubbing at my cheeks. "There is no way that bitch is going to win. If Morgan killed Linda, she will answer for the crime."

When we emerged from the portal in the lair, I went straight to Beau. The colonel stood as I approached, gently dislodging the luminescent form of his faithful hound, Duke, who leaned against his master's knee.

Putting my arms around him, I said, "Oh, Beau. I don't know what to say."

Rodney, who lay curled under his collar, stuck his head out to greet me. I felt the tickle of the rat's whiskers against my cheek when he leaned in to give me a kiss.

Beau's voice sounded heavy. "Miss Jinx, I felt her soul pass through me. We cannot allow lingering entanglements or unresolved business to draw her back. Linda cannot walk the earth as I have done."

Since Beau took possession of the Amulet of the Phoenix, it's been easy to forget that guilt over the death of the men under his command kept him from resting peacefully in his grave.

"You don't talk about that much," I said.

"Because you all came into my afterlife and gave me a way to be of use again in the company of people I love. There is no magic amulet that will blunt the sting of death for Miss Linda."

He was right. We didn't have spare resurrection bling on hand, but in that moment, I wished with all my heart that we did.

Chapter Eleven

DRAKE ABBEY

The compact mirror in Tori's pocket vibrated at just the moment the sun colored the morning sky in rosy hues. Maeve and Davin were making breakfast. Connor hadn't emerged from the tent and there was no sign of Blair.

Tori walked beyond the courtyard to answer the call. She expected to see Jinx's face in the looking glass, but instead Barnaby's visage greeted her.

"Good morning, Barnaby. Did you dial the wrong mirror? I can get Connor if you need to speak with him."

"No. I wish to speak with you. I have never mastered Middle Realm time conversion. What is the hour there?"

"Honestly, I haven't even bothered to wear my watch since we've been here. The sun's been up about half an hour."

"It's early evening here. Jinx and Lucas departed for Briar Hollow a few moments ago. My granddaughter asked that I call and share grave news from the human realm."

Tori's face registered surprise and concern. "Why didn't Jinx call herself? Is everyone okay? It's not my mom, is it?"

Hastening to reassure her, Barnaby said, "All your loved ones are well. Jinx spent every possible moment here in the Valley with Addie. I feel confident she will speak with you later when she has gathered more information about the crime."

Although she dreaded the answer, Tori said, "Who was the victim?"

"Linda Albert was killed in the library shortly after she opened the facility."

Stunned, Tori said, "That's horrible. Does Sheriff Johnson have a lead on the killer?"

"The Mother Tree has communicated to Jinx that Morgan le Fay most likely played a hand in the deed."

Her mind working overtime, Tori said, "I'll wake Connor and we'll go straight to Briar Hollow."

"You are needed here first. If Morgan becomes aware of Nysa's existence she could attempt to use the whelp as leverage. We must accelerate our plans to move Nysa and her mother to the Valley."

Tori looked skeptical. "Of course they'll be safer there, but is Shevington ready to take them?"

"At present, no," Barnaby admitted. "Before you present this plan to the dragonriders, we must ensure the accommodations we have in mind will suit the dragon's needs."

"Do you want us to meet you at the Lord High Mayor's house or the university?"

"Come directly to the campus. We will be waiting in Moira's workshop."

"Understood." Tori hesitated and then asked, "How did Jinx handle leaving Addie earlier than planned?"

"My granddaughter did what was demanded of her. Although I am not privy to the details, she did apparently have a terse exchange with the Mother Oak."

Tori winced. "I'll bet that was fun. Okay. We'll be there in a few minutes. If it wouldn't be too much trouble, could you have a couple of Madam Kaveh's dark roast endless cups on hand?"

Barnaby laughed. "I am well-acquainted with my grandson's difficulty with abrupt awakenings. Moira has already dispatched Dewey to secure beverages and breakfast food."

"Good thinking! See you soon." Tori signed off and stared at the mirror in her hand. After a few seconds of self-debate, she placed a call to Jinx.

When her friend's face appeared in the silver surface, Tori opened with, "You've been crying."

Plopping onto the easy chair in her alcove, Jinx said, "I have had a day. Barnaby told you about Linda?"

"He did. How's Beau holding up?"

"Doing the stiff-upper-lip soldier thing."

Sitting down on a boulder, Tori said, "I was afraid of that. At some point he'll have to face his real feelings. How are you?"

Jinx gave an exaggerated shrug. "Oh, you know. I had a fight with the Mother Oak, abandoned my daughter, came home to a murder, and Festus roofied Willow's nanny."

"You have had a day. So the nanny's a bitch?"

"Assuming she wakes up, we'll find out for ourselves, but ole Grumpy Whiskers hates her."

"Like we couldn't have seen that coming. I just wanted to check in before I wake Connor up and head for Shevington." Then, remembering her best friend duties, she added, "And you didn't abandon Addie."

"Check on her, okay?"

"You know I will, Jinksy. We'll come home as fast as we can."

Letting her composure crack for a second, Jinx said, "Hurry."

"We will. Hang in there."

Tori stowed the mirror in her pocket, stood, and looked out over the Sea of Ages.

"Blessed Moon you are the All Mother," she whispered,

"giving life from your body. All Father Sun, you are born to die and live again. Bless our friend Linda and see her safely to the Summerlands."

When Tori and Connor entered Moira's workshop on the top floor of the alchemy building two floating endless cups greeted them at the door.

"Thank the gods," Connor mumbled, grasping his tumbler like a lifeline. "Good morning, Barnaby, Moira."

The alchemist laughed. "It's supper time here."

Connor groaned as they crossed the room to the seating area by the windows. "Can't we do something about the time discrepancy between the realms?"

Barnaby looked up from the folder of papers in his lap. "How do you suggest we do that?"

Dropping into a chair across from his grandfather, Connor replied, "The Rivers of Time have been restored. Shouldn't that make a difference?"

"I hadn't considered that as a factor," Barnaby admitted. "I'll make a note to take it up with Miranda Winter and the Temporal Captains."

Tori gave Moira a quick hug before claiming one of the chairs for herself. "You'll have to excuse him," Tori said. "He has a bad case of what humans call jet lag."

"I anticipated this problem," Moira laughed. "I've added something to your coffee to help your bodies manage the transition, especially since you must cross the temporal barriers multiple times in the coming hours."

"Multiple times?" Tori said. "I thought we'd be leaving for Briar Hollow from here."

"We need to relocate the dragons before the day ends in the

Middle Realm," Barnaby said. "After we consult regarding the arrangements, you must return there and convince the whelp's parents to agree to the move. "

Connor sat forward in his chair. "The dragons live in close fellowship with their riders. If we're going to convince Giallo and Eingana, we need to provide quarters that will feel familiar to them."

At a wave of Moira's hand the air over the rug rippled and coalesced into an image of Fiona Ryan's back garden. The old woman sat quietly sipping tea at a wrought iron table reading *The Londinium Times* under the illumination of a floating lantern. Nearby a line of disgruntled dwarves leaned on their pickaxes.

Tori couldn't keep from laughing. "Those guys look miserable."

"Dwarves don't like their leisure time interrupted," Barnaby said. "Fiona has offered the use of her garden shed so that Nysa and Addie can be together. Moira and I will expand the structure to the dimensions you specify. What we cannot do with magic, the dwarves will accomplish through manual labor."

"Hold on," Tori said. "Do you really think it's a good idea to house dragons in Aunt Fiona's garden?"

Barnaby frowned. "Why wouldn't it be?"

"Because we're talking about Aunt Fiona. She's almost as bad as Aunt Clara."

Now thoroughly perplexed, Barnaby looked to his wife. "Do we know anyone named Clara?"

"She's referring to a 1960s television program that embraced an entertainment genre referred to as situation comedy," Connor said, brightening at the chance to discuss human culture. "The main character, a witch named Samantha, had an aunt called Clara whose spells always went awry."

Tori put a hand over her eyes and groaned. "Talking to you people can be like pulling teeth, you know that?"

When the furrow in Barnaby's brow deepened, she held up a hand. "No, dentistry has nothing to do with our current situation. What I'm trying to say is that Fiona tends to come up with bright ideas that go spectacularly wrong."

"Ah," Barnaby said. "Well, Lauren Frazier is in charge of security. Stanley lives next door, and Sgt. Periwinkle is most capable."

"Great," Tori muttered. "A water elf, Bigfoot, and a fairy walk into a bar... "

"Stanley doesn't drink," Barnaby said. "His species reacts poorly to intoxicating beverages."

"As much as I'd like to hear about a Bigfoot bender," Tori shot back, "I still don't think this is a good idea. And don't one of you dare say 'what could go wrong' because that's bad luck in any realm."

Now Connor looked perplexed, "But you said... "

Silencing him with a glare, Tori said, "What are the dimensions of the shed?"

A series of lines and numbers materialized around the structure. Connor studied the living diagram. "We'll need space for three dragons. Giallo will want to visit on a regular basis."

While he and Barnaby launched into an architectural discussion, Tori leaned toward Moira. "Are you good with this plan?"

The alchemist nodded. "The physical proximity will be beneficial for Addie and Nysa. I did have a private conversation with Lauren. She approves of having the child and the whelp living under more contained circumstances."

Tori's brows shot up. "Contained? You've met Addie. Contained is not a word I would use for her and I wouldn't describe Aunt Fiona as much of a disciplinarian."

"Young witches are difficult to discipline," Moira admitted, "but we are pressed for time. I'm sure the arrangement can be made to work."

"Well," Tori said, "that makes one of us."

Chapter Twelve

To Blair's embarrassment, half the morning was gone when she awakened with a feline stretch. Beside her bunk she found a covered plate and a note from Maeve.

"Will be on the grounds gathering field stones. Join me when you're ready."

Blair found the courtyard deserted except for Brick Deaver who stood at his workbench using a straightedge and pencil to mark blueprints.

"Good morning, young miss," he called. "Mistress Maeve asked me to keep a pot of coffee warm for you."

Accepting the offered cup, Blair sat on one of the stone benches along the wall to eat her breakfast. "What are your men working on today?"

"Your great beasties are helping the boys clear brush away from the grounds and the base of the cliff. We're uncovering more paved walkways and I want to set about replacing the damaged pavers. My bricklayers are working on the south wall..."

While the foreman droned on with pleasure, Blair finished her meal and helped herself to a second cup of coffee.

"You ran far under the rays of the moon," Giallo's voice said in her mind.

"Good morning, you big lout," she telegraphed back. *"Are you having a good time incinerating plants?"*

"The work provides amusement. The Mayor and his Lady used the portal to go to the Valley of Shevington this morning."

"Do you know why?"

"The Lady received a call in her looking glass. They left within minutes, but assured the Foreman they would return."

Blair waited for the talkative Deaver to pause for breath. "I'm sorry to interrupt, but where are Connor and Tori?"

"Mistress Tori received a message early this morning from Barnaby Shevington. The Lord High Mayor said they would return later in the day."

Sensing that the foreman was about to resume his construction lecture, Blair stood and stretched. "Thank you for the progress report, but Maeve left a note with my food asking that I join her."

"Of course!" Deaver beamed. "She offered to be of help in the day's labors. I asked if she minded gathering field stone. You'll find her in the open grass between the Abbey and the water."

Exiting the courtyard on the side of the building facing the Sea of Ages, Blair scanned the grounds until she spotted Maeve working beside a growing pile of stone.

Closing the distance between them Blair had to admit that she hadn't felt so energized since they left the Land of Virgo. When she came within earshot she called out, "Thank you for my breakfast."

Maeve looked up, sweat glistening on her skin. "Well, there

you are. I thought we might have to throw a bucket of cold water in your face to get you out of bed."

Blair ducked her head as a pink flush filled her cheeks. "I was out until dawn."

"Good. You look yourself again."

Stripping off her leather gherkin and rolling up her sleeves, Blair began to retrieve stones, which she added to the cairn Maeve had already assembled. "I made the mistake of asking Deaver what his men were doing today."

"I did the same thing when he arrived from Shevington," Maeve said, hefting a rock the size of a loaf of bread. "That one doesn't let the grass grow under his feet."

"Or anyone else's from what I can tell. I assume we are gathering stones in this area for a specific reason?"

"Deaver brought some kind of device with him from Shevington and used it to scan the grounds. A series of walled gardens once covered this area. He plans to reassemble them."

"Where's Davin? He didn't feel like picking up rocks all day?"

"He chose to supervise the dragons at the base of the cliff. We agreed that having a rider there would be a good idea. Deaver's men are still scared of our mounts."

"Only a fool would not fear dragon flame."

"Especially when the dragons are showing off and competing for how much brush they can destroy in a single breath."

"Is Nysa with them?"

Maeve straightened, shielding her eyes with her hand. "No, she's there in the grass."

Following her friend's gaze, Blair spotted the crimson whelp chasing butterflies. As they watched, Nysa tripped over her talons and tumbled into a patch of flowers with a happy giggle.

Though the ruby dragon was still no larger than a terrier, she moved with increasing strength and agility. Pulling herself upright, Nysa watched a brilliant blue butterfly flit toward the next patch of blooming flowers.

Rising experimentally on her haunches, the whelp awkwardly spread her wings. She executed a failed series of hops and flaps before her body put the necessary moves in sequence.

"She's got it now," Maeve said as Nysa rose inches off the ground and skimmed six feet of meadow before landing in a clump of clover.

Blair shook her head. "Giallo and Eingana are going to have a time with that one. I don't think she should be flying for at least another month."

"Maybe it's the effect of being in the Middle Realm. She could be experiencing enhanced development."

"That's why we're here. To expand the boundaries of archaic husbandry. I hope Nysa won't be the only whelp to get that chance."

Maeve put a hand on Blair's shoulder. "Other riders and their mounts will come from the Citadel. Give them time. It's no small thing to leave the mountains where you've lived your whole life."

"You left."

"Somebody had to come after you and keep you out of trouble," Maeve said with mock gravity. "I could hardly leave poor Giallo to deal with you on his own."

"A favor for which I am most grateful," the dragon's voice said in both their minds.

"Quit eavesdropping and get back to work," Blair ordered. "And stop scaring the workmen for the fun of it."

"You are in danger of becoming a pitiless drudge, a sheòid."

Laughing, both women returned to their work, but Blair's mind was still on Maeve's words. "If you came to keep an eye on me, why did Davin leave the Spica Mountains?"

"To keep an eye on *me*," Maeve replied, her lips curving into a smile. "He would go to far worse places if I asked it of him."

The Citadel riders had been making private wagers that Davin and Maeve would announce their betrothal during the next rainy season. Blair wondered how long it would take now that they were free agents in the Middle Realm.

"He's a good man," Blair said. "Perhaps even good enough to wed my friend."

"All things in their good time. What do you think of the Lord High Mayor and Tori?"

Dusting off her hands, Blair said, "He is a gentle soul. I fear she is a troubled one."

"What makes you say that?"

"Last evening when she came after me, she made pointed observations about the demands of leadership."

Maeve frowned. "Judging from the positive effect of her words on you, why is that a matter of concern? As best friend to the Witch of the Oak, I would think Tori well placed to understand such pressures."

"She is, but her references to herself carried the ring of bitterness. She referred to herself as a 'sidekick.'"

"What does that mean?"

"If she were a dragon rider we would say that she flies at the wingtip of the Witch of the Oak."

"As I fly on yours," Maeve said. "That is a position of trust and honor."

"It is, for each flyer, but Tori carries a wounded heart. I find her changed from our meeting in the Land of Virgo."

"Changed how?"

"Burdened by a great weight. I think it has something to do with her late father."

"How did he die?"

"I asked her the same question. She answered with a single word—'foolishly.'"

Maeve winced. "That does taste of bitterness."

"If the chance presents itself, I would hope to speak to her at greater length—to repay the kindness she showed me."

Maeve's eyes moved over Blair's shoulder. "Perhaps you will have that chance. She and the Lord High Mayor have returned."

Chapter Thirteen

Within minutes of our arrival in Briar Hollow, Darby blinked in with plates of hot food. We'd missed supper in the lair, which in brownie reasoning meant we hadn't eaten for days and stood poised on the brink of starvation.

I went into my alcove to take a brief mirror call from Tori. When I came out, my mother and Bertille Bergeron were sitting at the table with Lucas. "Hi," I said, bending to give my mother a hug. "It's good to see you."

"You too, honey," Mom said, squeezing me hard. "I know it's been a tough day."

"And then some," I agreed. "Hi, Bertille."

It would have been rude to come right out and say, *"What are you doing here?,"* but with a witch as intuitive as Bertille, I didn't have to voice the words for the sentiment to come across.

"Bertille's store was burglarized Sunday night," Mom explained. "She thinks there may be a connection between the incident and Linda's murder."

Taking my place beside Lucas on the other side of the table, I picked up my fork and said, "What brings you to that conclusion?"

"Sheriff Johnson came from the murder scene at the library to investigate what happened at my shop," Bertille said. "He thinks I had a break *in*, but according to the store mice it was really a break *out*."

Since one of our best friends is a rat, the rodent part of the statement didn't faze me. But what the heck had Bertille been harboring inside her store. "Excuse me?"

"The shop mice insist that a monster pushed its way out of a book, blew into a rage, trashed my store, and then escaped into the alleyway."

Lucas and I exchanged a sidelong look. Creatures emerging from books sounded like Seneca's area of expertise and suggested a connection to Morgan and Nevermore, the Land of Books.

"Did the mice say which book?" Lucas asked.

"No. They were on the counter eating cookies I left out for them. The volume came off a shelf by the front window. Sheriff Johnson won't let me back into the store until tomorrow morning. I'll try to find out the title then, but the place is a complete wreck."

Without warning, Festus vaulted onto the table, snickering when we all jumped.

"Would it hurt you to give us a heads up before you do that kind of thing?" I asked, using my napkin to wipe splattered gravy off my blouse.

"Yeah," the werecat said with deadpan seriousness. "Offering advance warning is against the feline code of ethics."

"Why do I even bother?" I grumbled. "Did you leap up here for the fun of it or do you have something to contribute?"

Affecting a diffident sniff, Festus said, "I always have something to contribute. The situation in Bertille's shop sounds like the perfect excuse to field test my 2RABID prototype."

Silence greeted the statement until Mom said, "Okay, I'll bite. What's a 'too rabid?'"

"You remember the RABIES tag Chase and I used on Chesterfield's shop?"

He was referring to a Registry-issued device called the Residual Active Base Imprint Energy Scanner—RABIES for short.

Festus loved the idea of the gizmo, which relied on a mixture of magic and technology to display the imprint of all activities in an area for the past 72 hours.

He hated that using it involved wearing a collar with a dangling silver disc. The werecat described the look and feel as "too damned domesticated" for any self-respecting feline.

Unbeknownst to us, Festus, with help from BEAR tech genius Stank Preston, had designed a second generation model. At Festus's direction, Lucas retrieved a ruggedized field case the size of a paperback book from the war room and placed it on the table.

"One of the biggest drawbacks of the first generation RABIES was the need for a second person to outfit the wearer with the device," Festus said, assuming a professorial tone. "Check this out."

The werecat executed a well-placed paw smack on the latch. The case snapped open to reveal an interior lined with thick foam. The padding protected what looked like a pair of behind-the-head earphones.

"Ladies and gentlemen, allow me to introduce the first field-ready iteration of 2RABID."

Using his paw again, Festus slapped the device and ducked his head. The unit rose out of the case and settled on the back of his neck with the two "headphones" positioned behind his jaw on either side.

"How the heck did you do that?" I asked.

"There's a proximity scanner built into the lock," Festus replied. "The 2RABID uses the same fairy-dust powered engine as a GNATS drone. The built in AI calculates the distance and trajectory to the user and engages the autopilot."

Lucas let out a low whistle. "That's smart. Ironweed revolutionized Fae tech when he figured out how to harness fairy dust."

In a rare show of magnanimity, thin though it might have been, Festus said, "Ironweed may have revealed the potential, but Stank and I have a far more elegant approach to tech development, starting with voice control."

Clearing his throat, he said, "Reba, engage."

LEDs embedded in the 2RABID glowed purple.

I couldn't stop myself. "You named your 2RABID 'Reba?'"

"Yeah," Festus said. "We needed something with soft vowels and distinct consonants. You know, like Alexa. It's the trigger word."

It was also the name of a red-headed, barrel-riding country singer from Oklahoma, but I decided not to go down that rabbit trail.

"Got it. What exactly does Reba do?"

As soon as I said the name, the purple glow returned, along with a lecture from Festus. "We don't say her name unless we want her to do something. Let me handle this."

Putting my hands up in deference, I said, "By all means, Q. Demonstrate your spy bling."

Festus gave me an arch glare. "Reba, activate scanning beam."

"Beam activated."

A light shot out of both sides of the device, merging six

inches in front of the werecat's snout. It flared out to a field roughly ten feet wide extending some fifteen feet into the lair.

The light struck the hearth and activated a ghostly image of Festus curled up asleep with Willow tucked under his chin.

"You old softie," Kelly said. "No wonder Willow idolizes you."

Juggling embarrassment with pleasure at receiving a compliment from my mother, Festus growled, "Reba, condense scan radius to five by three."

"Beam retracted."

Now the 2RABID revealed a wavering image of Darby down on his hands and knees using a sticky roller to get cat hair off the Persian rug.

"What an incredible device," Bertille said with such open admiration Festus's chest instantly puffed out. "We should be able to see exactly what happened in my store and corroborate the mice's account."

"I like you," Festus said. "You catch on quick."

"Uh, question?" I said.

"What?"

"Obviously if we're alone in the store your gizmo will work just fine, but how is having the 2RABID talk good for stealth ops?"

"My bad," Festus said. "Reba, initiate silent mode." Then to prove that it worked, he swiveled toward the table. "Reba, extend beam ten feet."

The scan field lengthened to reveal the image of my father diving into a massive bowl of ice cream slathered in chocolate sauce.

"That man!" Mom said. "No wonder he had to let his belt out a notch. And I bet I can guess who's serving up those midnight snacks."

"Don't get mad at Darby," I said, going to the brownie's defense. "He worships Dad. Darby would never tell him no."

"Oh, I know," Mom said. "Jeff will get an ear full for manipulating his friend, too."

Festus scratched at his left ear. The motion disengaged the 2RABID, which floated back to its nest of foam. The instant it settled in place, the case snapped shut and locked.

"So what do you say?" Festus asked Bertille. "Field trip to your place?"

The bookstore owner looked at me. "I think it's a wonderful idea. What do you think, Jinx?"

When I tried to answer, a yawn came out instead of words. "Let's table the investigation until morning," I suggested. "This has been a day from hell. We'll make a plan at breakfast. You're welcome to spend the night in one of the guest rooms, Bertille."

"Thank you," she said. "I'll accept that offer. Getting an early start tomorrow sounds like a good idea and frankly, I'm a little nervous to be out and about in Briar Hollow at night until we know what's really going on."

Looking back, my operational call proved the wisdom of "don't put off until tomorrow what you can do today" since Tuesday was about to present us with a whole new slate of complications.

Chapter Fourteen

SHEVINGTON

A circle of floating lamps surrounded the table in Aunt Fiona's garden. While Connor reviewed supply requisitions from the stables, Tori worked on an alchemy lecture.

She held out her hand and summoned one of the endless cups from Madam Kaveh, prompting Connor to observe, "You shouldn't be drinking coffee at this hour."

"Practice what you preach, Mr. Mayor," Tori said. "You haven't let that cup get six inches away from your hand since we got here."

Connor grinned as he folded a memorandum into the shape of a bird. With a gentle toss, he sent the document skyward. The wings fluttered and headed into the night.

"I'm a busy chief executive," he said, "who has been playing with dragons for days instead of tending to his paperwork. This is a good chance to stay awake and get caught up."

"Well," Tori said, lifting a paragraph off the screen and suspending it beside the computer, "not to burst your happy java bubble, but the coffee switched to decaf two hours ago. Was that memo for Ellis?"

'Yes. I'm bringing him up to speed on the dragons. We'll have to get Eingana to agree to inform Ellis before she flies to the upper valley to hunt. The sight of a full grown dragon in the sky over their paddock could disrupt the unicorn breeding program. What are those paragraphs for?"

"Material for the mid-term. Since I don't know what will be happening or where we'll be at test time, I want to get the exam written ahead of time."

"Good thinking," Connor said as he yawned and stretched. "These time changes are going to be the death of me."

"Oh stop," Tori said. "Your body still thinks it's early morning in the Middle Realm."

"My eyes tell me it's the middle of the night in Shevington and we're trapped listening to a gang of dwarves singing off key while they work."

Without looking up from her keyborad, Tori sang, *"Heigh-ho, heigh-ho, it's home from work we go."*

Connor stared at her. "What in the name of the gods was that?"

She raised her eyebrows. "You're kidding, right? Snow White? Walt Disney? The seven dwarves? I thought you were supposed to be a student of human popular culture."

Flipping open his notebook Connor scribbled a few lines. "Can I get that on NetFlux?"

"Net*Flix*," Tori giggled. "Try Disney+. Jinx hooked Addie up with an account. Adeline has the username and password. You might as well entertain yourself since we're stuck here until the dragon habitat is ready."

Connor settled in with his movie and Tori went back to her writing. Barnaby had left them to oversee the finishing touches on the shed reconstruction. They hadn't told Addie that she might see Nysa the next day, but the child's serene expression when she kissed them goodnight told Tori the little girl already knew.

Sometime around 3 a.m. the stout dwarf in charge of the work crew stomped over, dripping wet, and announced the project complete.

Struggling to keep a straight face, Connor said, "I see you tested the fire suppression system."

The dwarf's bushy brows furrowed into a scowl. "Very funny. I struck a match under the damn thing and got half-drowned for my trouble, but it works. Now quit playing with your toys and inspect the place so we can get some sleep."

The shed, which had been transformed into a cozy stone barn, passed with flying colors. After the dwarves marched into the night, Tori wrote a note for Aunt Fiona and slid it under the back door, then she and Connor walked through the darkened streets to the portal near the stables.

"Do you want to give Jinx a call before we go back to the Middle Realm?" he asked.

"I hope she's asleep. She looked exhausted when I checked on her earlier. If everything goes according to schedule, we'll be back in Briar Hollow for breakfast. We do have a murder to solve."

Connor caught hold of her hand. "We really haven't had time to talk about that. I'm so sorry. I know you enjoyed visiting with Linda when she came into the store."

"Everyone loved Linda," Tori said in a thick voice. "When Barnaby told me about her death, my first thought was to go straight to Briar Hollow and turn the place inside out until we found the murderer, but that's probably exactly what Morgan wants. So, we do this the right way. First we make sure Nysa and Eingana are safe, then we help catch a killer."

They finished their walk in silence. Tori had apologized for her behavior during the Las Vegas trip, but since then Connor couldn't shake the feeling that she'd been trying too hard to seem normal. The news of Linda's death hadn't helped.

Jinx advised him not to push, and Connor trusted his sister's instincts, but Tori was definitely keeping something from him.

When they stepped through the portal and into the abbey courtyard, however, Connor's mind instantly switched to a different set of worries. "I should check in with Brick," he said, taking a step toward the foreman's worktable.

Tori caught his sleeve and pulled him back. "Nice try. You're coming with me to talk to Blair."

"But Brick might need more supplies for the restoration."

"I haven't noticed Brick having any trouble asking for what he needs. What's wrong with you? The dragon husbandry program at the University was your idea."

Connor flushed. "I thought we'd have proper facilities to offer—not a hastily expanded garden shed. Don't get me wrong. The dwarves did a great job, but one small barn doesn't represent the best Shevington has to offer."

"Get your civic pride under control, Mr. Mayor," Tori laughed. "Eingana will be more than satisfied living in Fiona's garden because it will make Nysa and Addie happy. Honestly, I wish we could hire those dwarves out in the human realm. We could charge the earth for that kind of rock work."

He looked blank. "But why? Rocks are free."

Tori leaned closer and kissed him. "Sometimes you're too cute."

Though delighted by the spontaneous affection, Connor had no idea what she meant. "I am? What did I do?"

Chuckling, Tori steered him clear of Brick Deaver, who greeted them with a hearty wave. "We'll talk about the state of your cuteness later. Right now we need to find Blair."

Overhearing her, Deaver said, "She and Maeve are stacking

stones with the lads. You'll find them out front about half way to the water."

When they stepped outside, the speed of the workers' progress stopped them short. Stone walls edged a series of paved paths that had once connected adjunct buildings.

Red flags delineated the outline of recently unearthed foundations, and neatly mowed grass replaced the wild tangle of weeds that had obscured the grounds.

"How could they have done all this while we were gone?" Connor asked.

Tori glanced at her watch, which was set to Briar Hollow time. "How long were we gone?"

Counting on his fingers, Connor said, "Eight or so hours in Valley time and maybe four here? I can't keep up with all this realm hopping."

"Me either, but we're early enough in the day that Blair and the others will still be fresh. This deal we've cooked up might be a harder sell at the end of the day. I wouldn't want to face Giallo in the mood he was in last night."

"He was worried about Blair. You said yourself she was harming herself by not shifting."

"She was," Tori agreed. "Giallo felt her distress—and she's going to be able to feel his when we announce we want to take Nysa to the Valley today."

A shout from the field caught their attention. Blair stood beside Maeve and an enormous pile of rocks. She waved her arms to get their attention.

As Connor and Tori started across the open ground, he said, "I wish I understood more about the bond between riders and their dragons."

"That will be one of the added benefits of having dragons in Shevington. You'll be able to get to know them better."

Grinning from ear to ear, he said, "I hate the reason, but

man, don't you love the sound of that? Dragons in Shevington. It's a dream come true."

Unfortunately, Giallo didn't share that enthusiasm. Half an hour later with the group once again gathered at the stone benches, smoke curled from the drake's snout. *"Show me again."*

Tori rotated the holographic image of Fiona's garden shed. "We expanded and reinforced the building. There's room for all three of you to sleep when you stay over, Giallo. You'll have free range of the skies and can hunt in the foothills at the far end of the Valley."

The drake studied the projection with open derision. *"One breath of fire and that pathetic hut will be gone."*

"That's why we went with stone walls and added a fire suppression system," Connor offered. "At worst you'd singe some of the interior."

"There will be no fire," Eingana said in a firm voice. *"We have already agreed to this plan, husband."*

"We did not agree to move our daughter with less than a day's notice."

"We wouldn't ask you to do this if we didn't think Nysa would be safer in The Valley," Tori said. "She and Addie will be together, which is a good thing. Right?"

When Giallo didn't answer, Eingana tried to cajole her mate. *"Think how unhappy you would be if denied the companionship of Blair McBride."*

Giallo snorted. *"I think only of the peace and quiet such circumstances would entail."*

Blair, who had been leaning against one of the trees shading the area uncrossed her arms and pushed off the trunk with her shoulder.

"He doesn't mean that," she said, "and he isn't opposed to the plan. He just can't face the idea of leaving his child in a place so far removed from his watchful eye."

"There's a lot of that going around," Tori said. "Jinx didn't like moving Addie to the Valley either, but Giallo, you don't have to leave Nysa. You and Eingana are welcome in Shevington if that's what you decide would be better."

"I am free to stay there," Eingana said. *"I have no rider. Giallo's place is here."*

Blair stepped closer to the drake and ran her hand along the curve of his jaw. *"We'll go every day to see Nysa,"* she told him along their private connection. *"I know it breaks your heart to do this, but there isn't another way."*

"We will take part in bringing Morgan le Fay to justice?"

"Do you really believe I would miss that fight?"

A rumbling laugh rose in his chest. *"No, a sheòid, I do not."* Then, broadcasting his words so everyone could hear, the drake added, *"Very well. We will go to Shevington's Valley and see this hut with our own eyes."*

Chapter Fifteen

With Nysa's relocation to Shevington decided, the group returned to the Cloisters. Tori and Connor started to break down their makeshift camp while Blair went to her quarters to pack her saddlebags.

She was folding a set of fresh clothes, when Maeve spoke from the doorway. "May I come in?"

"Of course," Blair said, pointing to the lone chair. "Thanks to Brick and his carpenters, I can even offer you a place to sit."

Maeve accepted the invitation. "I don't mind telling you that I'm jealous of your trip to Shevington. Connor's stories make the Valley sound like a wonderous place."

"We may stay the night there. Giallo will feel better about the separation if we don't leave until he's assured that Eingana and Nysa are settled. The next time we visit Nysa, you'll have to come with us and see the city for yourself."

"I'd like that," Maeve said, sniffing as a breeze moved through the room carrying with it the scent of smoke. Wrinkling her nose, she asked, "Is Giallo still belching dragon fire?"

"And sparks," Blair sighed. "He agreed to this plan because he has no desire to quarrel with Eingana, but he doesn't like it.

Pray that he restrains himself. Setting their new home on fire the moment we arrive would not make for a good first impression. Normally he has better self-control."

"He's never been a father. I didn't think he would agree to this plan at all."

"Neither did I," Blair admitted. "After the meeting broke up, Giallo still tried to talk Connor into letting us wait one more night, but Eingana put her foot down."

Maeve shuddered, "Thankfully I missed that exchange. Stay in the Valley as long as you need to ensure Giallo is satisfied with the arrangements. Brick will keep us busy while you're gone."

"That man is a taskmaster. Another day of his 'wee chores' and you may wish you were back at the Citadel flying the swamp patrol."

The two friends fell into an easy back and forth about the Abbey renovation and Blair's plan to begin morning and evening patrols. She wanted to gain a better sense of the terrain around the grounds and map the mountains and shoreline to address weak spots on the perimeter.

Nothing they'd yet learned about Morgan le Fay suggested the sorceress had immediate plans to venture into the Middle Realm, but the precaution of taking Nysa to Shevington had them all on edge.

"Then it's settled," Blair said, buckling the straps on her bags. "You and Davin will fly the Sea of Ages tonight, and tomorrow Giallo and I will join you to survey the foothills."

When she moved to sling the pack over her shoulder, Maeve said, "Wait. There's something I want to discuss with you before you go."

"Is something wrong?" Blair asked, putting her things on the floor and sitting on the edge of the cot.

"No, but I have been thinking about the bonding between Addie and Nysa."

"What about it?"

"Can we really be certain that Addie is the first witch to be dragonborn?"

The question took Blair by surprise. "Why would you ask that?"

"Thanks to the Witch of the Oak and her associates we understand the truth of why the Ruling Elders sent our flight to the Spica Mountains."

"Yes."

"But how can we know what more was hidden from us? How can we trust that we've been given a complete history of drakon-culture? We're not only taking on the task of rearing the next generation of dragons without unnatural restraints, we're also taking part in training a witch as a dragon rider."

"And you would feel more confident in that task if some guide existed to give direction to that training."

"Wouldn't you?"

After a moment of indecision, Blair lowered her voice and said, "I planned to wait until we returned to speak of this, but Giallo remembers an extensive library here at the Abbey."

That news brought Maeve to the edge of her chair. "Really? Where was the building? We've found the outlines of numerous foundations."

"Giallo says the archive was housed underground. Only a select few scholars were allowed access to the books and documents . Giallo was only a whelp when he was taken from the Abbey. He doesn't know the exact location, but he believes the collection might still be intact."

Her eyes now gleaming with excitement, Maeve said, "When did he tell you this? And what are we going to do about it?"

"He told me during our argument last evening. He's

convinced that we will never uncover the Abbey's mysteries using our human eyes."

"We do see better at night in weretiger form," Maeve agreed. "Maybe that's why all the riders in our flight are tiger shifters. There could be all manner of secrets hidden on these grounds. Did you notice anything unusual last night?"

Blair shook her head. "No, I kept my big cat caged for too long. When I set her free, she wanted only to run and stalk the dark places. I did find evidence of ruins as far away as a mile from here though. There is no question that Drake Abbey has more to reveal."

Reaching into her jerkin, she pulled out a folded piece of paper. "I sketched what I could remember before I fell asleep last night."

Maeve studied the drawing. "Before the flights dispersed in time to scatter the Temporal Arcana, perhaps they secreted the records of our culture here at Drake Abbey."

Looking up from the paper she said, "Blair, the patrols can wait another night. Davin and I must shift tonight and begin the search for the library in earnest."

At the portal in the courtyard Tori addressed the Attendant. "Fiona Ryan's garden in Shevington, please."

"Destination acquired"

"Okay, I'll go through first. Then the dragons. Connor, you and Blair bring up the rear."

Giallo balked. *"Your plan is flawed. We need a larger means of entry."*

"Nice try," Blair said, "You've seen the portal expand. Quit stalling."

Beside Eingana, Nysa giggled. Her father turned his

ponderous head and pretended to glare at the whelp. *'Do you doubt your sire's wisdom, you insolent child?"*

At that fake admonition Nysa fell over laughing and holding her sides.

"Wow," Tori said. "She's *really* terrified. You're some harsh disciplinarian, Giallo."

The drake grumbled low in his throat. *"We waste time. Let us begin this journey."*

Laughing Tori stepped into the matrix and emerged beside Fiona's prize rose bushes. She moved aside and made room for the dragons as they lumbered through the portal.

Nysa barely cleared the energy field before Addie rushed forward and tackled the whelp with a joyous cry. Aunt Fiona bustled along in her wake waving her hands in welcome.

"You'll have to forgive my grand-niece. She's been talking non-stop about Nysa since Connor told us that you all were coming. You must be Blair, and this is Giallo and you're Eingana. Goodness gracious you two do have a beautiful daughter! Now, come along with me and let me show you what the dwarves did to my garden shed. You all are just not going to believe what a dragon palace they created for you. Addie! Nysa! Come on babies, come with us. "

Looking stunned by the effusive, non-stop greeting, Blair and the dragons followed Fiona into the shed.

"Well," Connor said looking at Tori, "so much for being worried about an awkward arrival."

Laughing, she said, "You should know Aunt Fiona better than that by now. Give her another 15 minutes and she'll have Giallo eating out of her hand. I'd say our work is done here for now."

Chapter Sixteen

THE LAIR

When Lucas and I went into our apartment, my eyes immediately fell on the nursery door, which stood ajar. The interior, illuminated by the dragon nightlight Amity found for Addie, glowed softly.

I knew I shouldn't, but I went into the room and picked up the blanket from the crib, burying my face in the soft yarn. A few seconds later, I felt Lucas move behind me. His arms encircled my body and I leaned against him still holding the blanket.

"You're not beating yourself up again, are you?" he asked.

"No," I said, breathing in our baby's sweet scent, "just missing her. I wish we could see what she's been up to today."

Word to the wise. If you make wishes in a fairy mound, be prepared for things to happen. The blanket in my hands tugged to be set free. When I let it go the rectangle floated about four feet away and stiffened into a makeshift screen.

The image that appeared showed a flurry of activity in Aunt Fiona's garden. A gang of disgruntled looking dwarves appeared to be remodeling the shed under Tori and Connor's direction.

The sun hung low on the horizon, but enough light remained to illuminate Addie's golden curls. She sat on Stan's lap watching the workers and asking questions, which the Sasquatch patiently answered.

When my aunt appeared to take Addie inside, our daughter threw her arms around Stan's shaggy neck and kissed him on the cheek. Then she toddled over to get hugs from my brother and Tori.

My chest tightened when Tori kissed Addie's hair before passing her off to Aunt Fiona. "Look at her," I said. "That baby is surrounded by people who love her."

"Are you just now catching on to that?" Lucas asked. His breath tickled at my ear and made me laugh.

"No," I said. "I'm just now catching on that we need everyone to help us keep her safe and that I've been whining about being a bad mother instead of getting on with things."

"You don't whine... much," Lucas said.

"Gee, thanks a lot, bub."

"Again with the 'bub' thing?"

"Quit acting like a bub, and I'll quit calling you one. Come on. Let's go to bed. I'm exhausted."

He followed me into our bedroom. As we changed into our night clothes, a thought suddenly occurred to me. "Hey," I said. "Why isn't Greer out there reading by the fire?"

"Because she's in Lundenwic," Lucas said, throwing back the covers and climbing into bed. "Brenna's with her."

The baobhan sith and the Reborn Witch in the seediest town in all the Middle Realm? How convenient that Lucas forgot to mention that.

"Okay," I said, joining him. "What are you up to?"

"I'm not up to anything but falling asleep," he said, yawning as he pulled me closer. "But they're trying to get a lead on Morgan le Fay."

Under normal circumstances learning that kind of information at bedtime would have guaranteed a night of insomnia, but

I couldn't fend off the fatigue that had been tugging at me for hours.

As I fell asleep with my head on Lucas's shoulder, I said a silent prayer that whatever Greer and Brenna were doing in Lundenwic, they would be safe.

The Devil's Hoof, Lundenwic

As Brenna and Greer walked through the warren-like streets of Lundenwic, the local citizenry shrank into darkened doorways and grimy alleys.

"Are they more afraid of you or me?" Brenna asked from beneath the cowl of the dark cloak she wore.

"I would venture to say we instill equal amounts of foreboding," Greer replied, shooting a feral grin at a man lounging under a flickering gas streetlight.

The vagrant pulled his collar high around his neck, gave a nervous tip of his filthy cap, and scurried away.

"You like doing that," Brenna accused.

"I do," Greer admitted. "A reputation for ruthlessness eliminates the need for so much small talk."

"Neither of us lack for reputation," Brenna said with an ironic snort, "on either side of the law."

They paused at the corner across the street from a witches pub called *The Devil's Hoof*. "When did you last see Melinda Owen?" Greer asked.

Brenna considered the question. "Sometime around the witch hunts under James I, when she and the others of her coven quit the human realm for Lundenwic."

"You will find her little changed in 400 years."

The round woman who met them at the pub's entrance wore a black robe and cape. She smiled when she recognized Greer.

"What brings you to my doorstep this cold, dank night?" she asked. "And who's your friend?"

When Brenna threw back her hood the buzz of voices fell silent. "Hello, Melinda. Fare thee well?"

"It's true," the witch gasped. "I see it in your eyes. You've regained your natural powers."

"I have."

"Rumor says you fell through the fires that separate the realms."

"I did, and I would not recommend the experience."

"You swore fealty to the Witch of the Oak the day Irenaeus Chesterfield died."

"Yes."

Melinda shifted her body to ensure every listening ear could pick up what she said next. "Then you're welcome at *The Devil's Hoof,* and those that bear grudges from the old days best take heed of that fact."

After a minute, chairs scraped against the warped floorboards, tankards were raised, and conversations resumed.

"Thank you, Melinda," Brenna said. "We are not here to cause agitation."

"Why are you here?"

"That," Greer said, "is a topic best raised in private."

Calling out to the bartender, Melinda said, "Seamus, a bottle of whisky and glasses in my office, and stoke the fire while you're at it."

The trio made their way through the crowded pub ignoring the stares and whispers as they passed. At the rear of the building, they ducked through a low, heavy-beamed doorway into a small cave of a room.

Bundles of dried plants hung from the ceiling. The book cases sagged under the weight of ancient tomes bound and strapped in leather. A wood fire blazed in the grate where three chairs sat arranged around a low table. The tray resting on its surface held a bottle and three glasses.

When Melinda took her seat a black cat appeared from beneath the desk and curled in her lap.

"Is that Lucifer?" Brenna asked.

Stroking the animal's sleek fur, Melinda said, "It is. He's a bit long in tooth these days, but still the best familiar in the three realms."

As if to confirm the assessment, the cat fixed its glowing green eyes on the sorceress and began to purr.

"Yes," Brenna said, "I recognize you, too. Thank you for your forgiveness, Lucifer."

Melinda tilted her head and listened. "He says you've changed."

"I have," Brenna agreed. "In more ways than you can imagine. I work in an apothecary with my descendants, Gemma and Tori. They are both exceptional witches and alchemists."

"You are proud of them."

"Immeasurably."

Moving her gaze to Greer, Melinda asked, "Did the Witch of the Oak send you?"

"Her husband," the baobhan sith answered. "We must speak of dangerous things, Melinda. I would ask that you protect our privacy."

The witch raised a plump hand and murmured, *"Bullam faciendo scutum pro audientia narratio tutum locum."*

A bubble for the making, a shield for the hearing, a safe space for the talking.

The darkness in the corners crawled forward and knit together until the three women sat within the confines of a secure cubicle. Content with the closeness of the arrangement, Lucifer put his head on his paws and closed his eyes.

"You were always a no-nonsense spell caster," Brenna said. "A practical witch."

"Practical magic always wins in the end," Melinda said. "Now, have the two of you brought trouble to my door?"

"I sincerely hope not," Greer said. "We are here to ask if you have knowledge of Morgan le Fay."

At that, the black cat's eyes snapped open and his fur stood on end.

"Settle down, Lucifer," Melinda said, running a hand along the cat's back. "What I know of the Goddess of the Crows is common knowledge to all the Fae. She faced the Witch of the Oak at the Battle of Tir na nÓg and was handed her broom for her troubles."

Brenna chuckled. "I am sorry you were not there to see it, Melinda. Morgan arrived with all her sisters and they were no match for those who stood with Jinx Hamilton."

"Aye," Melinda said. "The young Witch of the Oak has caused quite a stir throughout the realms. She does not handle issues in a conventional manner."

"For the first thirty odd years of her life, Jinx believed herself to be human," Greer said. "Her patterns of thought are not thoroughly Fae, but I have found that oddity to be a strength rather than a detriment."

"Then why be concerned about Morgan le Fay?" Melinda asked. "If the Witch of the Oak defeated her once, she can do it again."

Only the sound of the crackling flames and Lucifer's purring broke the silence until Brenna said, "A child has been born, one who came into the world in alternate time and wields the wand of Merlin. She is to the dragons bound."

Melinda leaned forward in her chair, the flickering fire highlighting the eagerness of her features. "The Dragon Witch? She was thought to be the stuff of legends. Does the aos si confirm this as truth?"

"Myrtle senses the power within the child," Brenna said. "Although Addie grew rapidly in the Land of Virgo, she is but a toddler. She has not yet heard the call of her quest in life, but she listens for it."

"Does the girl possess the tools of Merlin?"

"The sword and the wand, yes, but not the pentacles. Guinevere's tarot cards remain lost."

"There is more," Greer said. "Seneca of Blackfriars believes Morgan to be in league with the Master Publishers of Nevermore."

"If that is true," Melinda said, "Morgan would attempt to make use of the Compass of Chronos."

"To what end?" Brenna asked.

Their hostess made a derisive sound. "Come, Brenna. You do not need metaphysical schooling from me. Morgan would employ the Compass for one purpose only, to rewrite history so that she, not Arthur, gained the primacy of Camelot."

"So that is how the realms would collapse," Greer mused. "Time would not end, it would be reset with a new narrative."

"Correct," Melinda said, "and not a story in which any of us would recognize ourselves or the realms as we know them. What moves has Morgan made thus far?"

"We believe her to be behind the death of a human woman within reach of the fairy mound in Briar Hollow," Greer replied. "A woman known to Jinx, but not an intimate associate."

"I have no knowledge of these things," Melinda said, "but I can tell you this. Morgan never betrays her hand with direct action. If she seeks access to the witch child, she will first deprive Jinx Hamilton of her greatest strength. I would construct my defenses to that end."

Chapter Seventeen

DRAKE ABBEY

At the end of the work day Brick Deaver and his crew left for the Valley. Maeve and Davin shared a simple meal and then sent their dragons skyward to fly surveillance patterns over the abbey grounds.

After the great beasts lifted off the flagstones, their riders stood beneath the empty frame of the vaulted window and watched the moon rise.

"Are you ready to do this?" Maeve asked.

"Ready?" Davin laughed. "I'll take an adventure over burning brush and hefting rocks any day. Besides, I'm always ready to shift and run in the night with you."

"Behave yourself," Maeve scolded, but she was smiling.

"If Blair discovered foundations a mile away, we have vast ground to cover in search of this mythic library. Do you have a plan?"

"Instinct tells me we should begin in the labyrinth."

"Why?"

"Think about how we lived our lives at the Citadel."

He let out a scoffing sound. "We were warriors in training

with no conflict on the horizon. At least here we're building something."

"That's true," Maeve conceded, "but we were also trained as scholars. We assumed intellectual pastimes were meant to combat the boredom of a lonely posting lost in time. Now that I've seen this place, I think education and study were always part of drakonculture."

Scrubbing at his jaw, Davin said, "Master Kian tried to make us believe dragon riders lived apart from Fae culture, but he may well have lied. Even in ruins the ghosts of a thriving community haunt this abbey. I would like to know the truth about the place drakonculture once held in the Three Realms."

"Such knowledge may be a double-edged sword," Maeve warned. "If we discover that truth, we will have a responsiblity to take up any mantle cast aside in the name of deception."

"That's why we followed Blair, isn't it? To discover the truth about our heritage?"

"Among others. We could not let our friend face an unknown world alone."

Drawing her close, Davin said, "I hope Blair cherishes your loyalty as much as I do."

"She does. I am her wing woman."

"A position that demands exceptional intuition," he said. "If you are correct and our antecedents were warrior scholars, then a place of contemplation like the labyrinth would be a likely location to disguise the entrance to a secret library."

Maeve's smile flashed in the dim light. "You should not go to such lengths to disguise the brightness of your mind, my love."

"A man who pretends to be glib can learn much," he said. "Let us test your theory."

They kissed in the moonlight before stepping apart and turning their thoughts inward. Calling to the big cats slumbering within, the riders brought the flame of shifter magic upward along their spines until the energy infused their eyes.

Both melted downward, clothes falling away as their bodies morphed. Within seconds two tigers nuzzled one another's whiskers, thick muscle visible under black-striped, umber coats.

Leaning his forehead against Maeve's, Davin said in a husky voice,"You are even more beautiful in your true form."

She answered with a rumbling purr. "And you are a rogue no matter the body you inhabit. Focus on the task at hand. There will be time for play later."

Together the weretigers padded out of the courtyard. Seen through their enhanced night vision, the lines and contours of the abbey's grounds appeared in stark shades of luminous gray.

Breaking into an easy lope, the cats covered the open ground with brazen confidence as smaller creatures scurried for cover.

Maeve jogged to a stop at the stone that marked the start of the labyrinth. "Let us follow the path to the center of the maze. If nothing reveals itself, we will move into the undergrowth."

She took the lead on the circuitous path, letting conscious thought bleed away in favor of sharper, more primal senses. Her eyes scanned the ground and traced the outline of broken statuary scattered throughout the long-neglected garden.

Nothing unusual happened until her paw struck the mandala at the center of the maze. Constructed of tiny bits of colored rock, the medallion featured a tiger rearing on its hind legs, forepaws wrapped around a dragon.

On first glance, the scene depicted a fierce battle, but closer examination showed the two creatures locked in a tight embrace. The instant Maeve touched the symbol, a shaft of light broke through the scudding clouds.

The beam struck a worn sculpture of a sleeping dragon half obscured in a patch of weeds. The wind picked up, brushing over the tigers' coats as a voice whispered, "Set free the one who sleeps."

Davin growled low in his throat. "I do not like this."

"Calm yourself. We are alone. There is no danger in having a closer look."

He followed as Maeve approached the sculpture. Both cats circled the dragon. "How do we set free that which is carved in stone?" he asked.

"Folded wings cannot fly. Let us see if these will open."

Placing her forehead against the sculpture, Maeve leaned into the left wing. Davin copied her move on the right. Their combined strength caused the dragon's eyes to open with a mechanical snick.

Both weretigers jumped when a scraping sound echoed in the empty garden. As they watched, the dragon unwound from its crouched position, stepped off the pedestal, and moved aside. Settling on the grass, the wings and eyes closed again and the creature turned to stone.

The shaft of light now revealed a rusted iron handle in the center of a heavy metal plate. Examining the possible entrance, Davin said, "We will need hands, and perhaps tools, to open that."

"All true, but more importantly, we cannot investigate further without Blair present."

"Should we leave this discovery exposed?"

Moving beside him, Maeve nuzzled his ear. "I can only guess, but I believe the morning sun will solve that problem for us. Now, what were you saying about running in the night with me?"

Shevington, O'Hanson's Pub

Stan downed the last of his ginger ale and signaled the bar maid for another round. "Would you like anything else, Blair?"

The dragonrider pushed away an empty plate that had held a Scotch egg and a charcuterie board. "I couldn't eat another bite if I tried, but I would like a cup of hot tea."

After the Sasquatch passed on the order he said, "Well, was the Lord High Mayor right about the food?"

"I have to be honest with you, Stan. I found the idea of a sausage wrapped hard boiled egg fried in oil disgusting when Connor suggested it, but that was delicious."

Her shaggy companion let out a barking belly laugh. "He'll be delighted to add another convert to his list of conquests. I've seen Connor put away half a dozen of those things and never blink."

"You don't care for Scotch eggs?" Blair asked, accepting a steaming mug of tea from the waitress.

"My people are vegetarians."

"Are there others of your kind here in the Valley?"

"No," Stan said, a hint of sadness in his voice, "but my great-grandfather was the chief of the Tsul 'Kalu who negotiated a peace with Barnaby when he and the first settlers arrived in America from England."

When Blair looked confused, he said, "That's what the Cherokee called us. Our language wouldn't sound like anything but grunts, hoots, and yowls to you."

"How long have you lived in the Valley?"

Flicking a bit of lint off the sleeve of his tweed jacket, the Sasquatch said, "I was raised in Shevington, but my brethren prefer to clomp around the woods in the human realm scaring people and beating on trees."

Blair frowned. "Why on earth would they do that?"

"It's the whole ridiculous cult of the 'missing link' nonsense that's sprung up since people have started going out in the forest and trying to take pictures of us," he said, wiping his facial hair with a napkin. "I've done my best to encourage younger Sasquatch to come in out of the wet and cold, but it's hard to compete with the allure of reality TV."

The dragonrider shook her head, "I'm following the drift of your words, but I clearly have a great deal to learn about the modern world."

Stan patted the back of her hand with one massive paw. "I far prefer staying in the Otherworld. The Fae are accepting and broad-minded. I'm afraid too few humans can boast of those qualities. I can't even begin to tell you how many of my people dodge bullets, er, projectiles from human weapons on a regular basis. The young ones see outwitting hunters as good sport, but I think their behavior borders on suicidal lunacy."

After Blair finished her tea, they climbed the stone steps to the top of the city wall and walked through the illuminated gardens. Stan proved to be a genial tour guide, pointing out the lights of the fairy barracks, the soft luminescence rising from the Merfolk city at the far end of the valley, and the unicorn foals frolicking in their moonlit paddock.

As the pair descended the wall near Fiona's cottage, Blair said, "I have to bring my friends Davin and Maeve with me the next time we visit. They will find Shevington to be wondrous."

"It's a good place to live," Stan said, shortening his steps so she could keep up. "Connor has made an excellent chief executive. Ever since the University opened there are so many more wonderful cultural opportunities. If you can stay another night there's a performance of a new student opera at the auditorium. I can't say much for the tenor though. For a gnome he has a surprisingly nasal voice."

"I wish I could," Blair said, "but Giallo and I must return to Drake Abbey. The reconstruction is in full swing and Jinx may need our help with Morgan at any moment."

They stopped at Fiona's back gate and looked into the garden. Nysa and Addie chased fireflies in the yard while Fiona chatted with Giallo and Eingana.

Seeing the wistful look on Blair's face, Stan said, "Try not to think of leaving them here as being separated. You're part of the family now. We'll take good care of them the same way we're looking after Addie. This arrangement won't always be necessary. The return of drakonculture to the Otherword marks a new beginning."

Nodding toward the giggling child and the ruby whelp, he added, "I think those two are going to change the world."

Giallo spoke in her mind. *"He speaks truth,* a sheòid. *Guided by the knowledge that lies hidden at Drake Abbey, we will all be part of building a new future."*

"So you're satisfied for Nysa to stay?" Blair telegraphed back.

"I am satisfied. Protection surrounds the children at every turn and they are happy to be reunited. For us, work awaits."

Chapter Eighteen

THE LAIR

The next morning at breakfast we found most of the usual suspects gathered at the table. Lucas offered to fill our plates from the buffet, so I took my place and wished everyone a good morning.

Willow sat between her parents dining on what appeared to be pâté served in an elevated crystal bowl. "That looks good," I said.

"*Oh!*" Glory gushed. "Darby is the most *wonderful* uncle. He stayed up all night researching proper feline nutrition."

The brownie appeared at my elbow with a silver coffee pot. As he filled my cup, I said, "That was sweet of you."

Brightening at the praise, Darby said, "It was a most interesting exercise, Mistress. I have been discussing a proper diet with Master Festus. He is not receptive to the information even though I am quite certain I am accurate in my recommendations."

On the other side of the table the werecat, who was pawing through the morning news on his iPad, bit into a thick, greasy slice of bacon. "You tend to your blood pressure, Short Stuff, and I'll tend to mine."

"But Master Festus, the veterinarian has only to place a small cuff at the base of your tail... "

A murderous look came into the ginger cat's eyes. "I don't *get* high blood pressure, I *give* it."

That pushed Darby's literal mind right over the cliff of incomprehension. "But why would you wish to gift someone with a chronic cardiovascular disease?"

The werecat's ears went flat. Intervention time.

"Thank you, Darby. This is a wonderful breakfast, but would you mind getting me some apricot jam for my toast?"

Elated to be asked to do something extra for me, the brownie dropped the dangerous topic of Festus's vital signs and popped out.

"Dad," Glory said. "You really have to set a better example for W-i-l-l-o-w."

The kitten looked up, "Uh, Mom. Just so you know. I can spell, read, and I'm pretty good at quadratic equations."

A struggle played out on Glory's face—a comic mixture of horror and pride. "That's wonderful, sweetheart," she finally gulped.

"And don't pick on Festus," Willow added, giving her grandfather a look of complete adulation. "He is like the single coolest werecat in all the Realms. He *rocks*."

Chase put a hand over his eyes. "Bastet's whiskers, Dad. How did you manage to brainwash this child in less than 72 hours?"

"Natural talent," Festus beamed. "The kid's a keeper."

Seizing on that word to put in a request, Glory said, "Speaking of keeping things, Dad, can you watch Willow? Chase has to open the shop, I need to check in at the *Banner* office, and Miss Myerscough is still... indisposed."

Rube, who was reading a *Guardians of the Galaxy* comic book at the end of the table snickered.

"That will be enough out of you," I warned.

The raccoon gave me a bright-eyed grin. "Me and Festus ain't to blame this time, Jinx. You wanna bust somebody's chops for slipping Mrs. M. a mickey, you gonna have to take it up with your mom over there."

I didn't have to ask if he was telling the truth. The funny look on Mom's face confirmed the allegation.

"Now *you're* in on trying to kill Miss Myerscough?" I asked.

Using her knife to cut into the omelette on her plate with unnecessary force Mom said, "No one is trying to kill Miss Myerscough... yet."

"Wait a minute," I said. "You told me you barely met the woman before Rube drugged her."

"That's true, but she woke up early this morning."

"*And?*"

"After ten minutes listening to her rant, I put her right back out again."

Festus and Rube could no longer contain themselves. Both laughed until they cried, with Willow joining in.

"Did you see the way that old bag hit the floor?" Rube gasped, slapping the table with his paw. "She went down like a sack of taters."

"And the way her fur sorta *poofed* out when she hit the rug," Festus howled. "It was perfect."

Willow chimed in. "Uncle Rube took a picture. Show her."

The raccoon slid his phone down the middle of the table. It came to a stop in front of my plate displaying the image of a gray Persian lying face down on the rug in front of the fire all four legs splayed out in a classic "splat" position.

I gaped at my mother. "You drugged Willow's nanny?"

"Don't be ridiculous, Norma Jean," Mom said as she poured cream in her coffee. "I bespelled her. Festus is right. She's a meddlesome, cantankerous old biddy. I'll wake her up when all of this is over."

Looking to Myrtle who sat at the head of the table I said, "You approve of this?"

To my utter astonishment, the aos si replied, "I am in no position to tell the Roanoke Witch how to use her powers. I defer to Kelly's wisdom in this matter."

That's when realization dawned. "*Myrtle!* You don't like Miss Myerscough either."

"The woman is an insufferable bore. Perhaps under more normal circumstances we will be able to cultivate a rapprochement with her. For now, she is better off having a nice rest. So long as Willow stays with us here in the lair she'll be safe. The fairy mound is up to the task of containing a rambunctious werekitten."

"Don't you think Chase and Glory should have some say in this?" I demanded.

"Oh," Glory said, "it's fine. Really. Whatever Kelly and Myrtle think."

She wasn't fooling me for a minute. "You're scared to meet the nanny."

"Terrified," Glory said, bobbing her head for emphasis, "absolutely, completely, totally terrified."

"And you?" I asked Chase.

With a serene expression he said, "A caring husband should defer to his wife."

"Good one," Lucas said, reaching over the table so they could exchange a high five.

"Honestly," I said with exasperation. "What am I going to do with you people?"

"Thank us," Rube answered. "Mrs. M. ain't no walk in the park. Besides, she could use her some beauty rest. *Bad.*"

I shouldn't have joined in the laughter, but I couldn't help myself. "Fine, but when Miss Myerscough wakes up, you hooligans are going to be on hand to help me explain." Then, switching subjects, I said, "Glory, I thought you emailed your column to *The Banner*?"

"When we got home Sunday night I sent the file and attached a wedding picture," she said, "but Mr. Anderson hasn't answered. That's not like him, but the *Banner* computers aren't always reliable, so I'm going to walk it over later."

As Bertille joined us at the table, I said, "Hold off on that until you hear from me, okay? We're headed to the bookstore to figure out what happened there. I'd feel better if everyone stayed close to the fairy mound until we have an answer."

"Oh, that's fine," Glory said. "The column isn't due until 5 o'clock. Willow and I are going to do some online shopping for her room." She reached over and scratched the kitten's ear. "There is a little girl in there, after all."

"Yeah," Willow said, "and it sucks that I can't shift on my own yet."

A chorus of voice greeted the remark with, *"Language!"*

The kitten struck a defiant pose. "Festus says 'suck' all the time. Why can't I say it?"

"Because you're not old enough to be as *colorful* as your grandfather," Glory said, giving Festus a pointed look. "He says all sorts of things you don't need to be saying. Now finish your pâté so I can teach you how to use your father's credit card."

Connor and Tori came out of the portal as we were preparing to leave for Bergeron Books. I gave her a short rundown of the situation. "You want to come with us?"

"No, I'm going to check in with Mom and then analyze the hairs Beau collected at the crime scene."

Drawing her to the side and out of the colonel's range of hearing, I dropped my voice. "Sorry to put you straight to work, but could you hack the coroner's computer and get a look at the results of Linda's autopsy?"

"No problem," she said. "I'm on it."

"How's my baby girl?"

"Overjoyed to be reunited with Nysa. Those two are thick as thieves. Reminds me of us. That is if I could belch fire and fly."

With a straight face I said, "I learned a long time ago not to put anything past you."

Tori shot me a grin. "Smart woman." Nodding toward Beau, who was sitting on the hearth talking with Connor, she asked, "How's he holding up?"

"So so. The more he's with people the better. I told Darby to plan a big supper for everyone."

Tori glanced around the lair. "Where's Mom? I expected her to be here."

"She's got the apothecary to herself today. Brenna and Greer are in Lundenwic trying to get intel on Morgan. Lucas said they should be back in a couple of hours."

When Tori went off to play mad computer scientist, Bertille, Rube, Festus and I walked out of the lair. I carried the 2RABID case and Rodney, who was coming along as head rodent translator, rode under my collar.

We followed a shining white line that guided us through the new tunnels the fairy mound supplied so we could cross the square unseen.

As we walked, Bertille warned us about the swamp stench in the bookstore; her description didn't even come close.

Bergeron Books looked like the aftermath of a tornado and smelled like a toxic waste dump. I half expected a reporter to step out of the rubble with statistics on wind speed, storm surge, and level of biohazard.

While I cloaked the front windows so we could work in private, Rube coughed and covered his snout with one black paw. "Geez freaking *Lou-eez*! Lady, you gotta invest in better air freshinator, 'cause *day-um*."

He was right. Presented with the choice of conjuring gas masks or ventilation, I went with airflow. Speaking the words of a hastily conjured spell, I sent the backdoor creaking open, then raised a breeze with a wave of my hand.

The miasma in the shop solidified into a noxious, smoky river that flowed toward the alley. When the last tendril exited the building, I shut the door. "There. That should help us concentrate."

Nodding at Festus, who sat on the rug with his tail curled around his front legs, I said, "Okay, this is your show. Do your thing."

The werecat moved to a clear patch of floor. "Bertille, what time did you lock up on Saturday?"

"I closed at 5:30 and then finished some paperwork in the office. I was home by 7 o'clock."

Festus nodded and spoke to the 2RABID. "Reba, scan energy imprint at maximum duration range and display activity."

"Scanning."

A beep sounded and the pale images of a gang of mice scampered through the beam.

"Those are the store mice," Bertille said. "They live behind that cabinet. There's a hole in the baseboard."

Rodney tapped me on the shoulder and pointed.

"Yeah," I said. "Go on and introduce yourself. We're going to want to hear their side of the story, too."

The rat ran down my arm, leaped onto a pile of books, and disappeared under the cabinet.

Another beep from the 2RABID drew my attention back to the scan field. A book on a shelf near the window rocked and moved closer to the edge.

"Reba," Festus said, "magnify motion area. Isolate that book and pause."

"Magnifying and isolating."

The title came into focus. *The Man-Wolf* by Leitch Ritchie.

"We're getting up to our tail stripes in wolf books around this place," Rube said, digging in his waist pack and pulling out a candy bar.

"That book was not in my inventory when I moved to Briar Hollow," Bertille said. "It's rare, especially in the United States."

"You check every book when you moved in?" Rube asked, wiping chocolate off his whiskers.

"Well, no," Bertille admitted, "but I took inventory before I left New Orleans."

"Lotta miles between North Carolina and the Big Easy," the raccoon said. "How do you know somebody didn't slip the book in when you wasn't looking?"

Bertille's first impulse was to argue, but then she had to admit Rube was right. "I shipped my books through a literary freight company. The whole process took two weeks."

More than enough time to add one book—or more—to the load.

"So," Rube said, popping open a soda can. "We could be looking at one of them sentimental books the Black Bird told us about."

"The word," Festus said, "is sentient, and there's only one way to find out. Reba, resume scan."

Chapter Nineteen

DRAKE ABBEY

"You searched *one* location and found the library?" Blair asked, unable to disguise her astonishment and jealousy. "How is that possible?"

Davin puffed out his chest. "Sheer talent."

"Pay him no mind," Maeve said. "We benefited from sheer luck—and we can't yet say we've discovered the library. We've seen only a handle on what appears to be a hatch leading to a subterranean chamber."

"Which can't possibly be anything other than the library," Davin said. "You said yourself we should start in the labyrinth because contemplation and scholarship go hand in hand."

The three of them sat around the fire in the cloisters sharing a morning cup of tea. They had waited ten minutes after Brick Deaver left on an inspection tour of the Abbey worksite to begin their conversation.

Maeve's intuition impressed Blair. "That was good thinking. What made you notice the hatch?"

"Nothing," Maeve admitted. "We could easily have walked right past it. My paw happened to strike the center medallion.

When it did, I heard a voice that said 'set free the one who sleeps.'"

Suspicion filled Blair's eyes. "I don't much care for the idea of a disembodied voice orchestrating our actions."

"Agreed," Davin said, "but you know how hard it is to stop her when she's curious about something."

Setting her mouth, Maeve said, "I'd say my curiosity worked out rather well this time."

"It did," Blair admitted. "Did you locate the source of the voice?"

Maeve's brow crinkled. "To be honest, I didn't even think about trying until just now when you mentioned the idea. Davin was suspicious in the moment, but I had no apprehension about following the words as directed."

"Following them to what?"

"A sculpture of a slumbering dragon half covered in weeds. We nudged the wings open. When we did, the figure moved aside and revealed the hatch. This morning, as soon as the sun rose, the stone dragon returned to its normal position."

Using a rag to protect her fingers, Blair lifted the kettle and refilled their mugs. "Do you suppose that means that only a weretiger can activate the mechanism in the sculpture?"

"Possibly," Maeve replied, blowing on the hot liquid in her cup. "But with three of us on hand, I don't see that as an issue."

"Three may be sufficient to find what lies hidden here," Blair said, "but we will need a full wing if we hope to restore drakon-culture to its proper place in the realms."

"Perhaps," Davin suggested, "if we can offer the Citadel riders proof that an archive of our culture exists in this place, more will be moved to follow us to the Middle Realm."

Blair gave the fire a frustrated poke raising a column of sparks. "Which would mean dealing with Master Kian again, a man utterly lacking in even the pretense of imagination or vision."

"Before you set the cloisters ablaze," Maeve said soothingly, "it would be best to discover what lies beneath the labyrinth. Shall we return tonight and find out?"

Tossing the stick in her hand into the fire, Blair said, "Indeed we will, and in the company of our new friends. Our alliance with Shevington University must be transparent. Fiona Ryan instructed me in mirror communication last evening. We should speak with Connor and make him aware of this discovery."

Taking a folding mirror from her pocket, Blair placed the call, stumbling slightly over the words of the summoning spell. The silvered surface wavered, then caught the proper swirling pattern.

When the mirror cleared, Connor's boyish face looked out at them, worry etching his features. "What's wrong? Are Giallo and Eingana unhappy? Do we need to make changes to their housing?"

"No, no," Blair assured him. "All is well. Giallo and I have returned to the Abbey. We left Nysa and Addie chasing one another around the garden while Eingana sunbathed on the grass."

Relieved, Connor said, "Thank the gods. Do you need something or are you just taking the mirror for a test run?"

"Yes on both counts. I have quite a tale of discovery to share with you."

Connor listened with growing excitement. "A whole library filled with materials about drakonculture? This could be the find of a lifetime. How do you want to proceed?"

"Judging from the behavior of the statuary, we speculate the door can only be revealed at night. When the sun sets, we will confirm that theory. I assume you and Tori wish to be here."

Repositioning his mirror to show Tori hard at work behind a

maze of bubbling beakers, Connor said, "Yes we want to be there, but there's a lot happening in Briar Hollow. I need to confer with Jinx before I can tell you when we can leave for the Abbey. Let me give you a call back, okay?"

"Of course. We have more than enough to keep us occupied."

Connor signed off and Blair put the folding mirror in the pocket of her jerkin. "I like the Lord High Mayor," she said. "He has infectious enthusiasm and curiosity."

"He does," Davin agreed. "Tori taught me a human phrase to describe the Mayor's more animated outbursts."

"What is it?"

"He would have a good time at a rock fight."

Laughing, Blair said, "Indeed he would, and most likely scientifically classify the projectiles as they flew through the air." Then, clapping her hands together, she added, "So that's that. We have a full day before us. I'm sure Master Deaver has tasks aplenty to dole out. The more we labor, the less our minds will dwell on what lies in the labyrinth."

"Speak for yourself," Davin grinned. "I won't be thinking of anything else until the sun goes down."

"Me either," Maeve admitted, "but we should at least try to make ourselves useful while we wait."

Banking the fire, Blair said, feigning indifference, "After all, it's not as if anything major is afoot—only the future of drakon-culture."

"You're as bad as the Mayor," Maeve said as they went outside to join Deaver and his workmen.

"I may be worse," Blair admitted. "What we find tonight could change our lives forever. I wish Master Jaxon and my parents were here to see this."

Davin reached out and clasped Blair's forearm. As Blair returned the grip, Maeve stepped closer and caught hold of both their free hands.

"Master Jaxon, Adair, and Esme are with us always," Maeve said. "Their memory is the wind that lifts us skyward."

"Aye," Davin said. "What we do here, we do for them."

"For their memory," Blair said, tears filling her eyes, "and for those yet to come."

Talons scraped the flagstones as Giallo, Seoclaid, and Iathghlas formed a circle around them.

"And more there will be, a sheòid," Giallo said. *"One day my daughter will fly these skies with the witch child on her back. A new dawn comes."*

"Not unless we put our backs to it," Blair said, laughing and wiping her eyes. "There will be time enough for sentiment later. Now we work."

Chapter Twenty

BRIAR HOLLOW

By prior arrangement with the Attendant, Greer and Brenna arrived in the fairy mound without alerting anyone of their presence. Greer stood at the edge of the stacks and stared at Lucas until he felt the weight of her gaze.

She raised a slender finger to her lips and inclined her head toward the shelves. Lucas signaled his comprehension, waiting until the women were out of sight to gather up his tablet and an armload of file folders.

Connor glanced up from the makeshift desk where he was working by the fire. "Checking more references?"

"Yeah," Lucas said. "Leave it to Otto to send paper files from IBIS instead of feeding the information through Adeline."

"I'm sure Adeline would be happy to scan the materials for you."

"Naw," Lucas said. "I'm cooling my heels until Jinx and the others are done at the bookstore. Doesn't hurt me to do things the old-fashioned way once in awhile."

"Suit yourself. We'll have the fairy mound give you a shout if they get back before you're done."

"Thanks. Appreciate it."

Putting a row of shelves between himself and the lair, Lucas looked at the ceiling. "You want to give me a clue here?"

A glowing green line materialized on the floor. Lucas followed it to a secluded seating area where Greer and Brenna waited.

"Any particular reason we're skulking around the archive?" he asked, dropping the things he carried on an end table and taking his seat.

Greer made a tsking sound. "Laddie, I am too forthright by nature and far too old to skulk."

"And yet here we are hiding out to discuss something you don't want the others to hear."

"Expedience does not a skulker make. Brenna, if you please."

The sorceress curled her fingers in a sweeping motion. A privacy curtain descended at the same moment three coffee cups appeared. The drinks hovered in a patient holding pattern.

Reaching for the cup nearest his chair, Lucas said, "Skulking, privacy, and caffeine. This cannot be good."

"We have a great deal to discuss," the baobhan sith said, claiming her drink and sweetening it with whisky from a silver flask. "Comfort seems in order. Allow me to begin by summarizing our time in Lundenwic."

Lucas listened without reaction to Greer's description of their conversation with Melinda Owen until the baobhan sith used the phrase "Dragon Witch."

Then, he held up his hand. "Stop right there. Who or what is the Dragon Witch?"

Greer looked to Brenna who said, "She was believed to be the first of the tree witches, sworn to the service of Yggdrasil."

Lucas reached for his tablet. Tapping in a search query, he scanned the screen. "Okay. I see references to Norse myths about dragons living at Yggdrasil's base. They gnawed at the tree's roots in an effort to return the cosmos to chaos. No mention of a Dragon Witch."

That won him an arched eyebrow from his vampiric partner. "Come now, laddie. After all these years you reach for the interpretation of a myth rewritten for the benefit of humans and posted on the Internet? Have you taken leave of your senses?"

Lucas shut off the tablet, returned it to the end table, and steepled his fingers. "Fine. I'm going to be sorry I asked, but what's the real story?"

The privacy shield undulated as Myrtle crossed the barrier. "Pardon the interruption, but as you are speaking of the Dragon Witch, I thought it best I join the conversation."

Now even more suspicious, Lucas said, "How did you know we were here?"

"My dear boy, the fairy mound may allow an enchantment to keep your conversation from the others," the aos si said, snapping her fingers and conjuring a fourth chair, "but it most certainly will not withhold information from *me*."

Lucas chuckled. "Fair enough, but I'm starting to think the person who really needs to join this conversation is my wife. You know how Jinx gets when she thinks she's being kept out of the loop."

Myrtle dismissed his concern with serene confidence. "Nothing will be kept from Jinx. Greer and Brenna are not the only ones who have been abroad in the realms seeking information about Morgan and her purported alliance with the Master Publishers. I have undertaken investigations of my own."

Growing more serious, Lucas said, "Really, if this concerns Addie, Jinx should be here."

"At present we would do nothing but increase her already considerable anxiety."

"Just so you know," Lucas said, sipping his coffee, "you're not doing a heck of a lot for my nerves either. I respect you, Myrtle, but I'm not going along with hiding anything from Jinx. Especially if it concerns our daughter."

"Understood," Myrtle said. "You know that the child's welfare is foremost in my concerns as well. We ask only that you bear with us for a few hours. Greer, please continue with your account."

Setting her cup aside, the baobhan sith said, "Although Melinda knew nothing about Morgan's alliance with the Master Publishers of Nevermore, she offered a theory regarding how such an arrangement would be to Morgan's benefit."

"Which is?" Lucas prodded.

"That Morgan may seek to rewrite history so that she, not Arthur, is the hero of Camelot."

Lucas's face registered surprise. "Is that even possible?"

Myrtle answered. "Many things became possible when Jinx opened the Rivers of Time. Diverse threads of our experience appear to now weave a tapestry. The confluence of scriptomancy and key items among the Temporal Arcana could achieve previously unimagined results."

Scrubbing at his face, Lucas said, "Wow. It's hard to surprise me these days, but that came out of left field. You think Addie could be the Dragon Witch, don't you?"

"She may be more than that," Brenna said. "Merlin's tools are the wand, the sword, the cup, and the pentacles. Addie is the vessel of pure magic.."

A sick look came over Lucas's features. "She's the cup. How much power does my daughter possess?"

"More than we have imagined, and more than we have discovered," Brenna said. "She must never fall into Morgan's hands."

Lucas got to his feet and paced the length of the privacy shield. "That goes without saying. We have to tell Jinx."

"We have to tell everyone," Myrtle said. "In solving Linda

Albert's murder we have an opportunity to gain insight into Morgan's plans in greater detail and perhaps to thwart them "

Picking up his tablet, Lucas accessed the security grid for the square. "Let's see. Looks like Kelly went over to work with Gemma in the apothecary. Chase is in the cobbler shop and Beau is running the espresso bar. Jinx, Festus, Rube, and Rodney are at Bergeron Books and everyone else is in the lair."

"Why are Jinx and the others in Bertille's shop?" Greer asked.

"There was an incident there the night before Linda was killed," Lucas explained. "The store mice told Bertille a monster came out of a book and ransacked the place."

"I do not like the sound of creatures emerging from books," Myrtle said. "Not with the involvement of Nevermore in Morgan's schemes. Greer, would you be kind enough to join the investigation?"

"My pleasure."

Lucas looked at them like they'd lost their minds. "That's it? We just let everyone filter in for supper like this is a normal day?"

"It is to our advantage to give that appearance to anyone surveiling our movements," Myrtle replied. "Morgan has agents in Briar Hollow. Of that I am certain, but I cannot locate them. If she can shield her people from my awareness, her powers have grown exponentially, either by her own efforts or as a consequence of magical objects in her possession."

"Okay," Lucas said. "So we proceed with caution. What do you want me to do?"

"Go back to the lair and act as if nothing has occurred," Myrtle said. "The others will learn what we have shared with you soon enough."

Lucas's eyes went round. "You're kidding, right? I'm the

Director of the Division for Grid Integrity and you want me to go back out there and pretend to shuffle papers?"

"Patience has never been your strongest virtue, laddie," Greer said in a dry tone. "Mistress Owen said nothing that will alter our lives in the coming hours or increase the level of immediate threat to Addie. In addition to what we have learned, we need the information that may be uncovered at the bookstore. Your game of charades will not be a lengthy one."

"Fine," Lucas grumbled, turning on his heel and stalking away only to run headlong into the privacy curtain. "Would one of you take this damned thing down, please?"

Brenna drew the magic aside and Lucas left, all the while muttering under his breath. "Will he be all right?" she asked Greer.

"Lucas prefers to channel his fears into action. He does not enjoy waiting."

"Is that why you didn't tell him that Melinda said Morgan will seek to deprive Jinx of her greatest strength?" the sorceress asked.

"It is," the baobhan sith replied. "Only Jinx can know from whence that strength comes. In truth, she may not recognize that resource until the moment she loses it."

"A thought," Myrtle said, "that would preoccupy Lucas to the point of uselessness. We will need him and the resources at his command in the days to come. Now, if you will excuse me, I must contact Seneca and ask him to join us. This evening should prove to be exceptionally interesting."

Chapter Twenty-One

Later, Greer would tell us that she used the newly created tunnels to make her way to Bergeron Books. What we didn't know at the time was that her sharp hearing allowed her to be privy to our conversation long before she stepped into the room.

She arrived as Festus ordered the 2RABID to resume scanning the bookcase. "Reba, belay that order."

That kind of interference would have won a sharp rebuke from the werecat for anyone else. Instead, Festus said, "Oh hell. Now what?"

Rube offered up a more effusive greeting. "Yo, Red! Welcome to the party! You're looking all lethal lovely."

"Thank you, Reuben. Hello, everyone. Please forgive the abruptness of my entrance."

I'm always glad to see the baobhan sith back in Briar Hollow. She's like having a locked and loaded weapon on hand at all times. "Hi. Lucas said you were in Lundenwic. How did that go?"

"Well."

Greer knew I wanted more information. Her smoldering green eyes asked for my patience. Since I have complete faith that the baobhan sith always puts my welfare and that of my loved ones first, I gave it.

"Good to have you back," I said. "I assume Lucas told you why we're here?"

"He did," she said, surveying the chaos around us. "My curiosity compelled me to see the damage for myself. Am I to understand that you have located a copy of *The Man-Wolf* by Leitch Ritchie?"

"Yeah," Festus said, jerking his head toward the 2RABID beam, which was still focused on the volume. "We were about to see what popped out of the book and trashed the joint before you interrupted. What's up with that?"

"I am familiar with the novel," Greer said. "It is yet another origin story for the popular conception of werewolves in human society."

Rube up-ended his soda, burped, and said, "So, same old mangle-ated Hollywood story. Dude gets bit by a werewolf. Goes all furry. Hates howling at the moon 'cause he's got a dame who ain't into cross-species dating. Silver bullets fly. Wolf boy bites it, cue the hankies."

"Hardly," Greer said. "Leitch possessed more imagination than that."

Greer's comment didn't really surprise any of us, but Rube can never leave the obvious alone. "Sounds like you knew the guy."

"I did. He was a fellow Scot. A Glaswegian clerk turned novelist."

The raccoon furrowed his eyewhiskers. "I ain't following the part about glass wedges."

"Glaswegian. A denizen of the city of Glasgow. Leitch wrote *The Man-Wolf* sometime around 1831 as I recall. As Leitch was privy to my true nature, I supplied him with the necessary details to set his tale in the 11th century."

Any time the subject of Greer's private life comes up, I get queasy. Even though she doesn't leave a trail of corpses in her wake, the baobhan sith still mesmerizes unsuspecting men and drinks their blood. So far as I know, she's not in the habit of introducing herself as a centuries old Scottish vampire first.

No one else seemed ready to ask. I cleared my throat and said, "How did he find out what you are?"

"I told him. Although not a handsome man, Leitch was an excellent conversationalist. He awakened during our initial encounter and after a bit of back and forth was willing that we continue."

The great-granddaddy of all awkward silences descended over the room.

Greer laughed at our discomfort. "You are all adorably provincial."

So not a road I wanted us to go down. "Okay then. What can you tell us about the guy?"

Greer described Ritchie as the author of four successful novels and a number of short stories. The plot of *The Man-Wolf* involved a knight who goes on a drunken spree after being embarrassed in the presence of a beautiful woman.

On his way home through a dark forest he experiences a series of misadventures culminating in his transformation into a wolf. For the rest of the story, the knight's manservant tries repeatedly to return him to human form with comedic results.

"So what's gonna come out of the book?" Rube asked, "Sir Drinks A Lot, the dude who works for him, or the wolf?"

Bertille said softly, "The wolf."

I didn't like the look on her face. "Why do you say that?"

"Because I embarrassed a man in front of his friends and I think in his desire to regain his dignity, he did something extremely foolish."

"Like what?"

"May we see what the 2RABID finds before I answer that question?"

"Sure," I said. "Festus, do your thing."

There are times when I wish Fae tech would fail to deliver. Reba didn't. She was completely on her game, showing us the emergence of a half-man, half-wolf creature from the pages of Ritchie's novel.

But this was not an errant 11th century knight. The monster wore dress pants, expensive loafers, and a white shirt. The effect might have been comical, until the image of the beast threw its head back in a silent howl and flew into a rage.

Sensing that we'd seen enough, Festus shut down the scanner.

Rube, frozen with a half-eaten Snickers in one paw and a can of orange pop in the other gulped. "What in the name of the Trash Gods is that thing?"

"That," Bertille said, in a strangled whisper, "is a rougarou."

No one reacted to the foreign word until Greer said, "Do you mean a loup-garou?"

Rube swiveled his head between the vampire and Bertille. "Lou and Roo Garoo? We talking brothers here?"

Festus rolled his eyes, but the baobhan sith nurses a fond spot for the raccoon. "Reuben, 'lou-garou' is French for werewolf."

"No kidding. Them Frenchies don't never say nothing the easy way. That thing that came outta that book sure as shooting ain't no werewolf. I know werewolves."

Bertille agreed. "You're right. The rougarou is not a shifter like the werewolves you know. This creature is a man cursed by a witch to live half in one form and half in the other. In Louisiana, the rougarou is a sort of boogey man."

"That ain't very nice," Rube said, looking shocked. "I know the boogey man. His name's Burt. Bald as a cue ball. Looks more like a ferret with an overbite than what crawled outta the book."

Festus started to smack him, but Rube saw the blow coming. He dropped and rolled clear, coming to his feet beside a pile of cookbooks, soda and candy bar intact. "Too slow, Old Man. Coon here's got the moves. What'd I say this time?"

"As usual, something stupid," the werecat growled. "She means that parents in Louisiana tell their kids scary stories about this rougarou to make them behave."

Rube's eyewhiskers went up and he shuddered. "OHHH-HH!!!! You mean like *the Game Warden*. Ma used that one all the time. Scaring kids like that ain't gonna get nobody parental unit of the year."

"What's not nice is that while most people believe the rougarou is an old wives tale, it's actually the result of a curse cast by a black witch to condemn a human to live out their days as the creature we just saw."

Bertille's voice broke on the word human. We had wandered into personal territory. "You know this rougarou, don't you?"

That's when she told us about the gold cufflink Sheriff Johnson found at the library—a cufflink she believed belonged to her ex-boyfriend.

"The plot of *The Man-Wolf* could be the story of how Andre and I broke up," she said.

We listened as Bertille described her relationship with an art dealer named Andre Melancon. I didn't say so, but the guy sounded like a massive tool.

Bertille made the mistake of correcting him in front of his artsy friends. In a display of pure ego, he ghosted her for two weeks. When she went to his townhouse to try to make things right, she found the place deserted, ransacked, and reeking of the same stench that permeated her shop when we arrived.

"Sheriff Johnson found a single gold cufflink in the library engraved with a fleur-de lis," Bertille said. "I bought those cuff-links and had the custom engraving done as a gift for Andre. The rougarou that the 2RABID showed us was wearing those very cufflinks."

"Festus," I said. "Can the 2RABID show us that detail?"

"Of course. Reba, project an isolated image of the creature in your last recording."

"Projecting."

The rougarou appeared in the center of the store, frozen in mid-howl. For the first time I noticed the French cuffs on the white shirt and the engraved diamond-shaped gold cufflinks Bertille had described.

Linda Albert died in the jaws of that living horror. Even without the obvious clue of the *Sweet Adeline* sheet music, no logical scenario suggested the rougarou had been sent to Briar Hollow specifically to kill the local librarian—or that she would be its only victim.

There had to be a connection to Bertille's life in New Orleans.

During all of this back and forth, Greer walked to the front window and stared across the square. When it became clear she wasn't paying attention to our conversation, I said, "Greer, what is it? Do you see something out there?"

"Not see, feel," she replied with an expression of intense concentration on her angular features. When she looked at me again, the green fire of the baobhan sith burned in her eyes.

"We must return to the lair. Now."

Greer normally respects my leadership without question. She doesn't give orders like that without good reason.

Rattling the sack of *Doritos* in his paws, Rube said, "Spit it out, Red. We ain't up for no guessing games."

"Nor do I wish to play them. There is a master vampire in Briar Hollow."

Chapter Twenty-Two

A thousand protestations rose to my lips. Greer shut them down without either of us speaking a word. I have seen fear stop the baobhan sith once. Standing on a cliff in the Middle Realm she balked in the face of uncontrolled blood lust.

That day I said, "I trust you." How could I not trust her now?

"That's it," I said. "Pack up everyone. We're out of here."

Festus slapped the 2RABID case with his paw. The instant the collar settled into the foam, Bertille closed the container's lid, picked the box up, and headed for the basement door with Rube and the werecat in tow.

I bent down in front of the cabinet hiding the mouse hole and called to Rodney.

When his face appeared in the opening, I said, "Come on. We have to go home."

The rat refused, holding up three fingers and jerking his head toward the darkness at his back.

"The store mice will be safe inside the walls," I assured him.

Rodney crossed his arms and stared at me.

"Fine. They can come, too, but we have to get a move on."

He responded by executing a complicated series of up and down motions with his paws.

"The fairy mound made hidden tunnels for you, too?"

One pink thumb shot up.

"All right, but leave now. We'll see you back in the lair."

When Rodney turned and left, I did the same, my steps sounding hollow on the stairs. Greer followed, her movements silent and controlled.

No one said anything for the first hundred yards or so; enough time for my racing thoughts and screaming denial to shift into overdrive.

We toss the word "vampire" around for convenience sake, but in technical terms Fae species aren't that clear cut. Early in our relationship I asked Myrtle about the standard cinematic, blood-sucking, daylight-avoiding vampires.

She said they don't exist.

Greer had just announced that they not only do exist, but were camped out in my backyard.

The baobhan sith requires blood every month to six weeks. She doesn't live under a curse; nature designed Greer. Her family tree descends from the broader race of fairies.

The Strigoi, who live in the hills above Briar Hollow, survive on life energy, but have adapted to a diet of common household electricity.

All of that I can handle, but now, in the space of a few minutes, I had to get my head wrapped around a rougarou coming out of the pop-up book from hell *and* Dracula?

That foul ball smacked me so hard I couldn't even formulate my first question. Festus didn't suffer from the same paralysis.

"So what do you think?" he asked Greer. "Are the vampire and the rougarou working together?"

His tone was so blasé he could have been discussing the weather—which is why the werecat almost jumped out of his fur when I snapped, "Could everybody just slow down here and let me catch up?"

Ever helpful, Rube asked, "You want some nerve pills, Jinx? I got some good stuff stuck down in my pack for emergency situations."

"No, I do not want a *nerve pill*, you drug-dealing trash panda. I want Greer to explain what she is talking about, because Myrtle said specifically that standard vampires do not exist."

"Whoa," the raccoon said. "Getting kinda personal with the adjectives there, ain't you?"

Little did he know I hadn't even warmed up. "Pardon me if I'm sick unto death of every damn rule in the Fae world having an exception that lands square on my doorstep."

Festus trotted in front of me and stopped, forcing me to come to a halt or run him over.

"*What?*" I demanded.

"Take a breath, Jinx," he said without a hint of sarcasm. "All rules have exceptions. That's the way life works."

My next words sounded petulant even to my ears. "Bram Stoker is supposed to have based his novel on the Strigoi. Greer said so. This is too much. Casually tossing a vampire into the room is not fair."

The werecat would have been within his rights to laugh at me, but he didn't. "Leaving Addie in Shevington, losing Linda, and fighting Morgan isn't fair, but honey, we can take on a glorified swamp mutt and an off-the-shelf vamp on our worst day with one paw tied behind out backs."

The endearment hit me like a slap in the face. When Festus McGregor resorts to sweet talk with me, I'm totally off the rails.

"Sorry guys," I said, feeling my cheeks grow warm. "I got overwhelmed there for a minute."

"You're not the only one," Bertille said, squeezing my shoulder. "The rougarou was living in my store all this time. If I had known, Linda might still be alive."

"Don't think that way," I told her. "You didn't have so much as a clue that anything was wrong."

The bookstore owner's expression darkened. "I think I did have a clue. We all did. We just didn't realize it."

"What are you talking about?"

"The grimoire Stella Mae Crump bought," Bertille said. "What if that was a dry run to see how well I know my inventory?"

Crap. That meant Morgan or her agents had been at work in Briar Hollow for weeks. "Let's walk and talk at the same time," I suggested. "I'm going to feel a heck of a lot better once we're back in the lair."

A few steps farther down the passageway, I said, "Rube, I'm sorry I called you a drug-dealing trash panda."

"No worries, Doll," the raccoon said. "Offer still stands."

Although I couldn't see myself ingesting anything handed out by the black-masked bandit, nothing seemed impossible now. "I'll let you know. Okay, Greer. Who or what do you think we're dealing with?"

"The species of vampire I sensed on the square represents a divergence in the evolution of mankind. One thought to be extinct as my mother was believed to have killed the last of their kind centuries ago."

"Why did Katherine do that?"

"Because she found their delusional plans to become a master race superior to humans both tedious and annoying."

Rube, who was now walking on three paws so he could eat potato chips with the fourth said, "Ain't you bloodsuckers bound by some kind of peace treaty or something? Vamps don't kill vamps?"

"The Peace Accord of 1900," Greer replied. "That agreement

does not apply to the dark being I believe to be present in Briar Hollow."

I shivered for no apparent reason. A reaction that would have prompted Aunt Fiona to say someone had walked on my grave. "How were you able to feel him back in the bookstore?"

"We are distant cousins. The fire of the baobhan sith recognized the coldness of his heart."

"Which," Festus said, "takes us back to my original question. Are the rougarou and the vamp working together?"

"They could be," Bertille said. "A witch had to perform the spell to imprison Andre in the book, but any powerful being could release him with the correct incantation. I've also been taught vampires are a myth, but if one does exist, he could likely have breached the wards I erected."

"I sensed a *master* vampire," Greer said. "Such a creature would be at least a thousand years old and all but impervious to wards."

Alarm bells went off in my head. "Does that mean he could get into our shop?"

"Unless extraordinary precautions are taken, yes," the baobhan sith said. "For now, I believe the best course of action would be to have all of our people take refuge in the lair."

Bertille accepted the offer of sanctuary on the spot, but expressed concern about leaving the bookstore in its current condition for a reason that deepened my foreboding. What if the rougarou wasn't the only intruder hiding in the inventory?

With a hopping series of steps, Rube zipped his waist pack and with all four feet back on the ground made an excellent point. "You guys ain't thinking straight. If we's going by the movie rules, this vamp ain't gonna be looking to get a tan. Which means we're A-okay to be in the book joint long as its daylight."

I looked to Greer. "Is he right?"

"The vampire would not, as film lore suggests, burst into flames under the rays of the sun, but he would find the experience uncomfortable."

During the remaining walk to the lair, we worked out a plan. Festus would relinquish custody of the 2RABID to Greer that evening so she could scan the library.

I will be the first to admit I had no desire to watch the energy imprint of Linda's murder. If there were more clues to be found at the scene of the crime, I trusted Greer to spot them.

When we arrived in the lair, Lucas took one look at my face and said, "What's wrong?"

Going to my husband rather than blurt out the news and touch off a panic, I lowered my voice and said, "You're not going to like it."

"Tell me anyway."

He took the part about the rougarou pretty well. The master vampire detail not so much.

"I'll get some agents to New Orleans. This Andre Melancon had to have crossed paths with someone powerful to get himself turned into a rougarou. That someone could lead us to the vamp."

Festus's paws fairly flew over the screen of his iPad. "I'm asking Ironweed to double the GNATS presence in Briar Hollow and give us some drones with real fire power."

Behind us the portal crackled. Seneca flew out of the matrix, cut straight across the lair, and landed on the mantle. Edgar followed, his head swiveling to take in the details of the fairy mound.

"Oh boy," Rube muttered. "I ain't seeing no good coming outta this."

Cocking his head, Seneca looked down at the raccoon. "An apt observation as always, Reuben. The aos si invited us. It would appear events in Briar Hollow are gaining momentum with Ms. Bergeron's emporium playing a central role."

Amity chose that exact moment to emerge from the stacks. She all but crowed in triumph. "I *knew* it! I told you people from day one there was something suspicious about a voodoo queen coming to Briar Hollow."

No one could blame Bertille for bristling at that accusation given the events of the last 24 hours. "For the love of Hecate! How many times do I have to tell you? I do not practice voodoo."

"*Harumph!*" Amity snorted. "You're from Louisiana. The whole state is a swamp of questionable magic."

"The only part of that statement you got right is the swamp," Bertille said, eyes flashing. "I did not bring bad fortune to Briar Hollow on purpose."

"That's right," Amity said, warming to her topic. "Try to weasel out of responsibility for unleashing a crime spree on an unsuspecting community. Just the sort of behavior I would expect from the likes of Cajun bayou trash."

As static flashes of electricity crackled over Bertille's fingers, Seneca tried to calm the waters. "Ladies, this squabble will accomplish nothing. We must work as a coherent unit to unearth hidden dangers in our midst."

Amity wheeled on him and unleashed more venom. "I do not need a mite-infested blackbird who isn't fit for the stew pot telling me what to do." Then, pointing at Edgar, she said, "And why is he here?"

Edgar stammered, "Perhaps you are unaware that my short story *The Murders in the Rue Morgue* is considered to have pioneered the genre of detective fiction. I wish to assist with the investigation in the interest of repaying the many kindnesses shown to me."

Before Amity could fly off on another tangent, an earsplitting blast pierced the air. The room fell silent and everyone looked toward Tori who was standing at her alchemy bench holding an air horn with her mother looking on.

"Everybody knock it off," she ordered. "I have news."

"It better be good," I said, "because I have news, too."

Through long years of experience, Tori has learned not to play chicken with me. "You go first."

"Dracula's cousin is in town. Your turn."

Tori has a good poker face. Without batting so much as an eyelash she said, "There's a library at Drake Abbey hidden under a dragon sculpture that only comes to life at night for a weretiger."

From his perch, Seneca ruffled his wings. "Now you see, we are making progress on all fronts."

As much as I hate to agree with Amity Prescott about anything, I found myself wondering for the first time what raven fricassee might taste like.

Chapter Twenty-Three

Seneca's attempt at optimism didn't slow Amity's roll. "We do not have time to be concerning ourselves with lizard libraries," she snapped. "There's a murderer in this town and it's *her* fault."

"No," I said through gritted teeth, "it's not, and I don't want to hear you say anything like that to Bertille again. Do you *need* something, Amity?"

The older witch swelled at my rebuke. "Myrtle sent me a message that we would all be gathering for supper tonight. I haven't had a customer in hours because all anyone wants to do is speculate about Linda's murder, so I decided to come over early."

Behind me I heard Tori mumble under her breath, "Lucky us."

Stealing a look at my watch, I couldn't believe we'd barely reached the noon hour. Since I had no intention of dealing with Amity for another six hours, I gave her an assignment I made up in the moment—pull all references in the archive about a creature called the rougarou.

Lucas backed me up. "Would you mind, Amity?" he asked,

laying the charm on thick. "We're trying to keep Beau occupied upstairs. He doesn't need to be underground right now. It will only make him more depressed."

Above us the fairy mound grumbled in protest. Ignoring the chunks of dirt that landed on his shoulders, Lucas kept going. "We could really use your help."

Our irascible neighbor fell for my husband's act like a ton of lead bricks. "Of course, Lucas. I would be delighted to help *you*."

She intended for me to catch the emphasis on the last word, which I did, but I backed up Lucas's strategy all the same.

"Thank you so much, Amity," I said, shoving an inventory tablet into her hands. "A job like this requires someone utterly trustworthy,"

With that, I propelled her into the stacks with a promise that Darby would find her with a hot lunch delivery.

As Amity's figure retreated in the distance, Tori stepped beside me. "Want me to scramble the card catalog to keep her out of our hair until supper?"

"Do it," I said, "but don't get her so lost we have to go looking for her."

"Gotcha." She tapped a set of instructions into the FaeNet terminal. "There. The pad will make sure she enjoys some nice, long *scenic* detours."

Even Seneca looked relieved. His feathers settled into smooth, ebony lines and his talons released their tight hold on the mantle. Looking down, he realized he'd gouged the wood.

The raven healed the damage with a few words of Latin. "My apologies. That woman grates on my nerves."

"Join the club," I said, waving Edgar into a chair by the fire. "Please don't take anything Amity said personally," I told the author. "She's an equal opportunity crank."

"No apology necessary," Edgar replied, taking out pen and

paper. "She's a marvelous character study. I must use her in my next story."

I refrained from saying Amity and the horror genre were made for one another.

Next I turned my attentions to Bertille. "Are you okay?"

Even though her stormy eyes told a different story, the bookstore owner said, "Fine. Amity is a piece of work."

"That she is," I agreed. "Let's inject food into this situation. Darby!"

The brownie appeared beside me. "Yes, Mistress?"

"Could you make a sandwich platter? I know we're going to have a big supper, so just something light. And please take a hot dish to Amity. She's working in the stacks."

Our helpful friend's idea of "light" would have fed a small army, but concentrating on eating took the temperature in the room down from Amity's impromptu tirade.

Seneca pecked at a bowl of mixed grains on the hearth beside Greer who had asked for tea. Tori and Connor split a massive sub with fringes of lettuce and meat spilling out of the bun. Festus opted for roast beef, and Rube took a little bit of... well, everything.

Lucas and I sat on the sofa with a plate of chicken salad sandwiches between us. "Okay, Tori," I said, "tell us about this library at Drake Abbey."

Using a napkin to wipe her mouth, she said, "Only if you spill about Dracula's cousin."

For the next 45 minutes we traded details. She described the discovery of the concealed hatch in the labyrinth. I ran down our experience at the store. At some time during my recitation, Glory and Willow arrived and helped themselves to lunch.

With all of the recent developments now on the table for group discussion, Glory said, "Maybe I shouldn't be going to the newspaper office if there's a bad vampire in town."

Festus, who had asked for his plate to be put on his desk, alternated between chewing and arranging the new drone placements. Ironweed had wasted no time answering the were-cat's emergency request. GNATS pilots now blanketed the square and patrolled the streets three deep on all four sides.

"You're not going anywhere, Pickle," he said, "and neither is anyone else until we get a better idea what's out there. I agree with Greer, we need to circle the wagons here in the lair. Laurie's at a restaurant convention in Memphis, so she's safe."

I took out my phone, speed-dialed Adeline, our in-house AI and dictated a group message to be sent to everyone.

"When you come for supper, plan to stay the night. All movement after sundown restricted until further notice. Everyone sleeps in the lair. Go about business as usual for the afternoon, but come here ASAP after work. Full report from Festus to follow."

The werecat shot me an arched eyewhisker. "Gee, thanks. You know how much I hate writing mission reports."

"Consider it an exercise in personal growth," I retorted. Looking to my brother, I said, "Okay, so you two want to go to Drake Abbey?"

Connor almost jumped off the hearth. "We *have* to go to the Abbey. Can you imagine the wealth of information that could be contained in a library like that?"

Seneca turned his back to the fire and spread his wings to warm himself. "*I* can most certainly imagine. The collection could provide valuable insight into the dispersal of the Temporal Arcana."

"We have plenty of time to get to the Middle Realm and back for the meeting tonight," Tori said. "For once the time changes line up. If we leave now, we'll arrive at the Abbey at dusk."

Sidestepping away from the flames, Seneca said, "If I may, Edgar and I would like to accompany you. My knowledge of Fae esoterica could be of use in evaluating what lies beneath the hatch."

"That's a good idea," Lucas said. "They can share what they find with the whole group tonight."

Connor looked at me like he was asking for permission to stay out past curfew. "Oh good Lord," I said. "Go already, but don't be late or I'll sic Gemma on both of you."

That threat hit home. Connor wolfed down the last bite of his third sandwich, and said, "Will do! We'll be back on time, sis. Promise."

He and Tori threw their things in two messenger bags and headed for the portal with Seneca and Edgar close behind.

Lucas, Festus, and Rube left for the war room while Glory and Willow went home to pack. That left me and Greer alone by the fire. We both turned when footsteps sounded on the stairs. Mom came down first, with Beau behind her.

"Hi," I said. "Who's minding the store?"

"Your father," Mom said. "He closed our place and came over after he got your message."

While she helped herself to a sandwich, Beau sat down on the hearth. Duke, who had been asleep under his master's desk during our conversation, trotted over and settled at the colonel's feet. That's when I noticed the word "mortuary" on the cover of the folder in his hands.

"What are you working on, Beau?" I asked, pretending I didn't know.

"Miss Linda's final arrangements. Sheriff Johnson called to inform me that no family survives to assume the responsibility for her service. The body will not be released for several days, but the Sheriff thought it would be prudent to have the details in order and asked if I would take on the task. Of course, I said I would. I have just returned from consulting with the mortician."

No wonder he looked grim. "How did that go?" I ventured.

When the colonel looked uncertain about how to answer, Mom said, "What is it Beau?"

"While I realize there are more pressing matters at hand, I have examined the materials supplied to me and am grappling with a conundrum. I would be most appreciative of assistance."

"What can we do to help?" she asked.

"In my day, dear lady, there was no choice of a burial receptacle. Rich and poor men alike went to their eternal reward in wooden coffins." He removed a slick catalog from the folder. "I do not know how to choose. The caskets are all elaborate and shockingly expensive."

"Don't worry about the cost," Mom said. "Pick what would be right for Linda."

Beau fixed his eyes on the design in the carpet. "Do you think it would be disloyal to my late wife if we were to lay Linda to rest next to my obelisk? No one will question my right to the use of my 'ancestor's' plot."

It took two tries before I could get the words out to answer. "I think your wife would expect no less from the kind and gallant man she married."

"Thank you, Miss Jinx," he replied with such heartbreaking grief I wanted to rush over and give him a hug. "I believe if Miss Linda had ever known the truth about my existence, the gesture would have pleased her."

What would have pleased Linda would have been to marry Beau and spend the rest of her life talking books and history with him. Unable to give her that dream, Beau was trying to do the best he could for the poor woman after her death.

Mom went to our friend, sat beside him, and put her hand on his arm. "It's a beautiful gesture, Beau. Would you like me to go with you to Linda's house tomorrow and pick something for her to be buried in?"

Swallowing hard, Beau said, "I would be most grateful, Miss

Kelly. Left to my own devices, I fear I would be at a considerable loss."

"I'll come along, too," I offered.

Understand, I did have a genuine desire to support Beau, but I also wanted to get into Linda's house. Even though she died at the library, we needed to have a look around her place in case the killers had been there as well.

Little did we know that the next day would not only bring more death to Briar Hollow, but also put one of our own solidly in the sights of the master vampire.

Chapter Twenty-Four

T he scent of dust and disuse rose from the rectangular opening in the labyrinth. The dragons' nostrils flared as they pawed at the ground with their talons.

Maeve stared at the stone steps and shuddered. "It's like looking into an open grave."

Beside her Blair said, "What did you expect when we opened a hatch in the dark of night?"

Seneca, perched atop the statue of the sleeping dragon, observed with acerbic accuracy, "A night under the rays of the full moon cannot be dark."

"You're a lot of help," Tori said, leaning over the gaping hole. She snapped her fingers and conjured a glowing ball of light.

Pushing the orb forward and down with the flat of her hand, she illuminated a set of eight stone steps and a landing. The first tread of a second flight signaled a turn toward the right.

"What do you think?" Tori asked. "Should we go down?"

Without hesitation Blair said, "No. The hatch could close as quickly as it opened."

Still studying the stairs, Tori said, "Connor?"

"When the statue moved aside I heard a grinding sound, like

a series of gears. I think the statue triggered the mechanism. It's probably weight sensitive."

Squatting beside Tori, Davin said, "I don't think so. Maeve and I watched the hatch close this morning. The cover came across the opening first, then the statue reassumed its position."

"If I were writing this scene," Edgar said, "I would most certainly trap my protagonist beneath the earth."

Tori looked up. "Do you have any idea how many nights of sleep your stories have cost me in my life?"

Delight animated the author's usually taciturn face. "How kind of you to say that, Tori. Thank you."

"We could use some of the timber from the building site to wedge the door open," Davin suggested. "That would make entering the opening safer."

Connor snapped his fingers. "Wait! We have another option."

"What?" Tori asked.

"GNATS."

Davin let out a derisive snort. "How can a common insect be of any use?"

"He's not talking about a bug," Tori said. "GNATS stands for Group Network Aerial Transmission System. The fairy troops in Shevington developed the drones for surveillance purposes."

When the dragonriders regarded her with blank expressions she said, "Let me rephrase that. The fairies have a bunch of tiny flying things that we can send down into this opening to have a look around. We'll be able to see what they see."

Circling the hole to get a better view, Blair asked, "Are these drones safe?"

"Oh," Tori laughed, "the drones are totally safe. Waking up the guy in charge of sending them here may not be. That's your job, Mr. Mayor."

"Me?" Connor said. "Why do I get to be the one?"

"You're Ironweed's boss," Tori replied, standing and holding out a pocket mirror.

"Lucky me," Connor mumbled. He took the mirror, stepped away from the group, and chanted the calling spell.

The silver surface flashed to life with a burst of static punctuated by an angry voice. "You better have a *damned* good reason for waking me up at this hour!"

The image coalesced on the visage of a scowling fairy with close-cropped hair and a purple beret perched at an awkward angle. Major Aspid "Ironweed" Istra glared sleepily into his mirror and then recognized Connor.

Reining in his annoyance, the fairy said, "Sorry, Mr. Mayor. I thought you were my imbecile adjutant. What's up?"

Ironweed listened as Connor broke down the situation at Drake Abbey. Now fully awake and all business, the major said, "You're thinking this hatch has been rigged with booby traps?"

Tori leaned into the mirror's line of sight. "Hey, Ironweed. Enchanted security measures are certainly possible. None of us are looking to get crushed to smithereens. Loan us a couple of drones to have a look see?"

Scrubbing at his face, Ironweed said, "Two-thirds of my damn drones are in Briar Hollow looking for vampires. Give me fifteen minutes. I'll send you whatever I can spare. Whose tablet am I broadcasting to?"

"Mine," Tori said. "I'll be online by the time you're ready."

Minutes later, a GNATS drone came in low and hot, shooting past the group gathered in the labyrinth. Maeve ducked and swatted when the tiny craft whined past her ear.

"Sorry," Tori apologized. "Pilots like to show off."

Maeve cut her eyes toward Blair and Davin. "I am somewhat familiar with the phenomenon."

Davin paid no attention to the good-natured jab. His eyes

stayed glued on the drone. Letting out a low, appreciative whistle, he said, "That guy is good."

"Don't say that so loud," Connor said as the craft came to a hovering stop over the open shaft. "GNATS pilots are also notoriously self-impressed."

Tori thumbed on her tablet and began touching icons. A tinny, but familiar voice came through the device's speaker. *"Unicorn Man, this is Red Dragon One. And your damned right I'm self-impressed because nobody flies one of these things better than yours truly."*

Frowning, Tori said, "Red Dragon One, this is Hot Coffee. Ironweed, is that you?"

"Roger that, Hot Coffee. Gotta get out from behind a desk sometime and show my troops what a real pilot looks like."

"By that you mean a real pilot sitting in the flight center in his pajamas?"

"Cannot confirm or deny, Hot Coffee. Are we ready to do this thing?"

"Roger, Red Dragon One. Engage video feed."

"Video feed engaged, Hot Coffee. Initiating approach."

Casting around for a place to prop up the tablet, Tori settled on the furled wings of the sleeping stone dragon. "Okay everybody. Gather around. The show's about to start."

Ironweed switched on the drone's four high intensity LED spotlights as he made his slow descent. The stone walls showed no evidence of traps or triggering mechanisms.

Everyone jumped when a floating window popped onto the screen. Adeline Shevington sat in total blackness surrounded by multi-colored columns of data.

"Pardon the intrusion," the AI said. "I monitor the drone feeds in the background. When Ironweed's personal craft came online in the middle of the night, the activity piqued my curiosity. May I be of assistance?"

"You're always welcome," Tori said, before attempting to explain Adeline to Blair and the others. She finally settled on, "She's our resident information specialist."

Fascinated, Maeve asked, "Do you know anything about the history of the Abbey library?"

"I do not," Adeline said, "but I will be happy to analyze what Ironweed sees in real time if I may have direct access to the GNATs cameras."

"Be my guest," Tori said. "Red Dragon One, passing flight control to Cyber Witch."

"Roger, Hot Coffee. We are a go for Cyber Witch."

Under Adeline's direction, the drone moved down the stairs and executed a right turn. Flipping up the intensity of the lights, Ironweed showed them a circular chamber. Symbols adorned the walls.

"What are we seeing, Adeline?" Tori asked.

"Representations of the Mother Trees, along with markings associated with the Temporal Arcana. I detect nothing dangerous, but much of interest. You may join us if you wish."

With Blair's agreement, Tori manifested a cloud of glowing orbs. The group went down single file leaving the dragons to stand watch above. At the base of the stairs, Tori spotted a row of wall sconces, which she ignited one after another using an incendiary spell.

The brighter illumination revealed greater details of the chamber. Advancing curiously, Connor touched an intricate carving of the Mother Oak. "Look at this workmanship," he said, running his fingers along the tree's rough bark rendered in stone.

He gasped and jerked his hand away when the branches pulled off the wall and the leaves shimmered into three-dimensional life.

"What did you do?" Tori asked.

"Nothing, I just felt the texture."

As they watched, the remaining eleven trees freed themselves. Everyone looked up as a scraping noise echoed off the stones. A panel in the center of the ceiling slid away and a holographic model of Yggdrasil lowered itself from the arched ceiling.

The roots of the World Tree reached for those of the Mother Trees forming an intricate interlacing of light and stone.

"Do you understand what's happening?" Blair asked Tori.

Craning her neck, Tori said, "It's a model of the Coven of the Woods. The big tree that dropped out of the ceiling is Yggdrasil, the World Tree. The carvings represent her daughters, the twelve Great Trees that form the Grid."

With the roots of the trees now joined, mid-air hollows appeared at the base of each trunk.

"That's the Hourglass of the Horae," Maeve said, pointing to one of the transparent niches.

"And that," said Seneca, inclining his head toward another, "is the Copernican Astrolabe."

The group ducked on instinct as beating wings sounded above their heads. Twelve holographic dragons descended from the opening in the ceiling, each coming to rest in the branches of a different Mother Tree.

Only then did the thirteenth creature enter the chamber, a brilliant ruby draikana that assumed her place on Yggdrasil's lowest branch. As her talons touched the World Tree, the stones between the Mother Tree carvings melted away revealing rows of bound volumes extending like spokes of a wheel and receding as far as the eye could see.

"Holy literary allusion, Bat Man," Tori breathed. "I feel like I'm in an Indiana Jones movie."

Seneca clacked his beak. "An apt popular cultural reference, but what has been revealed here constitutes far more than a cinematic set piece."

Tori looked down at the raven. "Okay, Black Bird, give. What is all this?"

The bird's obsidian eyes glittered in the wavering light. "The place where the threads form the whole. The Great Trees, the dragons, the Temporal Arcana. We have discovered what I believe humans would call the mother lode."

Chapter Twenty-Five

THE LAIR, JINX

W e've hosted meetings in the fairy mound that make that whole *Lord of the Rings*/Council of Elrond assembly look like grandma's knitting circle. But even in the midst of crisis, we've always managed to maintain a degree of order. Not that night.

There's something you have to understand about Southerners and the Fae who love us. Any life event from weddings to supernatural murders triggers the same reaction: cook and consume ridiculous amounts of food.

Darby laid out a buffet worthy of the best Baptist church funeral. Don't ask me how or why a centuries old brownie knows when to whip up a green bean casserole topped with fried onions, but he does.

Only Greer maintained an air of detachment. She filled a plate for Festus, poured a dram of whisky for herself, and assumed her usual place by the fire, watching the rest of us with tolerant bemusement.

Considering the events of the last few days, we weren't so much celebratory as infected by nervous energy. Eating and talking gave us something to do besides worrying about stray rougarous and vagrant vampires.

When the portal crackled to life sending Tori and Connor bursting into the room, I had my hands full—plate on one side, serving spoon of potato salad on the other.

Gemma glanced at her watch and said, "Cutting it a little close, aren't you?"

Before either of them could answer, Seneca flew of the matrix, barreled across the lair and landed on the mantel. Edgar drew up the rear. The author immediately cornered Beau and began to talk with animated gesticulations.

Tori made a beeline for me, but I could only make out scattered phrases through the overall din. "*Whoa!* Slow down, Tori," I yelled as my friend tried to babble out what I assumed to be an account of their evening in the Middle Realm.

Myrtle came to our collective rescue with signature directness—she silenced every voice in the room. One minute we were all talking, the next the next we looked like beached fish; mouths open and moving, but emitting zero sound.

"While I appreciate your enthusiasm," the aos si told the group, "the resulting cacophany makes communication impossible. If you have not done so already, please secure your meal and be seated. When you are all in place, I will restore your ability to speak, at which time I would greatly appreciate a more contained level of exchange."

I have no proof, but I'm convinced Myrtle taught grade school during some phase of her long life. We followed her directions like errant children who had been punished for bad recess behavior.

Satisfied that we'd all gotten the message, the aos si returned our ability to speak, going around the room and calling on each of us to offer individual reports. The resulting conversation lasted until the wee hours.

Even after the last person stumbled off to bed and Lucas lay beside me snoring softly, my mind turned over the tsunami of information that discussion unleashed.

Before my husband fell asleep, I'd demanded to know how he could close his eyes with all we'd just learned.

"Now we know what we're fighting," he mumbled. "It's the not knowing that keeps me up. Get some rest, honey."

Right. Rest. Not happening.

We now possessed multiple data points that allowed us to correlate a big picture. We faced far more than Linda Albert's murder—more than Irenaeus Chesterfield threw at us—even greater complications than the scheming Reynold Isherwood created.

And all of it circled back to Addie.

The holographic representation of the Coven of the Woods in the Drake Abbey library confirmed Melinda Owen's suspicions about my daughter's true identity.

Lying in the dark, I remembered the moment when Myrtle assembled those scattered pieces for us. I reached for Lucas's hand and held on for dear life.

"Within each of the Great Trees beats the heart of a dragon," the aos si said. "I am old, but the events of which I speak occurred long before my birth and are familiar to me only in legend. When I was a child, I heard stories of the days when a dragon guarded each of the Mother Trees under the direction of the Dragon Witch who rode astride a scarlet draikana."

Rapid-fire images flashed through my synapses.

Myself standing in the temporal channel that carried me and Glory home from Elizabethan England.

A window that showed me another version of my life.

Myself walking with a toddler in the big meadow below Shevington.

That child, my daughter, now slept peacefully in Aunt Fiona's cottage.

Myrtle and Brenna believed that when I opened the Rivers of Time, I activated a new matrix of potential outcomes. That included Addie's birth, her possession of Merlin's wand, and her bonding with a red dragon whelp.

Tradition holds that Merlin's wand came from a shaft of English Oak, but according to Myrtle the tiny magical stick my little girl treated like a toy sprang from the inner core of Yggdrasil. The mark of the dragon on the shaft was the sigil of the Dragon Witch.

The memory of the Mother Tree's voice pierced my thoughts. *"You were the vessel that brought her into this world, but Addie's tasks in life are her own to fulfill."*

Morgan wanted to place Merlin's tools—and perhaps even the Temporal Arcana—in my daughter's hands, and use her to engineer a reset of the timeline that formed our reality.

For the first time Myrtle told us the ancient origin myth of the Grid. A flight of dragons led by a red draikana once guarded the cohesion of the realms. When the Fae matured sufficiently to assume that responsibility, the dragons selected points of power to form a watchful network.

There, one by one, they sank their hindquarters deep into the earth, piercing the realms, and became the Mother Trees. The cardinal tree, Yggdrasil, assumed her station in Tír na nÓg.

No one knew what became of the Dragon Witch. Time obscured her identity and fate. But during long years of exile in the frozen northern lands, Morgan le Fay came to understand the complex combination lock whose tumblers were the trees, the Temporal Arcana, and drakonkind.

Morgan needed Addie to return herself to Camelot, assume the throne that had been Arthur's, and develop a new narrative for the Three Realms under her dominion. Myrtle couldn't tell us if even a semblance of our lives would exist in that twisted alternate creation.

"The Dragon Witch can be our downfall," the aos si explained, "or she can be our savior."

Our savior.

A tiny little girl who liked to fly kites, babbled about dragons incessantly, and displayed an impish sense of humor so like her father's it filled my heart with pure joy.

One central question remained. Why had Morgan set her plan in motion by killing an innocent human woman in Briar Hollow, North Carolina?

Myrtle did have an answer for that question, one that chilled me to the bone. Morgan wanted to hamstring me—deprive me of my greatest strength, weaken me so that I would be less capable of defending Addie.

"What do we do?" I'd asked Myrtle.

"We protect your greatest strength," she replied.

There was just one problem. No matter how hard I searched my heart and mind, I couldn't name what that strength might be.

Chapter Twenty-Six

Around 6 a.m., I abandoned what had been a short, fitful sleep. Going to my alcove, I placed a mirror call to Aunt Fiona who carried the glass into the garden.

Addie barely slowed down enough to say hello, but at least I started the day with the sound of her infectious giggling. When I went back into the lair, Festus and Seneca had joined Greer at the hearth.

Darby hadn't put out breakfast, but everyone had coffee. Under normal circumstances I would have found the tableau comical.

Seneca dipped his beak in the steaming liquid, throwing his head back to let the dark brew run down his throat. Festus absently lapped at his china bowl, reserving the bulk of his attention for the iPad at his feet.

Greer took one look at me, went to the urn, and brought me a perfect cup of coffee. "Did you get any rest?" she asked, pressing the mug into my hands.

"Not much," I said, falling onto one of the sofas. "Good morning, everyone."

"Morning," Festus mumbled without looking up. "How's the kid?"

"Good. Playing with Nysa in the garden. Aunt Fiona said they're making ice cream this afternoon."

The werecat glanced up. "How the hell can you manage to look that depressed about ice cream?"

I didn't have enough caffeine in my system to discuss parenting with Festus McGregor. "She's safe. That's all that matters. What are you two doing?

Seneca wiped his dripping beak on his feathers and said, "Attempting to allocate resources. Festus feels an acceleration of The Blacklist Temporal Arcana Taskforce's mandate is in order. I advocate a thorough examination of both Bergeron Books and the Drake Abbey library for sentient volumes. My sons would not have involved themselves with Morgan unless the arrangement benefited their plans."

"Both of those things need to happen," I said, "but right now we have a rougarou and a vampire loose in town. We have to stop them before someone else dies."

Behind us Glory said, "Oh, Jinx. I'm scared someone already has—died, I mean. Mr. Anderson still hasn't answered my email and he didn't let me know that he got my column. Something's very, very wrong at the newspaper office."

The clock on the mantel, which we kept set to Briar Hollow time, read 7 a.m. Too early for the *Banner* office to be open, but not too early for us to have a look see. Festus read my mind.

"I'll get some GNATS drones over there," the werecat said, typing with his paws. "With the extra pilots Ironweed sent, we have more than enough fairy power."

"Pipe the feeds to the big screen," I said. "We all need to see this."

Lucas walked into the lair as the television descended from the ceiling. Giving me a quick kiss, he said, "What's up?"

"Glory hasn't heard from Larry Anderson. We're doing a welfare check."

As the GNATS pilot approached the *Banner* offices the craft's camera showed drawn shades and a "Closed" sign dangling from the door knob.

"That's not right," Glory said. "Mr. Anderson always opens at a quarter of seven so he can sweep the sidewalk."

Festus, who was now wearing his headset thanks to some help from Greer said, "You want me to tell the pilot to go inside?"

Breaking and entering wouldn't be necessary. The GNATS drone could slip through the keyhole. I started to give the werecat the go ahead, but then I caught sight of Willow who had bounded out of the guest room after her mother.

The kitten didn't need to see what I increasingly suspected we'd find inside the building: Larry Anderson's body. No matter how smart or how advanced Willow might be, she was still a child.

I looked at Lucas, who instantly understood my apprehension. "If something's wrong a drone camera won't give us the detailed information we need even in high definition," he said. "One of us needs to go over there."

"Let me do it," Glory suggested. "I have a key and no one will think a thing about seeing me let myself in."

In recent months we'd all stopped coddling Glory. Regardless of coming off as a ditz, the woman is capable and well educated, which didn't change the reality that in a supernatural fight she's about as effective as a wet noodle.

When I suggested Greer go along on the reconnaissance mission, the baobhan sith stood to leave only to be stopped by Chase's voice echoing across the lair.

"Not so fast. No one has discussed this plan with me. I do not want my wife going into a potentially dangerous situation."

I have intimate experience with Chase's protective streak. He had every right to be concerned about his wife, but Glory has come a long way. She was no longer the terrified, cursed woman sent into our store as a spy.

What I did may not have been fair, but the decision belonged in Glory's hands. "Greer won't let anything happen to her, but it's Glory's choice if she wants to help or not."

That elicited the response I expected. "Of course I want to help," Glory cried, "and don't you be telling me I can't, Chase McGregor. I'll be fine with Greer. We make a good team."

A statement dear to Glory's heart that had an odd ring of truth. She and the baobhan sith have forged an unlikely but real friendship.

Chase looked daggers in my direction. "That was dirty pool. I'm going with them."

This time, Festus laid down the law. "No, you're not. You're going to open the cobbler shop like usual. The town gossips don't need more fuel for their wagging tongues. If we all go rushing over to the *Banner* and Linda's killer is watching us— which I suspect he is— we'll be giving him the kind of validation sick creeps like that love."

When Chase started to argue, Festus softened, but not much. "I'll have the drone follow Pickle and Red from the instant they step outside. They'll both be wearing headsets. We'll get Adeline to route the feed to your phone so you can watch. If you see anything you don't like, I won't stop you from going over to the newspaper office."

That mollified Chase enough that he changed direction and headed for his shop, pausing on the way to kiss Glory and rub Willow's ears, but he was still grumbling under his breath when he rounded the corner to the connecting passageway.

~

When Greer and Glory stepped onto the sidewalk, the baobhan sith scanned the square. "Local activity normal, Big Tom. Proceeding to target."

"Roger that, Red Hot."

Rather than cut across the courthouse lawn, which would have allowed anyone in the newspaper office to see them coming, the pair walked toward the corner grocery.

After a few steps, Glory tapped Greer on the shoulder, pointed to her earpiece, and mouthed, "Turn it off?"

"Big Tom. Glory and I need to speak of a matter of feminine concern. Please cut our ear pieces until we reach the objective."

An explosion of profanity came across the channel. *"You two aren't out there to chitchat about dish patterns."*

"Very well. If you wish to hear your daughter-in-law speak in intimate terms about her honeymoon... "

"WHOA!" Festus yelped. *"No! God, no! Muting your mics now!"*

Glory giggled. "Greer, you're going to give him a hairball."

The baobhan sith shrugged. "Since we do not have far to walk, an expeditious strategy seemed to be in order. What did you wish to speak to me about?"

"I'm so sorry to do this in the middle of a mission, but with so many people in the lair right now, I didn't know when we'd have a chance to talk just the two of us."

"I understand. Is something troubling you?"

For a minute Glory looked like she might be having second thoughts and then the words tumbled out. "Festus is what's troubling me. I don't think he should have told Chase no in front of Willow like that."

She paused for breath and then, lower lip quivering, added, "And I don't think I'm going to be a good wife because I should have realized that when it was happening and stood up for Chase."

"You have been married less than a week. It seems premature to judge your long-term marital skills based on a single incident."

"Chase and I have been together a whole lot longer than a week and I haven't said a word about Festus always trying to put him in the corner like Baby in *Dirty Dancing*. That's a movie."

"I am familiar with the reference. Festus was correct in asking Chase to go about his normal business at the cobbler shop. The fewer disruptions to catch the attention of the local citizenry, the better. However, I may be able to ameliorate your self-recrimination to a degree. I do not believe Festus's stern behavior toward his son is without purpose."

"What do you mean?"

Pausing to check for traffic, the two crossed the street before Greer answered. "Chase showed bad judgment in regard to the Malcolm Ferguson incident."

That statement surprised Glory so much she almost tripped. "How can you know about what happened back then? That was before you came to Briar Hollow and when I was still stuck on the side of that awful cup."

"Awareness does not always require proximity. The DGI began to surveil Jinx the moment she came into her magic. Not to be indelicate... "

Glory made a dismissive gesture. "It's okay. Chase was in love with Jinx back then, but now he loves me."

"The two of you enjoy a far more balanced relationship than the one he experienced with Jinx. Chase allowed his feelings to cloud his judgment in those days. As Festus would put it, circumstances necessitated that Chase be 'benched' until he could adjust his perspective."

Glory skidded to a halt. "Oh! That just makes me so mad! Sometimes Festus is *impossible*. Chase has excellent perspective. He has better perspective than anybody in the whole world, and I don't mind saying that right to Festus McGregor's furry face."

Bemused, Greer put her hand on Glory's elbow and propelled her down the sidewalk. "That will not be necessary. Festus intends to offer Chase the position of Tanist to Clan McGregor."

With a blank look, Glory asked, "Is that good?"

"Chase will be second in command of the clan. He cannot be the protector of the Daughters of Knasgowa so long as his father holds that responsibility. However, to continue with the sports metaphor, Chase will be 'back in the game.'"

"Oh my goodness gracious! Chase will be thrilled to death. When is Dad going to tell him?"

"At the first opportunity, which I suspect will be when Chase speaks to his father about having been told to stay in his shop today."

Giggling, Glory said, "You see that conversation coming, too?"

"I do. Offended dignity of that proportion cannot be easily disguised. We have arrived at our destination."

No lights were visible at the edge of the drawn shade and the "Closed" sign was still in place. Glory shivered. "Something doesn't feel right."

"Indeed it does not," Greer replied, a faraway look in her eyes.

"Is it safe to try my key?"

"I believe so. There are no living beings inside this building."

"Does that mean there are dead people in there?" Glory asked, a faint ripple of green washing over her face. "Because, I don't like dead people."

"I smell stale blood, but that does not necessarily mean we will discover a corpse. Is there a rear entrance?"

"Yes."

"Will your key work in that lock?"

"I've never tried, but when Mr. Anderson gave me the key, he said it would."

"Then let us continue as if we are enjoying a pleasant morning stroll. At the corner, we will turn left. Shortly before we reach the alley, I will employ fairy dust to hide our movements."

As she finished speaking, a car pulled up at the curb and a woman got out. "Hi, Glory! I can't wait to read your column this week." Then, catching sight of the sign, the woman asked, "Is the *Banner* office closed?"

"Oh, hi, Laura Beth!" Glory gushed. "Your hair looks adorable today! Are you still going to Iradell to have it done? Oh, and where are my manners. This is my friend, Greer. She's related to Tori and her Mama. She's visiting all the way from Scotland. Can you just imagine?"

Primping at the compliment to her coiffure, Laura Beth said, "Hi, Greer. Are you related to that other Scottish lady who works in the apothecary? She makes the most wonderful soap in the world. My complexion has been tragic my whole life and Brenna fixed me right up."

"Brenna is my cousin," Greer said. "It's a pleasure to meet you."

Laura Beth squealed with delight. "Oh, I just love the way you Scottish people talk! You sound like that hunky man in that *Outlander* show. Did you read those books? They make me want to find some rocks standing up in a circle and dive right through back into time."

Without blinking, Greer said, "I do not think you would enjoy time travel."

Drawing her brows together as if thinking hurt, Laura Beth said, "How on earth could you know that?"

Sidling between them, Glory said, "Greer keeps her head poked in a book all the time. I bet she's read just about every story ever written about time travel, and you are so right about

Outlander. Did you need to see Mr. Anderson about something?"

"Oh my heavens, I almost forgot. I want to put a notice in the paper about our annual garage sale. Mama and I wouldn't miss selling junk to the neighbors for anything in the world."

"Of course you wouldn't!" Glory agreed with enthusiasm. "Now, you have to let me come over the night before so I can get the good stuff, you hear? I will not take no for an answer. Why don't you give me that notice and I'll make sure Mr. Anderson gets it."

"But don't I have to pay for it?" Laura Beth asked, reaching in her purse. "I can give you the money if you know how much the ad costs."

Making a tsking sound Glory said, "I don't know one thing about the advertising end of the business. I'll tell Mr. Anderson he has to run the ad for free because he made you wait."

"That is so sweet of you!" Laura Beth cried. "That's going to save me so much time. You all excuse me now. I have to switch cars with Jigger so I can take the truck over to the Baptist church and borrow the long tables from the fellowship hall."

As Laura Beth drove away, Greer said, "Jigger?"

"That's her husband," Glory explained. "He used to have a teensy problem with drinking too much but then he started going to those Triple A meetings and he's all better, but the nickname stuck."

"Why did you not share the news of your nuptials with her?"

"Oh," Glory said. "If I had done that Laura Beth would have kept us here an hour wanting to hear about every detail. I don't mean to be unkind, but she talks a lot. She's not self-restrained like me."

"*Bastet's whiskers!*" Festus swore in their ears. "*For starters, Pickle, you're as bad as Rube. Triple A does roadside assistance. You mean AA as in Alcoholics Anonymous. Jigger Millican is a moron*" *drunk or sober, and you wouldn't recognize self-restraint if it smacked you in the kisser. Now can we please get on with this?!"*

Rubbing at her ear, Glory said, "Gracious, Dad, you don't have to yell. We can hear you."

"Then move already!"

"Well, I never," she said in a huff. "We really have to have a talk about the kind of behavior you're modeling for your grand-daughter."

"Pickle... "

Taking control of the conversation, Greer said, "We're going through the back entrance. Do we have confirmation that the alleyway is clear?"

Over the open comm's link they heard Festus order a GNATS drone to make a reconnaissance run behind the building. As they turned the corner, the pilot radioed, *"All clear, Big Tom. Repeat, the alleyway is all clear."*

Greer threw a pinch of fairy dust into the air. The sparkling particles settled in a thin curtain.

"It's so pretty!" Glory breathed. "How does it work?"

"Anyone watching will see us continue down the street," Greer replied, cutting into the alleyway.

"But what about people who see the fake us? Won't they be suspicious when the sparkly stuff wears off and we disappear?"

"Only those who might have been watching when I dispersed the dust will see our images," Greer assured her, stopping in front of a metal fire door with *Briar Hollow Banner* stenciled at eye level. "If you will give me your key, I will go in alone."

"No," Glory said, drawing herself up. "I'll go with you. I owe that to Mr. Anderson."

Greer turned the key in the lock and pushed the door open. Faint light filtering in from the front windows cast the interior in mottled shadows. But even in the dim conditions, they both spotted the body of a man slumped over one of the desks.

"That's Mr. Anderson," Glory gasped. "Is he dead?"

Squatting beside the corpse, Greer snapped her fingers and ignited a bright green flame. "Quite dead and killed in the same fashion as Linda Albert."

"What do we do now?"

"You use the 2RABID to get as much information as possible," Festus said, *"and then you ruin Sheriff Johnson's day with a phone call."*

Chapter Twenty-Seven

Glory turned pale celery when Greer took out the 2RABID. "I can't watch Mr. Anderson be murdered. I just can't. He was my friend."

Through the earpiece, Festus said, *"We wouldn't ask you to do that, Pickle. There's a kitchen at the back of the office, right?"*

"Yes."

"Stay back there until Greer tells you to come out."

"Thank you, Dad," Glory said, choking on the words. "When you're not being awful, you're so very sweet."

Greer waited until Glory was safely out of the room to activate the scanner. "May I broadcast the feed to the lair?"

"Yeah. We had Rube take Willow up in the treehouse. He'll keep her there until I say she can come back."

The beam passed over the room illuminating the shadows but registering no residual energy.

"You can start any time," Festus said.

"I have already scanned the room once. No images appeared."

"That can't be right. Run it back the full 72 hours."

"Reba, increase scan to maximum time duration."

"Time duration increased."

The light brightened, but the results remained the same. "Festus, there are no residual energy imprints in this room."

"Not even Anderson going about regular business?"

"Nothing."

"That's never happened before."

"It would seem that the culprit has found a way to thwart your technology. What do you wish me to do?"

"How long do you think Larry has been dead?"

"I would estimate in the vicinity of 24-36 hours."

More profanity crackled through the earpiece. *"Have a good look around and then call the sheriff. If we wait any longer, Larry is gonna start getting ripe."*

A muffled gasp came across the line. *"Dad! That's not nice!"*

"Dead is dead, Pickle. You think you're upset now, wait until your boss starts smelling like three-day-old roadkill. And then there's the issue of the bugs... "

Interrupting before Festus could finish his grotesque thought, Greer said, "Instructions acknowledged, Big Tom. We are on it."

John Johnson chewed on his toothpick and stared at the red-haired woman dressed head to toe in black who was looking at him with cool green eyes. "And you are who exactly?"

"Greer MacVicar. My cousin Brenna Sinclair works in the apothecary with Gemma Andrews."

"Wouldn't that make you Gemma's cousin, too since she and Brenna are kin?"

"I descend from a different side of the family."

Rather than try to sort out the complicated ancestry, the Sheriff said, "Uh huh. You here visiting?"

"My work requires that I travel. I try to come to Briar Hollow whenever the opportunity presents itself. On this occasion I had the pleasure of returning to North Carolina with Chase and Glory after serving as maid of honor at their wedding."

At that news, the Sheriff's skeptical expression changed to a broad grin. "Well, son of a gun! Why didn't you say something Glory? Come here and let me give you a hug. Congratulations!"

With a happy squeal Glory allowed the Sheriff to lift her off the floor and swing her around. When he set her down, Johnson said, "Well, come on. Show me the pictures. I know you're dying to."

Pulling out her iPhone Glory launched into a long wedding narration. Peering at the Elvis impersonator who officiated, the Sheriff said, "That ole boy made it through last winter in good shape. He needs to get a bigger jumpsuit."

"Well," Glory said, "later in life Elvis did have a problem with his metabolism. The impersonator was striving for authenticity. After all, representing the King is his profession."

"Fair enough, "Johnson said. "Who's that guy giving you away? He looks sorta familiar."

Glory's eyes widened. "Oh, that's... "

"My brother, Fergus," Greer lied with ease. "He lives in Nevada."

"Do tell," Johnson said. "He looks like the cat that ate the canary in that picture."

"Brother is known for his droll sense of humor. I believe he had just made an inappropriate comment when that photograph was taken."

Johnson stared at the picture a few seconds longer and then said, "Okay, we need to get back to business. Tell me again why you all came over here."

"Well," Glory said, "I emailed a wedding photo and my column to Mr. Anderson and when he didn't answer, I got worried. Greer and I walked over to make sure that he wasn't sick or something. But the front door was locked, so we went around back and I used my key to get in. That's when we found him. It turns out what was wrong was much, much worse than him being sick."

Johnson rearranged his toothpick. "Yeah, I reckon you could put it that way."

Looking uncertain, Glory asked, "What's going to happen to the newspaper now?"

"The newspaper? Well, I suppose if Larry didn't leave it to anybody it'll go up for sale."

"That's not what I meant. This is the biggest news week in the history of Briar Hollow. Mr. Anderson would want the *Banner* to come out on schedule."

Casting a sidelong glance at the sheet-draped body, the Sheriff said, "I don't see how the newspaper is going to come out on schedule given the current condition of the editor."

"Why," Glory said, "*I'll* put it out. That is, if you'll let me be in here so I can do the necessary work."

Johnson looked skeptical. "Do you know how to publish the newspaper?"

Nodding earnestly, Gory said, "Mr. Anderson has been teaching me the business. I know I can do it. I *want* to do it. It's like a memorial."

"Well, we'll have to see about that. We're dealing with an active crime scene. You two go on home, and I'll let you know if you can come back into the building."

Glory and Greer exited into the alley and walked toward the apothecary. Festus waited until they had cleared the newspaper office to bellow through the earpiece, *"What in the name of Bastet's litter box are you thinking, Pickle? We're right in the middle of a crisis. This is no time for you to play Brenda Starr, girl reporter."*

Looking confused, Glory said, "I don't think I know Brenda. Is she from Briar Hollow?"

"Oh, for the love of the Great Cat! Brenda Starr *was a comic strip."*

"That was first published in 1947," Greer said. "As popular culture references go, your metaphor is rather dated."

"What. Ever. Forget about publishing the newspaper, Pickle. It's not happening."

"Now, Dad, you listen to me. We need to have a serious talk about your attitude... "

The Briar Hollow Sheriff's Office

"Novajean, I need a nap. Unless the courthouse burns down, I want an hour to myself."

Popping her gum, the Sheriff's secretary said, "Now, John, if the courthouse burns down that's the jurisdiction of the fire department."

"Fine. Then give me *two* hours."

Going into his office, Johnson closed the blinds and locked the door. Sitting down at the desk, he pulled off his boots and massaged his feet. If he stayed in law enforcement for the rest of his life he would never understand why the "look" demanded he clomp around like a cowboy.

Feeling under the top drawer, he removed a magnetic box. Using the key inside, Johnson unlocked the file drawer and pulled out a battery-operated kettle, a bottle of water, and a box of green tea.

He filled the kettle and waited until steam curled from the spout. Filling his cup, the Sheriff took a personal iPad out of the drawer while he waited for the bag to steep.

Following the discovery of Linda Albert's body, Johnson

emailed a buddy with the New Orleans police who owed him a favor. Now the Sheriff had a dead newspaper editor on his hands with the same bizarre neck wounds.

"This may call for more than green tea," Johnson said to himself, rummaging in his private stash until he came up with a small brown bottle of CBD. Dribbling the hemp extract into his drink, the Sheriff popped in a set of earbuds and hit play on his favorite *Thunder and Gentle Rain* ambient track.

His contact in Louisiana had replied with a fat PDF attachment that contained a collection of documents. Johnson started with a report on Bertille Bergeron.

The bookstore owner appeared to have been a solid citizen in the Big Easy. A few months before her relocation to Briar Hollow, however, Bergeron's boyfriend, Andre Melancon, went missing.

Sipping his tea, Johnson swiped the page and scanned the investigation summary. The detective noted signs of a violent struggle in Melancon's condo, but no blood. The premises smelled strongly of swamp water, a detail for which no one had an explanation.

Opening the Notes app, the Sheriff started a list.

(1) Who followed Bergeron to Briar Hollow?

(2) Why was Linda killed instead of Bertille?

(3) What does Larry Anderson have to do with any of this? Was he asking questions that got him killed?

Moving to the next page of the PDF, Johnson found a second crime scene report. The proprietor of a business described as a "metaphysical emporium" was discovered dead in his store from a "stab wound to the neck that mimicked the bite of a large predator."

Johnson frowned. Could Linda have been killed by some kind of strange weapon? He hadn't even considered that.

Reaching for the phone, he punched in a series of numbers.

When a man answered Johnson said, "Doc, you had time to look at my murder victim?"

"And a cheery good morning to you, too, John. As it happens, I just finished. Nasty business. If I didn't know better I'd swear a dog killed the poor woman. Bite pattern is canine, but there's no saliva in the wound."

"You know of a weapon that could make a mark like that?"

"Afraid I don't, John."

"Thanks, Doc. I hate to tell you this, but I'm sending you another body with the same wound. After you compare the two victims, can you go ahead and release Ms. Albert's body? She's got friends who want to see her laid to rest proper like."

"That shouldn't be a problem. We'll try to get her home to Briar Hollow this afternoon."

Signing off on the call, the Sheriff shoved the odds and ends on his desk aside and took a large rectangle of brown wrapping paper out of his secret drawer. Unfolded, the sheet revealed an intricate diagram covered with scribbles all color coded.

Lines connected groups of words, some circled, others starred. A wild array of arrows and coded symbols decorated the self-styled flow chart, a project Johnson began about three months after Jinx Hamilton inherited her Aunt Fiona's store.

Studying the chart, the sheriff ran his finger along the timeline from the young woman's arrival in town to the present day. Events transcribed in neat block letters jumped off the page.

- Hamilton girl and friend solve serial killing.
- Reports of unusual light disturbances in and around cemetery.
- Pete the Pizza Guy goes missing.
- One Brenna Sinclair buys building on square. Disappears.
- Gemma Andrews buys same building.

- Brenna comes back and goes to work for her. Supposedly related?
- Fish Pike found dead on bench in front of Jinx's store.
- Fall festival goers report strange dreams, fragmented memories of lightning storm.
- Anton Ionescu reported dead from electrical mishap in home.
- Three local ghost hunters claim attacked by "vicious tiny insects."
- Kelly Hamilton, Gemma Andrews wreck rented van. Claim to be moving furniture. Nothing in van. Blame crash on "white deer."
- Scrap Andrews dies of mysterious blood ailment as per death certificate.
- Some customers comment on Jinx displaying "robotic" behavior.
- Who is Glory Green?
- Who is Lucas Grayson?
- What is up with Chase McGregor's cat?
- Uptick in local raccoon activity? Why?
- Courthouse ghost spotted during divorce trial.

The most recent annotation involved the incident with supposed giant insects at Stella Mae Crump's house.

The Sheriff would have assumed Stella Mae was hitting the bottle if he hadn't personally bagged and tagged a grasshopper leg as long as a .12 gauge shotgun that was currently on ice in the evidence room freezer.

And now he had two dead locals and a break-in on the square in less than a week. Maybe the time had come to have a heart-to-heart talk with Jinx Hamilton.

Chapter Twenty-Eight

I n the interest of what Seneca called "personnel allocation," I decided to leave Festus in charge of monitoring the developing investigation at the newspaper office.

Honestly, by that point, I didn't have time to mourn Larry Anderson's death. I knew the man from working on the SpookCon committee with him and running the occasional unnecessary ad in the *Banner* in the name of good business relations.

Mainly, I felt for Glory. He'd taken a chance on her talents with the advice column. The reception buoyed her confidence and speeded her recovery from the abuse she suffered at Chesterfield's hands.

For that, if nothing else, I grieved for Larry, but that grief and my feelings about Linda's death took a back seat to stopping the killers in our midst—and Beau needed me.

Mom and I had promised him we'd help pick out clothes for Linda's laying out. I didn't want the colonel to think we'd lost sight of the importance of the murdered woman's funeral.

Bertille, Seneca, and Edgar left for Bergeron books to begin sorting through the inventory and Tori volunteered to run the store.

"Are you sure?" I said. "You must be dying to get back to Drake Abbey."

"Of course I want to go back," she admitted, "but we have to catch these bastards first. How are you doing on figuring out your greatest strength?"

She already knew the answer, so I didn't bother lying. "Lousy and terrified. How am I supposed to sort through everyone and everything around me and come up with one person, place, or thing?"

"You'll figure it out," she assured me, before switching topics and asking about Beau's state of mind.

Mortuary-related details absorbed all Beau's attention. On the short drive to Linda's house he and Mom discussed the service while I kept a watchful eye on the sidewalks for menacing strangers.

My mind rocketed from one wild scenario to the next. Linda was connected to Beau. Glory worked for Larry Anderson. Who would be next? When the talk in the car turned to caskets, however, the intricate details penetrated my preoccupied state and I tuned back in to the discussion.

If you've never been involved in picking out a casket, funeral homes don't hand out color swatches. Beau would have been happier if they did. My Prius hadn't cleared the square before he produced a slick catalog studded with sticky note bookmarks.

Pointing at a photo of a lavender coffin with a pale plum lining, Beau said, "Miss Linda wore a frock in a similar shade to the Easter services at the Baptist church. The color is lovely, but I fear the presentation could be overwhelming. What is your opinion Miss Kelly?"

Mom agreed that all purple might be too much, but suggested the lavender dress could work with a more understated coffin. Thankfully they didn't ask for my input because when Beau brandished the catalog I caught sight of the prices.

Even if we did intend to conjure the cash, $8000 was an obscene amount to pay for something going under six feet of dirt. Don't even get me started on the vault to go over the casket.

I'm not a huge fan of hermetically sealing a corpse in nesting boxes. It's not like the deceased will be exhumed and put on display at some future date.

But I kept those opinions to myself. Beau's feelings were far too fragile for me to wise off. As a Fae witch, I have an indeterminate lifespan, but I made a mental note to have a discussion with Lucas about what I did and didn't want for my own "arrangements."

The funeral planners were still going full steam when I pulled up to the curb and cut the engine.

"Should we be worried about someone being in there?" I asked, looking past Beau and toward Linda's white two-story cottage.

"According to Greer we're dealing with a standard vampire from fiction. Linda would have had to invite him inside," Mom said. "They can't enter a human dwelling on their own. If Linda had done that, they would have killed her here. We can get Festus to send a drone over to look inside if it would make you feel better."

"No. He has his paws full with the Larry Anderson situation. I think we'll be okay."

Even to my ears the words lacked conviction, but I opened the door with fake resolution and headed up the walk.

We let ourselves in with a key the Sheriff gave Beau. Going into someone's empty house has always given me the creeps. I'll volunteer to water the plants for you, but only during the day and preferably with backup.

In this case the someone was dead, which upped the freaked

out factor for me by several levels. Not mom. She charged right for the kitchen to find a pitcher to make sure Linda's ferns continued to outlive her.

Beau and I stood awkwardly in the living room, which was lined with oak bookcases. Judging from the presence of a matching card catalog, Linda indexed her home library the old-fashioned way.

The volumes beside Linda's overstuffed easy chair bristled with scraps of paper covered in notes written in the librarian's precise hand. Linda wasn't a casual reader. She engaged with the text and relished spearheading a book club known for the vigorous discussion of themes and ideas.

The eerie silence made me long to light the fire and inject a spark of warmth into the lonely setting. The bookcases continued down the hallway and into the kitchen, with additional free standing shelves there and in the dining room.

Having completed her fern rescue, Mom examined a curio cabinet housing a collection of inkwells and dip pens. "Books and words really were her life."

Beau ran his fingers along the edge of a framed photo of Linda and a group of women standing under a banner proclaiming, "American Library Association."

"She must have friends and colleagues in the profession who should be apprised of her passing," he said. "We must ensure that Miss Linda is appropriately remembered. Also, I believe it would be fitting to ask the members of her book club to serve as pallbearers."

My mind flashed on the memory of eight stalwart men, my father among them, struggling to carry Tori's Granny Mo up a steep slope to her final resting place in the cove where she'd lived as a young woman and then as a widow.

"Aren't most of the book club members women?" I asked.

"Yes," Beau said, "but to my surprise the undertaker

informed me that women increasingly take on this task. The ground leading to my obelisk is level, which will ease their labor."

Taking out her phone, mom started a to-do list, adding details as we moved through the house. We found a roster of the book club membership on Linda's desk and an old copy of *American Libraries* yielded contact information for the professional group.

When we climbed the stairs to Linda's bedroom we discovered a light, airy space. A beautiful handmade quilt covered the bed now bathed in sunbeams cascading through the skylight.

I imagined how nice it would be to lie in that four-poster and stargaze or watch the rain while the branches of the old hickory outside the window brushed against the panes.

Turning to ask Beau a question, I was surprised to see him standing at the threshold. "Are you okay?" I asked, thinking the grim visit might be too much for him.

"A gentleman should not enter the boudoir of a woman to whom he is not married," he replied, color rising in his cheeks. "It is not proper."

Beau has come so far in embracing a 21st century life, I forget that he's a man displaced in time. Moving to him, I caught hold of his hands. Under my fingers I felt his heavy gold Masonic ring.

Masons believe in honor and personal responsibility. Beau epitomizes those principles with heartbreaking sincerity. "Linda wouldn't be offended if you come into her bedroom," I told him. "You're being her good friend by taking this on."

He nodded and followed me over to the closet, moving with reluctant, halting steps. Rifling through the hangars, I pulled out the lavender dress. "Is this the outfit she wore on Easter Sunday?"

"Yes. She looked exceptionally lovely that day,"

I almost had a heart attack when a voice behind us said, "Thank you, Beau, but don't you think that dress makes me look heavy?"

A gasp sounded from the bureau where mom was rummaging for a scarf to disguise Linda's neck wound.

The librarian's ghost stood near the window. I could make out the outline of the hickory through her gossamer form. Seeing our shock, Linda said, "I didn't mean to startle you all. Welcome to my home."

Mom and I looked to Beau. He was, after all, the one qualified to be dealing with recently deceased spirits. "Why are you here, Miss Linda? Your soul should be at peace."

Linda put a somewhat more pertinent question to the colonel. "Well, if we're going to play twenty questions, why didn't you ever tell me you're a ghost?"

In Beau's defense, that is a difficult topic to work into a casual conversation.

"The circumstances of my current corporeality are complex," he stammered. "I have been entrusted with secrets that I am not at liberty to reveal."

"You mean that Jinx and her Mama are witches and a lot of magical activity goes on at the store?"

For as much as I hated to see Beau so discomfited, I felt nothing but relief that post-mortem Linda seemed clued in to the magical underbelly of life in Briar Hollow. There is no *Cliff's Notes* version of the Fae world and we didn't have time for lengthy explanations.

When the silence in the room stretched past anyone's comfort level, Mom suggested that we go downstairs and talk in the living room.

"Oh my goodness!" Linda exclaimed. "Where are my manners? I can't fix anything for you all, but if you want to make a pot of coffee for yourselves, I have some cookies that will go stale if someone doesn't eat them."

I agreed to make coffee just to give myself time to think. Clearly we'd dealt with ghosts before, and faced the prospect of asking a murder victim to describe how they were killed, but those people were strangers. We knew Linda—and Beau, whether he was willing to admit it or not, was in love with her.

When I came out of the kitchen carrying three cups and a small plate of cookies on a tray, Linda was sitting in her chair staring in dismay at the stack of reading material. "Is there some way that I can finish these books?" she asked. "Since I've been home I've tried to pick things up and I can't do it."

"You have not been on the other side for a sufficient length of time to cultivate such skills," Beau explained, "and I hope you do not remain among us long enough to do so."

The librarian looked hurt. "Aren't you happy to see me?"

Horrified Beau said, "Of course I am happy to see you, but I do not want you to walk the earth for decades as I have."

In a small voice, Linda said, "But we can be together now, unless you're seeing another ghost."

Poor Beau looked like he wanted the floor to open up and swallow him. "Miss Linda, I have been completely honest with you. I have not entered into a romantic relationship out of respect for my late wife, but if I were to do so, I quite assure you that you would be the lady to whom I would offer my affections."

That seemed to mollify the librarian. I suspected that she believed given sufficient time she could win Beau over. "Eternity" qualifies as "sufficient" by anyone's standards.

I shot Mom a pleading glance. We didn't need telepathy for her to get the message. *"Do something!"*

Clearing her throat, Mom said, "Linda if it wouldn't be too

distressing, could you answer a few questions about your arrangements for us? We want to honor your wishes."

"Oh, that will be fun!" Linda said. "And when we're done, we can talk about that thing that murdered me. We wouldn't want it to kill someone else."

That boat had sailed, but Linda didn't need to know that until she came home with us.

Oh, come on. You knew I was going to say that. We couldn't leave her there and indelicate though this might sound, Linda might be able to save us a heck of a lot of time.

Chapter Twenty-Nine

THE WITCH'S BREW, TORI

Tori ran a wet cloth down the length of the counter. "Do you think he's up for this?" she asked Jinx, casting a worried look in Beau's direction.

"He needs something to do other than beat himself up that he didn't walk into the library five minutes sooner."

"Poor guy. I hope planning Linda's service will give him some comfort," Tori said. She jerked her head toward the morning crowd and whispered, "It doesn't sound like word has gotten out about Larry."

"Good," Jinx replied. "Hopefully we'll be back before it does. Sheriff Johnson is getting cagey. He and his deputies rolled up behind the newspaper office in John's truck."

"Why would they do that?"

"Because the Sheriff has figured out that someone is probably watching and enjoying the effect the crime scenes have on the anxiety level in town," Jinx said. "Be careful if anyone comes in that you don't know."

Tori rolled her eyes. "Come on, Jinksy. I've known the 'don't talk to strangers' rule since we were like three."

"Good rules bear repeating. Call me if anything heats up over at the *Banner.*"

"Will do. Any idea when Linda's service will be held? People are wondering."

"No, but I should know more when we get back."

After Jinx, Kelly, and Beau went out the back door, Tori started unpacking a delivery. As she put paper cups and lids in the cupboards, she listened to the buzz of conversation from the morning coffee drinkers.

Part of her really did want to be at Drake Abbey, but she couldn't abandon the homefront during a worsening crisis. That would absolutely get her booted out of the Sidekick Hall of Fame.

While she worked, she caught snippets of murder theories that floated over the counter.

"I heard Linda was involved with someone in Cotterville."

Tori didn't say anything, but the groundless accusation made her blood boil. The gossips seemed to be blaming Linda for her own death. Typical.

"No, Lou Ann told me Linda took up with a married man at the last library convention she went to."

At that, Tori slammed a cabinet door harder than necessary to indicate she could hear what was being said. Linda didn't deserve to be the center of small-minded, salacious conspiracy theories.

The volume of the grisly chitchat dropped, but not before Tori overheard one last unfair supposition.

"I'll bet she got tangled up with somebody on the Internet like Fish Pike did. Look what that got him."

The town would never stop talking about crazy old Fish. Now Linda seemed to be doomed to enjoy similar infamy in local lore. Would anyone remember the years of hard work the poor woman had devoted to making the library an institution in the community?

A callous thought made Tori wince. As much as she hated the gossip, any of the theories circulating among the patrons would, in some way, be better than the truth.

Morgan le Fay had brought her vendetta to the streets of Briar Hollow as phase one of a grotesque plan to remake history to her advantage. Not one of the townspeople with their wagging tongues had any idea that a centuries old sorceress was probing the weaknesses in the fairy mound—any more than they knew their sleepy community was a power center in the Three Realms.

Lost in thought and preoccupied with emptying boxes, Tori almost didn't look up when the bell on the front door jingled.

A stranger stood framed against the morning light, the sun's rays making the highlights in his jet black hair appear almost blue. His style of dress looked out of place and old fashioned. Wire rectangular spectacles with purple lenses obscured his eyes.

The din of animated conversation died, but when Tori called out, "Good morning. Welcome to the *Witch's Brew*," no one looked up.

She realized too late that none of the patrons could see the man in the doorway. He was the dangerous stranger Jinx had been talking about, and Tori had just given him an open invitation to walk in and make himself at home.

Offering her a thin smile, the newcomer crossed the floorboards with silent steps, which should have been impossible since he wore leather-soled shoes.

"Good morning, are you the proprietress of this establishment?"

His voice carried a strange weight that made Tori's head feel tight. "I'm one of the owners. May I help you?"

Bowing, he said, "Allow me to introduce myself. I am Jean-Baptiste Dampierre. Might I trouble you for an espresso?"

From a great distance Tori heard the faint echo of Myrtle's voice. *"Do not allow him to draw you into conversation. Resist."*

"You're not here to drink coffee," Tori said. "What do you want?"

Dampierre's smile broadened. "Ah. I see that the aos si intends to intrude on our time. That is unfortunate. You ask what I want, but would we not make more progress if I were to ask what you want, Victoria Andrews?"

"I want you to turn around and walk out of this store."

"My departure will become inevitable before long. Already I feel Brenna Sinclair pushing against this intimate bubble I have created. Let us not waste these fleeting moments. Are you content to spend the rest of your life in the shadow of the Witch of the Oak?"

The question crawled into Tori's consciousness with seductive intent. She blinked against a tide of mounting confusion. "If you think I'm going to talk to you about Jinx, you're sadly mistaken."

"What has that commendable loyalty gained you? As we speak the Witch is abroad in the day searching for killers while you serve as barmaid to inconsequential humans. I can show you a different life. Your father had the imagination to reach beyond his sniveling humanity. Do you not wish to follow his example?"

"Make me proud, baby."

Gasping Tori shrank against the back wall. "Stop it. That is not my father's voice. He's dead."

"You are an alchemist. The barrier between life and death can be crossed if you will but set aside your so-called ethics."

Tori knew where Dampierre was trying to lead her, and she

wasn't going to follow. "Necromancy is an abomination," she said with conviction. "I refuse to explore the dark side."

"Think, Victoria. The curiosity that drew your father to Seraphina and Ioana courses in your veins. Do you not long to release that fiery passion? To discover the true extent of the abilities you hold in check out of deference to the Witch of the Oak?"

Scrap's pleading, disembodied voice returned. *"Don't you want to bring me back, Tori? You're my little girl."*

Clapping her hands over her ears, Tori cried, "No! I don't want to bring you back. Not at the expense of my soul."

The basement door flew open. One moment Brenna stood at the head of the stairs, the next she put her body between Dampierre and Tori.

"Leave this place, creature of the night, or suffer the consequences."

Dampierre brushed off the threat. "You will not battle me with fragile humans only feet from the field of play, but I will go. If you do not wish me to return, Reborn Witch, I suggest you erect stronger wards and instruct Victoria in vampiric etiquette. I am here because she invited me inside."

With an exaggerated bow he said, "We will meet again, Victoria. Our business has yet to be completed."

Turning on his heel, he strolled out of the store. The instant he crossed the threshold, the rumble of conversation returned. The customers showed no sign of having heard the tense exchange.

Brenna turned and put her arm around Tori, "Did he touch you?"

Trembling, Tori said, "No, he didn't get that close. He's right. I knew not to ask him inside and I did it anyway. He's the master vampire, isn't he?"

"Yes, and as we feared, he walked through our perimeter spells."

Trying to tamp down her fear, Tori said, "I heard Myrtle's voice in my head. She told me not to talk to him. Why didn't she do something to help me?"

Gesturing toward the counter, Brenna cast an illusion barrier between them and the customers and then drew Tori into a tight embrace.

"I am sorry, granddaughter. She has gone to Tír na nÓg. Only the aos si could make her voice heard across the realms. I broke through his mesmerization as quickly as I could. He's extremely old and powerful."

Against Brenna's shoulder, Tori murmured, "You left out scary, Grams."

"That as well."

The back door opened. Jinx took in the scene behind the counter and came straight to the espresso bar. "What happened? Are you okay?"

"We had a visitor," Tori said. "Of the bloodsucking variety. Grams scared him off."

"Hardly," Brenna said. "He chose to leave. We have a great deal of work to do to prevent his return."

The sorceress caught sight of Linda's ghost and raised an eyebrow. Tori followed her gaze. The spirit was standing beside Beau, whose hands were full of books.

"Uh, Jinksy? What the what?"

"She was in her house rattling around trying to figure out how to finish her reading list. We couldn't leave her there. Besides, she's the only witness we have to her murder."

"Yeah," Tori deadpanned. "Victims are handy like that."

"I will take over here," Brenna said. "Don't worry. The customers will not see you go through the doorway to the basement."

Tori cast a worried eye toward the front of the store. "Do you think he'll be back?"

"No," Brenna said, "but should he try, he will not get through me."

Taking off her apron, Tori handed it to her grandmother. "Thanks for bailing me out of trouble, Grams."

As she turned to follow the group downstairs, Dampierre whispered in Tori's mind, *"Next time, I will take precautions to ensure that we are not interrupted, Victoria. I know you are intrigued by my offer. You have but to ask and I will come to you."*

The chilling intrusion made Tori stumble. Jinx caught her by the elbow. "Hey, are you really okay?"

"Sure," Tori said, flashing her signature grin. "You know me. Always tripping over my own feet. Come on. We need to get Linda downstairs."

Dampierre's sinister chuckle filled her head and didn't go away until Tori stepped into the protective envelope of the fairy mound's magic. As she passed through the membrane, the vampire's seductive voice purred, *"You cannot hide beneath the ground forever, Victoria."*

Chapter Thirty

We had multiple reasons to get out of the store and into the lair. I trusted Brenna's obfuscation magic. The patrons wouldn't notice us, much less see Linda's ghost, but now that the master vampire had penetrated the store's defenses, I felt exposed and vulnerable above ground.

While we were still on the stairs, I stopped Tori. "What the hell happened up there?"

She tried to shrug off the encounter. "I did something dumb. Grams saved my butt. End of story."

That was nowhere *near* the end of the story.

Everyone has that one emotional reaction they don't handle well. I'm not good with the place between uncertainty and surprise. Tori doesn't want anyone to know when she's scared, but she wasn't fooling me.

Fear radiated off her in waves. That business about tripping over her own feet as we were heading downstairs was nonsense. If anything, I'm the clumsy one. She's as sure-footed as a goat, and as stubborn to boot.

She must have sensed that I was about to press her to tell me the truth. Shifting into fairy mound hostess mode, Tori chirped with bright enthusiasm worthy of Glory, "Welcome to the bat cave, Linda."

The librarian stopped on the landing, awed by the view of the lair, the endless shelves of the archive stretching into the distance, and the Wrecking Crew's tree house rising above it all.

"Are there any real bats?" she gasped.

"Not that we've seen," Tori replied, "but if you want some, I'm sure we can find a few."

Lucky for us, Linda has a sense of humor. She giggled, and then caught sight of the bookshelves flanking the fireplace. One minute the librarian was standing beside us and the next she was running her fingers over the antique spines.

Festus, who was sitting on his desk, let out an audible groan. "For the love of all that's feline! What the hell is she doing here? We don't exactly have time for a *Ghost Whisperer* revival."

Linda tore her attention away from the shelves long enough to gape at the talking ginger feline. *"You!"* she said, pointing an accusing finger at Festus. "I always suspected you were more than a run-of-the-mill alley cat."

Executing one of those slow "oh, you did *not* just say that" blinks, he drawled, "Well, that's a back-pawed compliment if I ever heard one. Looks like death upped your IQ, Linda."

Rather than being offended, the ghost considered his sarcasm with far greater seriousness than it deserved.

"I don't think being smarter has anything to do with it," she said. "I can just see and understand things now that were always right in front of my face."

Beau, in his role as tour guide to the newly deceased, said, "I experienced a similar awakening after my passing. Although I did not communicate with the living until Miss Fiona began to frequent the cemetery, I was aware that Briar Hollow and its immediate environs were home to beings whose abilities transcend those of mere mortals."

Still looking Festus over, Linda asked, "Are you always a house cat?"

Never give a werecat a chance to show off. Festus triggered the shimmering curtain of his shifter magic. Within seconds a tawny mountain lion with a gray muzzle answered the question.

"No, but if I walked around town looking like this some idiot would take a shot at me. I have a human form, too, but we don't know each other well enough for you to see me buck naked."

I would have expected the abrupt transformation to frighten Linda, but she didn't flinch. Beau, on the other hand, looked mortified.

"Miss Linda, please forgive Festus's overly forthright nature. He does not always think before he speaks."

"Damn straight I don't," Festus yawned. "That would be a hell of a waste of time since whatever comes out of my mouth is exactly what I mean to say."

Linda laughed. "I always liked you Festus, but it's a delight to meet you this way. You're everything I thought a talking cat would be."

Susceptible as always to flattery, the werecat said, "Okay, she can stay."

Returning her attention to the bookcases, Linda said, "These are very old." Then, realizing she was making physical contact with the volumes, she asked, "Why can I touch them?"

"The space beneath the store imparts a solidifying effect on noncorporeal beings," Beau explained. "That is why I brought your current reading material along. You will be able to hold and finish the books during your stay with us."

Then he coughed self-consciously and added, "We play host to a vast trove of fascinating materials. I would be happy to escort you through the holdings should such an excursion be of interest to you."

Tori caught my attention and raised her eyebrows. As stilted as their conversation might be, Beau and Linda were flirting with each other. When Linda answered him, her eyes shone with adoration.

"Oh, Beau! I would like that very much. What system do you use to catalog the materials?"

Festus made a hairball hacking sound, but I silenced him with a warning glare.

"A method of our own devising," Beau answered. "One that employs an artificial intelligence to cross reference the materials. Miss Glory and I rely on computer tablets to photograph and index the holdings."

Linda looked so excited she glowed like a Christmas tree bulb. "Beau, that's amazing! Things at the library have been so much more efficient since we began to use computers. I miss the card catalog, but that doesn't matter. We have to keep modernizing for the benefit of the patrons."

The poor woman didn't seem to have fully accepted that her tenure as local librarian had come to a definitive end.

Rather than be the harbinger of bad news, I let them have their book nerd moment. Looking at Festus I jerked my head toward the war room. Nodding, he jumped off his desk, shifting in mid-air and nailing a three-point landing.

"You're full of yourself today," I said.

"Jealous?" he asked with a flip of his tail.

"You wish," I muttered.

Tori, Mom, and I followed the werecat into the war room and closed the door. Beau would keep Linda well occupied. At the moment, I was far more interested in getting to the bottom of what happened between Tori and the master vampire.

The back-and-forth between Linda and Festus had given Tori more time to collect herself and hide whatever she was truly feeling. At my prompting, she offered up an unconvincingly dispassionate account of her encounter that only left me more worried.

I didn't have an opportunity to express that, however, since Festus threw a fit.

"What in the name of Bastet's litter box was Myrtle thinking running off to Tír na nÓg?" he fumed. "Brenna's going to have to up her warding game if this vamp just strolled through the front door. And why in the name of the Great Cat didn't you let us know what was going on right over our heads?"

"The vampire didn't just stroll in," Tori said. "I'm partially to blame for the security failure. I was preoccupied and welcomed him into the store before I realized he was bad news. If I hadn't issued the invitation, the wards might have held."

I could tell Mom was starting to have her own suspicions about the vampire's effect on Tori. "Don't be so hard on yourself," she said. "Any of us could have made the same mistake. "We have to get more information about this Jean-Baptiste Dampierre."

We all turned at the sound of the door opening. Greer strode in, the fire of the baobhan sith smoldering in her eyes. "That will be an easy matter. I am acquainted with Jean-Baptiste though I believed him to be dead. He qualifies as far more than 'bad news.' Tori, have you heard his voice within your thoughts?"

Tori didn't look away, but I know her body language. She was controlling her urge to escape Greer's probing attention. Tapping the side of her head with her index finger, Tori said, "Nope. Nobody home in here but me."

Looking back on that moment I should have listened to my gut, which told me that while my best friend wasn't exactly lying, she also wasn't telling the whole truth.

Later I would learn Greer had much the same reaction in the moment, but kept the suspicion to herself.

We would both live to regret that shared reticence.

Chapter Thirty-One

Tori's blithe assurances didn't fly with Mom either. She shot me a sidelong glance that I answered with an imperceptible nod. Tori and I would be revisiting the topic of vampiric encounters in private.

For the moment, however, I let my suspicions drop and turned to Greer. "How do you know what happened in the store?"

"I sensed Jean-Baptiste's presence, but also Brenna's confrontation with him. Glory and I were in the alleyway behind the apothecary. It seemed prudent to return home through the fairy mound."

The door banged opened again and Rube trundled in. "You ain't the only one that got the metal-physical 411 Red. *Day-um!* That bloodsucker had every hair on my striped backside standing straight up. Sorry turn of eventuals when a coon can't even get a nap around this joint."

With that, he scaled the leg of the conference table and stopped in front of Tori's chair. "You good, Doll?"

After she fed him the same fake line she used with us, Rube

proceeded down the middle of the table tossing a casual "yo, McGregor" in Festus's direction before coming to me.

"Hat Man wanted I should tell you that he dropped a dime on Otto at IBIS. The doc's got some ideas on how to axe the rougarou, so your hubby shoved off for Londinium. He'll be back for supper."

Axe the rougarou? Was I the only one who remembered that beast started out as a *human?*

Festus cut short my moral protestations. "Before we get our tails in a twist over Andre the Airedale, I would like to know how Greer got on a first name basis with a vampire her mother killed who is now working for Morgan le Fay."

The baobhan sith crossed her long legs and flicked a speck of dust off one knee. "I can assure you of one thing with complete assurance. Jean-Baptiste might work with Morgan, but he most assuredly does not work *for* her or anyone else."

The weight of that idea hit me hard. Myrtle's revelations from the previous evening left me with the impression Morgan operated as a solo arch villain. I assumed the rougarou and the vampire were henchmen, not partners.

My face must have betrayed my distress because Rube asked, "You okay, Jinx? Green for green you're giving the Glorster a run for her pizza-anchos."

"Pistachios," I said on reflex. "Greer, how *do* you know this Dampierre guy?"

Almost nothing makes the baobhan sith uncomfortable, but I thought I saw something akin to chagrin flit over her angular features. "In a young and rebellious stage of my existence I associated with Jean-Baptiste for the primary purpose of annoying my mother."

Tori wasn't about to let that admission go. "Are you telling us that guy was your teenage bad boy boyfriend?" she gasped. "And your mother killed him?"

Greer arranged her features in impassive lines. "Neither Jean-Baptiste nor I were teenagers at the time, but there was an... involvement of which my mother did not approve."

Well, that sure as heck tops hooking up with your high school ex at the class reunion. Not that I would know anything about that, you understand.

Beside me Rube unzipped his waist pack and took out a massive burrito wrapped in wax paper. "Geez, Red. I woulda thought your Mom knew dead from dead. This guy's like one of them cockroaches that drinks the *Raid* and starts moving the furniture."

"A droll but disturbingly accurate assessment of Jean-Baptiste's resilience," the baobhan sith demurred.

Rube unwrapped his snack unleashing a fragrant aroma that made me realize the food was warm. My mind gave over to a healthy case of shock and denial, switching from the disturbing topic at hand to the realization I missed lunch.

"How do you keep stuff hot in there?" I asked the raccoon.

Delighted by the chance to talk about his bottomless supply of edibles, Rube replied, "Ironweed ain't the only one putting fairy dust to good use. A guy gets tired of cold chow, you know. You want one?"

"Can I get it with guacamole?"

"Sure thing," he replied, diving deeper in the bottomless pack.

When I accepted the food I realized everyone in the war room was staring at me with horrified faces. "What?" I asked defensively. "I'm hungry."

And also in serious need of comfort food, but that wasn't up for sharing.

"For starters," Tori said, "don't let Darby see you eating anything he didn't cook and since when did you take up second-hand dumpster diving?"

"Hey!" Rube yelped. "What's wrong with dumpster diving?"

Tuning both of them out, I bit into my impromptu meal. My taste buds went into a happy dance over the explosion of flavors. "Rube, this is incredible."

"Thanks, Doll. Was you thinking a guy who likes his chow as much as I do couldn't cook?"

"I guess I took you for more of a forager."

He reached into his pack again and handed me a napkin. "Eating out ain't what it used to be. Too much tofu and vegan crap. Don't even get me started on the glutton-free glop."

"Gluten-free," I said, wiping guacamole off my chin. "I agree with you. Tastes like cardboard."

When Festus put a paw over his eyes, I realized that for once, I was the one responsible for letting the conversation wander down a gustatory rabbit trail. "Sorry. Where were we?"

"We were delving into Greer's sordid, checkered past with common run-of-the-mill vamp trash," Festus purred. "Did the two of you get matching coffins?"

I saw a frisson of green fire run through the baobhan sit's eyes, but she refused to let the werecat bait her.

"As I was saying, Jean-Baptiste appears to have survived his encounter with my mother, an odd occurrence since she tends to be efficient at eradication. Myrtle has gone to Tír na nÓg to discuss the matter with her."

"The two of them picked a hell of a time to go off and have a hen party," Festus grumbled.

"Please," Greer said. "Do say that to mother the next time you are in her company. It will be a most entertaining exchange."

The werecat made a dismissive sound, but I saw his ears lower a fraction. No one in their right mind wants to cross swords—verbal or otherwise—with Katherine MacVicar.

Rube finished his burrito, wadding up the wrapper and

using the corner of Festus's desk to bank the resulting ball in the trash can. "Okey dokey," he said, clapping his black paws together. "So who's the biggest big bad here? Morgan or this Damp-pear, dude? And what's the plan?"

When no one rushed to answered the question, the raccoon accurately assessed the implication of the silence. "Right. We ain't got no idea. Perfect. So now what?"

I looked at Festus. "Well, Mr. Head of Security, what's your take on the priorities?"

The werecat raised his good hind leg and scratched at his ear. "I don't think Dampierre will be back today, but I'd leave Brenna in charge of the store until closing time. Greer, do you have any idea when Myrtle will be back?"

"No, but I can place a mirror call to my mother."

Looking over at Tori, I said, "We should probably try to talk to Linda."

She answered with an audible groan. "I hope you have a good opening line for that conversation because 'hey Linda, how was your murder?' could come off as insensitive."

Chapter Thirty-Two

I rewarded Tori's remark with the sarcasm it deserved. "Ya think?" I asked. "Come on. Let's get this over with."

We both got up and exited the room, but I stopped Tori halfway to the lair. She took one look at my face and said, "Don't start."

"Don't hold out on me and I won't start."

That won me *the look*.

"I'm not holding out on you. I don't want to talk about being dumb enough to invite a vampire into the store. That's the kind of thing that gets a person kicked out of the Buffy Fan Club."

Seizing the moment, I said, "How exactly did that happen?"

Tori grimaced. "I was listening to the coffee drinkers gossip about Linda. They had all these theories that she was seeing someone, and that's what got her killed. I didn't have my mind on business."

Beating myself up for past mistakes ranks among my super-powers. I understood why Tori didn't want to dwell on the subject, but I would have fallen for the same distraction. We both have a short fuse for the local gossip mill.

"I can promise you Linda wasn't carrying on an illicit affair,"

I said. "She came right out and told Beau that she sees being dead as a chance for them to be together."

Ever a sucker for a happy ending, Tori said, "Well, why can't they be together?"

"Because Beau doesn't want her to walk the earth for decades the way he's done."

Tori looked like she could have happily kicked something. "Oh, come on! First it was respect for his dead wife and now it's 'sorry, honey, go into the light?' I'm starting to think Beau has commitment issues."

"Hardly," I said. "He has one priority—ensuring that Linda's soul is at rest. Beau never talks to us about the downside of being a ghost. Having the Amulet of the Phoenix helps, but technically he is still a restless spirit."

Taking up the mantle of afterlife feminism, Tori declared, "That's Linda's choice, not his. What's he going to do if Linda refuses to move on? Put her out in the cold to haunt on her own?"

As usual, Tori directed my attention to what should have been obvious. None of us had the right to tell Linda what to do —dead or alive. If she insisted on remaining in Briar Hollow, as her friends, we had to support that choice.

"Yeah," Tori said. "Didn't think about that angle, did you?"

"Honestly, no."

"Well, I wouldn't say Linda's future is a done deal by any means. Look at her. She's got it bad for our colonel."

Tori pointed toward the lair where the librarian was sitting beside Beau's desk. The two of them were caught up in rapt conversation over an illuminated manuscript Beau must have brought out of the collection.

Duke rested his head on Linda's knee. His tail beat out a steady rhythm on the Oriental rug. The coonhound was ecstatic to be in the company of another ghost who could give him an uninterrupted ear rub.

When we came into the room, Duke whined, which caused Linda to tear herself away from Beau and notice us. "Jinx! I cannot believe you've been hiding a collection of this magnitude under the store all this time."

"Don't blame me!" I protested. "The fairy mound was here long before I came along."

Linda let me off the hook, but only by redirection. "You're right. Fiona is the one I should be mad at. She could have trusted me to know about all these marvelous books. Will I get to see her now that I'm on the other side?"

The librarian looked to Beau for an answer. The colonel opted for a diplomatic dodge. "Alas, there is no way to predict who and what you may encounter in the afterlife."

If Beau didn't think Linda should know Fiona faked her death, I was willing to follow his lead. I suspected he didn't want his friend to get too comfortable in her Briar Hollow afterlife, but his efforts didn't appear to be working.

I sat down at Glory's desk, and Tori perched on the back of the sofa. "Linda," I said, "we need to talk about what happened to you."

Beau gave me a horrified look. "Miss Jinx, we have identified the responsible party. There is no need to put Miss Linda through such a painful recitation."

If she'd had a circulatory system, Linda would have blushed. "That's so gallant of you, Beau, but really, I don't mind. Living through it... well, dying through it wasn't pleasant, but I'm fine now. That thing can't hurt me again. What do you want to know?"

Moving to the FaeNet terminal, Tori called up the scans from the 2RABID and projected them as holographs. One scene showed the rougarou in Bertille's shop, the other caught the creature at the library's back door. Wisely, Tori opted to scale the representations down to about a quarter of the rougarou's true size.

"Well, would you look at that," Linda said, levitating off her chair and floating toward the models. "He almost looks like a cartoon monster when you see him like this."

None of us had expected Linda to be quite so conversational about her demise. The upbeat attitude made questioning her much easier. "Was he in the library when you went to work Monday morning?"

Sounding uncertain, Linda asked, "What day is today?"

"Wednesday."

She shivered, "It feels like I died only a few minutes ago."

Ever the proctor of all things post-mortem, Beau said, "That uncomfortable sense of immediacy will pass with time. I endured the sensation for some fifty years."

No wonder he wanted Linda to move on to whatever was next for her.

"But you were alone, Beau," she protested. "I have all of you to help me."

Tori arched an eyebrow in my direction that said, *See? I told you so.*

She was right, but addressing Linda's romantic notions would have to wait. "The creature that killed you is called a rougarou," I prodded. "Was it waiting in the library when you came to work?"

The ghost's brow furrowed. "I guess it must have been. Everything about the morning seemed normal. I got to the library on time, made my coffee, and checked our email. There was a funny message asking for a book about werewolves."

That bit of information touched off a furious burst of typing from Tori. The text of an email materialized beside the rougarou holograms.

Dear Ms. Albert,

I have been searching regional North Carolina libraries for a copy of Le Loup Garou *by Alfred Marchard in the original French. To my surprise and pleasure, I have discovered that your facility recently came into possession of the volume.*

Would it be an imposition to ask that you scan the first chapter and email the file to me? I believe there to be errors in the translated edition in my possession. I will, of course, pay for your time and trouble.

Best regards,
J. Jones

"That's the message that made me go into the stacks," Linda said. "I knew exactly where to find the Marchard book because the library only received the volume a couple of weeks ago."

Everything about the message screamed fake to me, right down to the signature. "Why would someone give a book like that to a local library?" I asked before it occurred to me Linda might take professional offense.

The instant the spirit drew herself up in indignation, and a frigid wind hit me full in the face, I realized my mistake.

"The Briar Hollow Public Library has an excellent reputation for the quality of our collection," she said. "We consistently rank in the top five for facilities of commensurate size in the state."

"I'm sorry," I said. "I phrased that question poorly."

"You most certainly did," Linda agreed, but then softened enough to add, "The Marchard book does stand out in the library collection, but primarily because we do not tend to shelve books that aren't in English."

"What made you decide to keep it?" Tori asked.

The librarian's features settled into an expression of guilt. "I've been trying to convince the library board to let me start a rare book room for years. I planned to take the Marchard book to the next meeting and use it to press my case. With all the old homes in this area, almost every estate sale would yield at least one book that should be conserved in a library."

"Is that why you were so happy when Miss Bergeron opened her emporium?" Beau asked.

"Oh, yes!" Linda said with enthusiasm. "I went right over and welcomed her to the square, and we had a lovely talk. She has some wonderful gems in her inventory."

The comment reminded me I needed to get over to Bergeron Books and check on the progress of the clean-up/investigation. "Who donated *The Man-Wolf?*"

"There was an unsigned note in the package. The donor said he found the book in a junk shop and wanted to save it."

"Does that kind of thing happen often?"

"More often than you might think. Some people can't stand to see old books float around unwanted or worse yet get thrown away."

While I'd been questioning Linda, Tori had continued to type at the FaeNet terminal. "I traced the IP address on the email to somewhere in Scandinavia," she announced. "I can't pinpoint the exact location, but I think it's Denmark."

More confirmation that Morgan had orchestrated the librarian's murder.

"Linda, are there any other details you can think to share that might help us stop the rougarou?"

She answered without hesitation. "I think he was hearing voices."

"Why would you say that?"

"I don't believe he wanted to kill me. He whined and tried to back up, but then he put his hands over his ears and started to nod like he was listening to someone. That's when he... did what he did, but his eyes were so sad."

From the moment the 2RABID showed us the rougarou and Bertille identified him, I'd thought of Andre as cursed. The idea that he might be aware of his crimes and that he could be an unwilling participant stirred even greater pity in my heart.

"There was a piece of sheet music tucked into the book," I said. "Did the rougarou do that?"

Linda grew wistful. "I must have already been dead by then because I saw it all like I was standing on a tall ladder. He has lovely hands."

"Who?"

"The rougarou. His nails are trimmed and buffed like he's had a manicure."

Glory cut short our conversation when she came into the lair juggling a laptop and a stack of bulging file folders. Rodney rode on her shoulder wearing his green editor's visor.

"What's all this?" I asked, vacating the chair so she could deposit the load on her desk.

Plopping down like she was exhausted, Glory said, "Sheriff Johnson doesn't know when I can get back in the newspaper office, but then I realized I have Mr. Anderson's passwords. He's been showing me how to get the *Banner* ready every week. I thought I'd see what I can get done from here if I can figure out how to access the newspaper's computers."

"I can help with that," Tori said. "We'll set you up with a virtual terminal into the *Banner's* network."

Rodney ran down Glory's arm and bounced over the file folders. He took the stairs two at a time up to his shelf office and pointed at the tiny laptop.

"Rodney's going to help," Glory explained. "He says together we can figure out the software."

Tori started typing. "Good idea. Two heads are always better than one. I'll get you both access to the system. It'll be just like sitting in Larry's chair working at his computer."

"I wouldn't want to sit in his chair," Glory said, putting on her red polka dot reading glasses. "That's where he was when he died. But if you can get us into the system, we don't have to go back in that room at all."

With a flourish, Tori hit a final keystroke. The screen of Glory's laptop changed to a picture of antique lead type blocks. "Oh!," she cried. "That's Mr. Anderson's wallpaper. Tori, you're a genius! Rodney are you in, too?"

The rat shot her a thumbs up and began to explore the files on Anderson's desktop.

Now all business, Glory said, "Linda, I'm so glad you're here. Can you help me with something?"

Brightening at the idea of being needed, Linda said, "Of course, dear. What?"

"We need to write your obituary."

Chapter Thirty-Three

Linda jumped on Glory's suggestion with enthusiasm. "Oh, thank you for asking me. Most of the obituaries in the *Banner* are so cursory in relation to the person's true accomplishments in life. How many column inches can you give me?"

"Well," Glory said, "you are a leading citizen after all. You write what makes you happy. We can always cut *Vittles with Vera* for the week. She's doing green bean casserole recipes again."

The librarian's misty features registered her disapproval of that news. "Well, as topics go, that one lacks imagination even for Vera. Every Southern woman worth her salt comes out of the womb knowing how to make a green bean casserole."

I whispered a silent prayer that Linda wouldn't quiz me on *my* culinary credentials. Thankfully, a bit of ectoplasmic accomplishment distracted her. She reached for a pen on Glory's desk and squealed in delight when she managed to pick up the writing instrument.

"Oh, Beau!" Linda cried. "Look! I'm getting better at this ghost business all the time."

The colonel offered fulsome praise, but I saw the truth in his eyes. He didn't want Linda to acquire advanced haunting skills. Maybe Tori was right and Beau did have a thing about commitment.

Oblivious to his reaction, Linda made notes on a yellow legal pad, consulting Tori about points of phrasing. Since the obituary project generated more laughter than I would have expected, I ditched my plan of asking Tori to accompany me to Bergeron Books. She needed a light-hearted, albeit macabre distraction.

After being forced to discreetly hide what could have been a major belch, I decided to abandon my trip across the square entirely. Rube's burrito had started doing a flamenco dance in my gut.

Since I couldn't admit to Darby that I'd eaten the raccoon's cooking, I went upstairs to check in with Brenna and locate a *Tums*.

Turns out a double homicide can drive a heck of a lot of business. I walked into a standing-room-only situation in the espresso bar. All the discussion centered on wild theories linking Linda and Larry's deaths. Not a one had a shred of validity, but that didn't slow the theorists down a bit.

I stayed with Brenna until closing time when we had to all but push the last protesting customer out the door. We both heaved a sigh of relief when I turned the lock and flipped the *Closed* sign around.

With my digestion somewhat returned to normal, I went straight to the war room and asked Festus to send a GNATS drone over to the bookstore. I wanted to check on Bertille, Seneca, and Edgar, and remind them of the approaching curfew hour.

The werecat touched an icon on the MonsterPad that dominated his desk. One of the dots moved over Bergeron Books, giving us an instant view of the store's interior.

Bertille and Edgar worked at returning scattered volumes to the shelves, while Seneca used his beak to peck information into an iPad.

Festus pawed the mic on his headset. "GNATS 11, this is Big Tom. Initiate intercom protocol."

"Roger that, Big Tom. Protocol initiated."

"Hey everybody," I said. "How's it going?"

My voice startled Edgar, who dropped an armload of books. Looking around with wild alarm, he said, "Jinx? Where are you?"

"Sorry, Edgar. I'm talking to you through the GNATS drone. GNATS 11, show Mr. Poe your location."

A faint red outline pulsed at the edge of the screen when the pilot turned on the craft's landing strobes.

"You are speaking to me through an insect?" Poe asked.

"Not exactly. Seneca will explain it to you later. Have you all found anything today?"

Bertille dusted her hands and pointed at the filled shelves. "So far everything we've picked up is on my inventory sheet, at least in terms of title. We're getting some outside help on checking the editions."

"How are you doing that?"

The screen split, and Adeline waved at me. "Hello, Jinx. I've opened channels into the BEAR archives, and the Fae reading room at the British Museum to cross reference the volumes in Bertille's store."

Take that, SIRI.

Festus's whiskers quivered. "Please tell me those are official channels Adeline?"

"Define 'official.'"

In an uncharacteristic, pleading tone, the werecat said, "Don't get caught. If Hortense Tyton finds out you're poking around inside her computers the pinfeathers will fly."

The barn owl in charge of the BEAR archives isn't known for her good disposition, but Adeline was undaunted. "Even as an AI, I am still a former Witch of the Oak, Festus. I outrank Hortense by several levels."

Blowing out a long breath, Festus said, "Just keep your activities quiet, okay? Hortense can't stand me. I have enough to worry about without getting into an interdepartmental cat fight. Bureaucratic politics are about as much fun as a lindwyrm with infected venom sacs."

"Which species?" Adeline asked. "Upright or undulate?"

The werecat's ears went flat. "*Not* the point, Adeline."

Addressing Bertille, I said, "Better wind things up and get on back to the lair. I don't think it would be a bad idea for everyone to get back to the fairy mound early tonight."

"Understood. We'll be there in the next half hour."

Back in the lair I found Connor sitting in one of the chairs by the fire opposite Greer and her omnipresent book.

"Hey, Big Brother," I said, sitting down on the hearth. "Where have you been today?"

"Back and forth between Shevington and the Abbey," he replied. "Barnaby and Moira spent the day in the library trying to get a sense of the size of the collection."

"How'd that go?"

"Fine, but the branches off the main chamber go on forever. We walked for an hour and still didn't find the back wall. Barnaby wants Seneca's help as soon as he's done here."

Tori joined us in time to hear what Connor said. "Mind if I tag along with the black bird?" she asked, sitting beside me on the hearth.

Before I thought, I said, "Do you think that's a good idea after what happened to you today?"

Connor sat up in his chair. "What happened to her today?"

"Down, boy," Tori said, laying a hand on his knee. "The

master vampire came in the store, and my second mom here has her tail feathers in a twist."

From across the lair Gemma said, "Your first mother would have appreciated being told about this sooner, too. Instead, I had to hear the news from Kelly."

Gemma and my mom came out of the stacks together. For an irrational minute I felt like I'd been caught red-handed doing something bad with only one chance to blame it on Tori. Gemma read my reaction and shut it down fast.

"Don't you even think about trying to back peddle your way out of this, Norma Jean Hamilton. I expect this kind of behavior from Tori, but you're supposed to be the responsible one."

Casting around for a response, I came up with nothing. My silence only fueled Gemma's growing ire.

"All week I've been playing along with this 'make things look normal' plan even though two people are dead on the town square. I do what you ask and keep the apothecary open, but you couldn't be bothered to tell me my daughter came face to face with one of the murderers? Explain yourself, young lady."

With that, she crossed her arms and waited. I looked at my mother who gave me the "you're on your own" face.

"Everything has just been happening so fast," I stammered. "Did you say hello to Linda?"

Cutting her eyes toward Glory's desk, Gemma said, "Sorry you're dead, Linda."

"Why thank you, Gemma," the librarian answered. "That's so nice of you. Don't forget you have books due before Saturday."

"It's on my calendar, but I appreciate the reminder." Then cutting her gaze back to me, Gemma said, "Try again, Norma Jean."

Six-year-old me took over and threw Tori right under the bus. "It was her idea."

"It was not!" Tori shot back. "We didn't even discuss keeping Dampierre a secret."

"The two of you are so skilled at collusion you didn't have to discuss it," Gemma said, "but since we're all here now we can have a *group* talk. Victoria Tallulah, you can start."

I listened as Tori went through an almost letter-perfect recitation of the same story she'd told in the war room. Her delivery improved with practice, but I still had a nagging feeling she was leaving something out.

She finished with, "And I was just talking about going back to the Middle Realm with Connor and Seneca, which should make you all happy because Dampierre won't follow me to the Middle Realm, right Jinksy?"

That was my cue to agree, but I couldn't. "How can you be sure about that?"

"Dampierre cannot use the portal network," Greer said. "The matrix has been programmed to reject his kind."

And *I* was the one in trouble for withholding information?

The baobhan sith's statement qualified as both good and bad news. Good to contain the vampire. Bad for giving Tori an excuse to go to the Middle Realm when I was convinced she needed to stay home.

"How did that 'programming' happen?" I asked.

"At the height of their power, vampires presented a significant threat to humankind. The Fae had no desire to facilitate their movement. The system, which we now call the Attendant, modified the matrix to prevent such an occurrence."

Let me address one seeming inconsistency in how we use the portals. Transdimensional mechanics make about as much sense to me as algebra. To this day, I've never had to solve for the value of X, and I assure you I don't tinker around with the portal matrix either.

My attitude toward the portal can be compared to how I use electricity. I flip the switch and expect the lights to come on.

But, it's not lost on me that having the dang thing mere feet from the lair would, at first glance, make us vulnerable to unannounced, unwelcome visits.

I've always had complete faith that will never happen because I've assumed the fairy mound polices all arrivals and departures thus protecting us from attack.

Greer destroyed that belief in favor of a better one. The portal network possesses self-awareness. The Attendant isn't a system helper, she is the system.

"Have you known that's how the network functions all along?" Tori asked.

Unflappable as always, Greer said, "No, I spoke with my mother while Jinx was upstairs and you were assisting Linda with the composition of her obituary. Mother and Myrtle are working with Bronwyn to understand how Dampierre has remained hidden for centuries."

"And they thought portal hopping might be the answer?" I said.

"Precisely," the baobhan sith replied. "Myrtle spoke with the Attendant to inquire about unusual energy signatures in transit hoping to detect a pattern. That proved fruitless, which is when the Attendant explained that the energy matrix would have ten-times the effect of the sun on Jean-Baptiste."

Good to know. I wouldn't mind shoving Dampierre through the nearest portal if the opportunity arose.

"Would it have hurt the Attendant to introduce herself sooner?" Tori asked.

"She does not appear to have thought an introduction necessary with a Time Witch."

"A what?" I asked.

Tori gave me a melodramatic eye roll. "Jinksy, she means you."

Yet again someone who thought I knew what I was doing when I opened the Rivers of Time. "Right. Greer, what else did your mother have to say?"

"She has no explanation for how Dampierre survived their encounter, but Morgan is, of course, the prime suspect in facilitating his continued existence."

"If Morgan kept him alive, why haven't we run into him before?" Tori asked.

"She could have employed any number of containment methods, including chaining Jean-Baptiste inside a coffin. He does not sleep during the day, but he could be restrained inside a casket with silver and Holy Water."

Gemma cleared her throat. "That's all fascinating, but we've wandered off topic here. Why am I only now learning that my daughter had an encounter with the vampire?"

"Because it was nothing, Mom," Tori said. "The guy's all smoke and mirrors. He can't even use a portal. I'll be fine at the Abbey."

That pushed Gemma's tolerance to the breaking point. "Come with me, Victoria. *Now*."

Groaning, Tori followed her mother into one of the guest rooms and closed the door. Dad and his fishing dogs arrived just in time to save me from a maternal lecture of my own.

While my parents talked about Dad's day in the sporting goods store, and Connor romped on the floor with the dogs, Greer looked over at me. "You are worried about Tori."

"Yes, I am, and I don't even know why exactly."

"I share your concerns."

Leaning closer and lowering my voice, I said, "You don't worry without a good reason. Tell me."

"Few beings can face a master vampire and emerge

unscathed. I sense a certain lack of truth in Tori's account of her meeting with Jean-Baptiste."

"Any idea what we should do about that?"

"We wait."

The next words out of my mouth burned like gall. "Can we trust her?"

Fire flickered in the baobhan sith's eyes. "I do not know, but there is one thing of which I am certain. Even if Jean-Baptiste has enthralled her, Tori will not hurt you."

"I'm not worried about myself," I said, my voice rough with unshed tears. "I'm worried about her, and all the rest of you."

"Together, we are a formidable force and we fight for our own. If Tori is in trouble, we will know it soon enough, and we will be there for her."

"And in the meantime?"

"As I said, we wait and watch."

Watch my best friend. A person I trust with my life—with my child's life. If Dampierre was inside Tori's head, he'd pay for that invasion with his miserable living dead existence.

Chapter Thirty-Four

A look of intense concentration carved deep lines on Greer's face. Dad's dogs stopped playing with Connor, tucked their tails between their legs, and dove under Beau's desk with Duke.

"What is it?" I asked the baobhan sith.

"She hears what we came to tell you about," Bertille said, emerging from the passageway. "The rougarou is howling."

Considering our current location, that made no sense. "Sounds from the square shouldn't be audible inside the fairy mound."

Seneca settled on the mantel. "Magic has been used to amplify the creature's voice. He appears to be everywhere and nowhere at the same time."

Though normally saturnine, Edgar looked animated. "Imagine the horrifying effect of the voice of a creature that moves always beyond the grasp of the searcher. What a marvelous motif for a story."

I made a mental note to have a talk with Edgar about the opposing meanings of "marvelous" and "horrifying."

Tori and Gemma came out of the guest room. "What on earth is that sound?" Tori asked me.

"You can hear it, too?"

"Yes, but Mom thinks I'm nuts," she said. "You hear it, right?"

"No, but according to Bertille, Andre has decided to serenade Briar Hollow. Sorry, but no one leaves the lair, not even for the Middle Realm. Dampierre is up to something. It's going to be a long night."

I had no idea; Andre howled until dawn.

Every dog in Briar Hollow joined in until the lonely, bestial symphony echoed off the mountains. Around midnight, Lucas and I went up to the store where we stood in the dark and listened.

The iPads in our hands showed us the feeds from the GNATS drones. House lights blazed all over town. The pilots zoomed on scenes of armed men and women standing guard on their porches with shotguns.

Sheriff Johnson and his deputies prowled the streets searching the shadows with handheld spotlights. They found nothing.

After one nerve piercing cry I shivered and pulled my robe tighter. "How long can the rougarou keep this up?"

"As long as his master orders," Lucas answered. "I don't like this, Jinx. The townspeople are barely over the giant insect scare. If their nerves get frayed enough, they're going to start using those guns to shoot at anything that moves."

I almost had a heart attack when Festus jumped out of the blackness at our feet. The werecat landed on the window sill and stared out at the square. "Which is what Dampierre wants—chaos in the streets. Chase and I don't dare shift and go out there hunting that glorified coon hound. We wouldn't make it a block."

"Bastet's whiskers!" I exclaimed. "Would it hurt you to warn us before you leap out of nowhere like that?"

"Watch your language," Festus said absently. "That sounds ridiculous when a biped says it."

While I struggled to get my heart rate back to something resembling normal, Lucas asked, "How are the others?"

"Jeff's dogs and Duke are still nervous wrecks. Even after Brenna cast a noise cancellation spell they can hear that damn thing howling. Those mice Rodney brought home aren't in much better shape. But that's not what's pissing me off."

Festus doesn't belong to the Canine of the Month Club so his reaction to the plight of the dogs didn't surprise me, but it did pique my curiosity. "What *is* pissing you off?"

The werecat's eyes flashed in the darkness and his tail lashed back and forth, "That howling Cajun cur is scaring my grandkid."

I love Festus, but there are moments when he reminds me how much with such force I want to scoop the old rascal up into my arms and kiss his scruffy ears—which would probably cost me a pint of blood.

"Maybe we should get Rube to take Willow to Shevington," I suggested.

"Not an option," Festus answered gruffly. "I don't want her thinking we're taking her back where we got her. Kid talks a good line, but she's still not a hundred percent certain she has a forever place with us."

He turned golden eyes toward me made luminous by the glow of the street lights. "And this is her home, not *his*."

The werecat jerked his head toward the window. "That mutt has to go. He might have been a man once, but he's not now. Brenna's been on the horn with Myrtle. They say the only person who can turn Andre human again is the witch who cursed him. Seneca says the same thing. We don't know the identity of that witch, and we don't have time to find out."

I hated to agree with the werecat, but with gun-toting, trigger-happy townspeople abroad in the night, I didn't have much choice. With hesitation, I asked, "Can Tori still hear him?"

"She can," Festus said, "which I don't like one damn bit. That vampire did something to her."

Well, there it was. Out in the open. "You think so, too?"

"Of course, I think so," the werecat said, "and so do you, you're just afraid to admit it."

"Lucas?"

"Yeah," he said, snaking his arm around my waist. "She's trying too hard to be herself. Something's not right and she refuses to be honest with us."

My loyalty flared. "It's not like we can force her to tell us what's going on," I said, all the while knowing that we could, but putting Tori through a magical interrogation session was not an option.

Still looking out the window Festus said, "If Dampierre can make that rougarou howl for hours, he can get into Tori's mind in the fairy mound. It's only a matter of time, Jinx. You're not thinking straight."

"Well, if you're so damned smart, what do you suggest?" I demanded.

"Honey," Lucas said, "The idea is to kill the disease, not the patient. We're not talking about doing anything to Tori. Dampierre is the problem. Right now he has Andre to do his dirty work. By getting rid of his henchman, we force the vampire to act on his own and then we take *him* out."

"Do you have a plan?"

"We could try drawing Andre to some isolated location where we don't have to worry about witnesses."

"What would be use for bait?"

From the basement door, Bertille said, "Not what, who."

She moved to stand with us, flinching as another undulating cry split the night. "Andre is under Dampierre's sway, but if we can locate him, he will follow me. Yes, I embarrassed him back in New Orleans, but I also hurt him. Under all that pride, he was in love with me. There's only one thing I can do for him now."

When her voice broke, Festus finished the thought. "Put him out of his misery."

"We'd have to separate Andre and Dampierre," Lucas murmured.

"Do that," the werecat said, "and Chase and I will take care of business."

I looked at them both with open horror. "You two aren't actually considering this plan, are you?"

"Do you have a better option?" Festus asked.

"No, but what makes you think Dampierre will just let us blow a dog whistle and lure Andre away from him?"

"He's not the only vampire in town," Festus pointed out, "and he has a history with Red. In case you haven't noticed, the woman can be distracting when she puts her mind to it."

A renewed round of howling made my skin crawl. "Can we please go back to the lair and table this discussion until morning?" I pleaded. "I've had all I can take for one day."

They agreed, but no one felt much like leaving the comfort of the area around the fireplace, not even Linda who couldn't feel the warmth, but craved it anyway.

Darby rustled up a supply of cots, but no one will remember that night as a slumber party.

We reverted to the primitive part of ourselves, pathetic creatures huddling around the flames praying the light would hold back the stronger beasts that stalked the night.

Poor little Willow didn't stop trembling until Chase shifted into mountain lion form. She curled up against his chest and with Glory on the other side stroking her fur, the kitten finally fell into a fitful slumber.

Chase and I made contact over the sleeping forms of his wife and child. I saw something new in those eyes; the dedicated, deadly protectiveness of a husband and father.

Unable to shut down his own guardian instincts, Lucas stayed awake playing chess with Greer. I claimed one of the sofas, wrestling with the blankets. Just as she'd done when I was a child, Mom smoothed the bedding and tucked me in, bending to kiss my cheek.

Looking up at her, I said, "You know about Tori?"

She nodded. "And so does Gemma. Go to sleep, honey. We've already decided to take turns keeping an eye on her tonight."

Tori and Connor had pushed two cots together against the bookshelves. She was asleep, but she twitched in time with what I assumed was Andre's continued howling.

I'm not sure how long it took me to doze off, but I came awake in an instant when Festus laid a paw on my arm. I started and jerked upright, but the werecat shook his head and pointed upstairs.

"What?" I mouthed, my heart thudding at the thought of the rougarou inside the store.

Festus put his mouth so close to my ear his luxuriant whiskers tickled my cheek. "John Johnson's upstairs beating on the front door."

Relief flooded through me followed by irritation. "So what?" I whispered. "We're closed."

"You're going to have to let him in, Jinx."

Studying the seriousness of the werecat's furry features, the hair on the back of my neck stood up. "Why?"

"Because he looked straight into a GNATS camera and said he's not leaving until he talks to you."

Chapter Thirty-Five

When I unlocked the door, Sheriff Johnson stepped inside without waiting to be invited. "Hi, John," I said, not bothering to mask the sarcasm. "Come on in."

"Sorry. I've been up all night playing animal control officer. I assume you heard the howling?"

Closing the door and turning the key, I said, "Me and everyone else in town. You want coffee?"

"God, yes."

He followed me into the espresso bar and plopped into a chair while I ground beans and pulled shots for two large lattes. I felt the sheriff's eyes on me as I worked, but neither of us spoke.

When the drinks were ready, I carried them to the table and went back for fresh pastries. Darby must have channeled his anxieties into baking; I found the cabinet full of still warm goodies.

Johnson bit into the apple fritter I set in front of him like he hadn't eaten in a week. He washed the food down with a healthy gulp of latte. "That's good. Thank you."

"You're welcome. What can I do for you, John?"

The sheriff reached into his back pocket and brought out a piece of brown wrapping paper, which he unfolded and spread on the table. As I traced the web of lines and read the annotations I felt the color drain from my face.

Making a feeble attempt at running a bluff, I said, "What's all this?"

When Johnson scrubbed at his face the stubble on his cheeks made a scritching sound. "Jinx, are we really going to waste time playing games with one another? We both know there's some kind of creature killing folks in this town. I'm here to find out what can be done about it."

I looked at the lawman—at the black circles under his eyes and the gray pallor of his skin. The man wasn't just tired, he was *bone* tired—and worried about the people he spent his life protecting. I owed him more than a fresh version of the usual smoke-and-mirrors approach the Fae take with humans.

"How much have you put together on your own?"

He waved a beefy hand around the shop. "There's something about this building. The old timers talk about the store. They say your grandmother and her mother before her could cure people, make them fall in love, heal their grief. Are you all cove doctors?"

"Not exactly. We're witches—members of a lineage called the Daughters of Knasgowa."

The instant I said the words a weight slipped off my shoulders. Hiding in plain sight takes a lot of energy. I wasn't ready to put up a billboard out on the interstate, but coming clean with John Johnson came with an unexpected benefit—absolution.

The Fae lie to our human friends for good reasons, but a lie is still a lie.

Johnson's eyes went round. "You all go all the way back to Alexander Skea's wife?"

That impressed me. "How do you know about Alexander?"

He tapped the chart lying between us. "Disturbance at Knas-gowa's grave right before people started seeing ghosts wandering around town. I did my homework and found out who she was."

I smiled. "You're not as slow-witted as you want people to think you are."

He smiled back. "Not by a long sight."

Behind me I heard the basement door squeak open. Festus sauntered in and offered us a plaintive meow.

"Don't bother," I told the werecat. "He's already figured most of it out."

Ditching the placid house cat act, Festus jumped onto a free seat. "Damn, John. You really are brighter than you let on."

The sheriff almost jumped out of his chair. Jabbing a finger in Festus's face, he cried in triumph, "I *knew* it! I *knew* there was more to you than napping out there on that bench all day."

Festus yawned. "Oh, please. You have no idea what there is to me. I've watched sheriffs come and go in this town. I'll give you this, you are the first one to get a freaking clue."

"Nope," Johnson said, "I'm not. Every Sheriff since the 1860s has made notes about this shop and about Jinx's people. I found the files when I took the job. Figured they were all crackpots, but then Jinx and Tori solved the W.J. Evers case. That's when I started wondering if something really was going on over here."

"Why?" I asked, sounding defensive. "Tori and I covered our tracks really well."

"You honestly think that?" Johnson laughed. "Jinx, honey, I hate to tell you this, but you are one lousy liar."

"She is, isn't she?" Festus said. "What does a cat have to do to get a cup of coffee in this joint?"

Moving woodenly, I got out of my chair and fixed the werecat a bowl of java. Relieved or not, the surrealism was getting to me. I could *not* be sitting at a table in my store talking openly with John Johnson while Festus McGregor offered color commentary.

Seated again, I said, "What are you planning to do with this information, John?"

"Nothing," the sheriff replied. "Best I can tell, you all spend your time trying to get in between the townspeople and the weird stuff no one wants to admit goes on around here all the time."

"Then what can we do for you?"

His demeanor turned serious. "You can tell me what's loose in Briar Hollow and how we can stop it, because if you'll have me, I'm in. Whatever was doing that howling killed Linda and Larry, didn't it?"

Taking my phone out of the pocket of my robe, I texted Lucas to come upstairs. When he joined us, I summarized our conversation with the sheriff.

"My husband also works in law enforcement. Lucas's jurisdiction is... broader than yours, and he handles these kinds of cases. It'll be faster to loop him in now."

"Sure thing," Johnson said, standing and offering his hand to Lucas. "I'm always ready to work with a brother officer."

Together, we told the sheriff what we knew. As we talked, he unclipped a pen from the pocket of his uniform shirt, flipped the piece of brown paper over, and took notes.

The point of the pen faltered when we got to the part about the vampire, but Johnson recovered and kept listening.

When we were done, he said, "I looked into Miss Bergeron's past in New Orleans. I knew about the boyfriend—not the part about him being this... " He consulted the paper. "rougarou. Do you all know that a storekeeper was killed down there with the same bite mark to the neck we found on Linda and Larry?"

It was my husband's turn to take notes. "No. When did this happen?"

"Sometime after the police found Melancon's apartment trashed and before Miss Bergeron left town. The guy owned some kind of magic shop. My buddy called it a tourist trap, but I'm guessing from the look on your face, he was probably wrong."

While Lucas thumb typed, I tried to explain. "A witch cursed Andre. Only that person could lift the spell and return him to human form. If the storekeeper your're telling us about was the practitioner in question, we really don't have any choice but to kill the rougarou."

Festus fixed me with an impassive feline stare. "A point I've been making for several hours now."

Johnson agreed wholeheartedly. "Thing is," he said, "you can't kill what you can't see. We covered every square inch of this town last night and so did those flying bugs of yours. Every time I thought we were closing in on the rougarou, the howls came from someplace new."

When Lucas set his phone down I caught sight of Adeline on the screen pushing columns of data around. Johnson saw her, too but didn't ask.

"We're working on a plan to separate Andre and the vampire," Lucas said. "One of our associates has a connection to him."

"The red-headed Scots woman?" Johnson asked. "Tall, wears black all the time, green eyes that give a man ideas?"

Festus let out an appreciative whistle. "Do they ever."

"I'll say," Lucas added.

Granted I had a bad case of bed head and was wearing a bathrobe, but I still had a pulse. "Um, excuse me. Woman sitting right here."

Lucas at least had the sense to look sheepish. "Sorry, honey, but you do have to admit Greer makes a visual impact."

"Fine," I said. "She's gorgeous. Moving on."

He may be new to the being-married game, but Lucas got the point. "Anyway. Greer thinks she can draw Jean-Baptiste off long enough for us to lead Andre out of town using Bertille as bait, but we have a problem."

"I'm guessing that would be every Jim Bob and Betty Sue in Briar Hollow being armed to the teeth and ready to shoot at shadows?" Johnson said.

"Exactly."

The sheriff drained the rest of his coffee, folded his chart, and stood. "Get your ducks in a row. Leave the would-be vigilantes to me. What time do you want to do this thing?"

Chapter Thirty-Six

Tori sat cross-legged on the daybed in my alcove and balanced her breakfast plate on one knee. When I told her we needed to talk alone, she tried to get out of the confrontation, but I all but shoved her through the privacy curtain.

"That's really something about John Johnson figuring us out, huh?" she said, pushing a fork loaded with hashbrowns into her mouth. "Ith hardth to believeth he caughth on."

"Gemma would smack you for talking with your mouth full," I said, "and I didn't ask you in here to talk about John Johnson. He told me I'm a bad liar."

She paused for a gulp of orange juice before agreeing. "You are a bad liar."

"You're worse."

This time the fork stopped halfway to her mouth. The potatoes fell off, hitting the plate with a wet *thwack*. "What do you mean?"

"The Sheriff asked me not to play games with him. I'm putting the same request to you. Dampierre got in your head and he's still there. Denying that will only make an already bad situation worse."

Tori put her plate aside and reached for her coffee. She cradled the cup, letting the hot brew warm her hands. "He's not in my head as long as I stay down here."

"And if you go upstairs?"

She shivered. "I hear his voice... and my Dad's."

No wonder she was all twisted back on herself. "What do the voices say?"

She stared at the floor. "Dampierre says my talents are wasted playing second fiddle to you. Dad wants me to bring him back from the dead so we can be together."

I don't know what I expected her to say, but the actual words knocked the wind out of me. After several seconds I recovered enough to say,"You don't play second fiddle to me."

Tori looked up and gave me a haunted smile. "Don't I, Jinksy?" Her voice sounded thin and hollow. "You're the hero of this story. I'm the sidekick."

Reaching behind me, I opened the top desk drawer and took out a tarot deck. Fanning the cards until I located the one I wanted, I handed the pasteboard rectangle to Tori.

"The Fool?" she said. "What are you trying to say to me, Jinx?"

"You see that dog nipping at his heel keeping him from walking over a cliff? That's you, Tori. The force of nature that keeps me on the correct path. You are not a sidekick, a second fiddle—a second *anything*. Dampierre is playing you, and that second voice is *not* your father. It's all a trick."

She studied the card. "That's how the Mother Oak described us to Myrtle, isn't it? When Myrtle merged with the tree to heal."

"Yes."

Without warning, Tori flipped the card back at me. I caught

it with a flash of anger. "What's wrong with you, Tori? Something's been bothering you for weeks."

"I told you," she said. "The Principle of Correspondence. My head and my heart aren't in the same place. You're growing and evolving. I'm not. I'm worried that because of me the bond between the Daughters of Knasgowa won't be formed in this generation."

"You're still worried about *that?*" I said. The question came out more frustrated and less sympathetic than I intended.

"Yes, Jinx, I'm still worried about *that,* and I'm worried about the character flaws I inherited from my father. Dampierre is using those things to manipulate me."

Leaning forward, I took her coffee cup, set it on the end table, and caught hold of her hands, "Then we turn the tables on the manipulative bastard."

"That won't set me on the right path."

I wanted to scream at her that she wasn't on the wrong path, but some inner voice silenced my protests. Only Tori could judge the quality of her journey. I didn't have that right, but neither did Jean-Baptiste Dampierre.

"Maybe silencing him won't set you on what you believe to be *your* correct path, but getting that bloodsucking backseat driver out of your head will be a damn good start."

Even though tears rimmed her eyes, Tori laughed and let me see a glimmer of the person I know and love. Seizing on that recognition, I pressed my case. "We have a plan and it won't work without your help. Are you game?"

"Jinksy," she said, squeezing my fingers, "I was born game, but you don't understand the strength of Dampierre's mesmerism."

"I don't care about his mesmerism. We're stronger. Now, you want to hear the plan or not?"

When we stepped out of the alcove, I dropped the plates I was carrying. Shards of china flew across the room. The rougarou stood in the center of the lair with my father's dogs clustered around his feet.

I raised my hand, blue flame flickering at my fingertips. As I moved to hurl the bolt, Mom stepped in front of the monster. "*Stop, Norma Jean!* That's your brother!"

In that fraction of a second, I managed to pull my shot, sending the energy ricocheting toward the mantel. Seneca squawked and ducked as an arm of fire shot up from the grate and intercepted the magic projectile before it singed his tailfeathers.

"Sweet Hecate!" I swore. "Would someone tell me what's going on here?"

Behind the mask of pale fur now covering his face, I saw Connor's eyes sparkle.

"*You!*" I said, pointing an accusing finger. "This was *your* idea."

Quickly sidestepping, Connor moved behind our mother and whined.

"Stop yelling at your brother," Mom said. "He volunteered to be temporarily cursed so we can test out the weapon *you* suggested we use against the real rougarou."

"That *I* suggested? Have you lost your mind?"

Lucas started forward. "Now, honey... "

"Don't you *'now honey'* me. I did not for one minute suggest that my brother be turned into a rougarou for the purpose of some kind of weapons testing."

"No," Lucas said, "you didn't, but you are the one who suggested we use a dog whistle to call Andre."

My mind flashed on our conversation in the darkened store

the previous night. "What I said was that we couldn't just blow a dog whistle and lure Andre away from Dampierre."

"Right," Lucas agreed, "but that gave me an idea, which I took to Brenna."

I looked at the sorceress. "You're in on this, too?"

She shrugged. "Someone had to cast the spell."

Well, of course. What was I thinking? "Somebody start at the beginning."

Lucas and Greer had done far more in the dark of the night than play chess. They'd concocted a plan that, when I settled down, I admitted was brilliant.

A dog whistle works in the frequency range of 23-54 kHz, above the capability of human hearing. Even though a rougarou does not exist as a natural being, it bears a close relationship to a dog.

What if a whistle could be designed that only the rougarou could hear? That would prevent a second night of howling, while still giving Bertille a way to draw Andre to her more quickly.

My husband and his co-conspirator took the theory to Brenna who developed the whistle, but with the stipulation that she needed test subjects. Enter my over-eager brother. Ever ready for an experimental adventure, Connor volunteered to let the sorceress curse him.

Since Dad's dogs recognized Connor's scent, they weren't afraid of him, only curious about the change in his form. While Tori and I had been talking in the alcove, the group in the lair had been testing the whistles—with the hope of finishing before we emerged.

"You were going to lie to me about Connor's involvement?" I asked the group in general.

"Not at all," Seneca said, "we merely reasoned that apologizing after the fact would be more expeditious than requesting permission."

I narrowed my eyes and glared at the raven. "Did you now. We'll discuss that 'reasoning' later. Does the whistle work?"

Brenna moved to Tori's workbench. "Whistles, plural. I enchanted six. The first five produced discernible reactions in your father's companions. This one, however, achieves our desired goal."

She raised a slim silver tube to her mouth and blew. Not one of the dogs so much as twitched a whisker, but Connor raised his head and whined, dancing in place like a race horse eager to burst out of the gate.

"Why is he so nervous?" I asked when Brenna lowered the whistle.

"The frequency enchantment includes elements of a summoning spell. Andre will not be able to resist following the sound. When Bertille has him in sight, she will move to the spot Festus has designated for the final encounter."

Turning to the werecat, I said, "And that would be where?"

"Knasgowa's waterfall. It's private and isolated. We know the ground like the back of our paws. That gives us the home field advantage."

Out of the corner of my eye I saw Connor roll over on his back and stick his feet in the air while Bobber jumped on his chest. "Brenna, would you please turn him back before he decides to lift a leg on the furniture?"

She chanted a series of words in what sounded vaguely like French. The hair on Connor's face retreated while his nose and mouth returned to normal. Putting his arms around Bobber to contain the dog's enthusiasm, Connor sat up and said, "See, Sis? I'm fine."

"I'll deal with you later, too."

"Mom said I could," he protested.

"Oh for God's sake, *whatever.*" Turning back to Festus and Lucas, I said, "What happens after Andre is no longer in the picture?"

"Death will break the curse, and return Andre to human form," Lucas answered. "The story will be that Sheriff Johnson got a tip, discovered the body, and found a diary, which Seneca and Edgar will have fabricated. The entries will indicate Andre followed Bertille from New Orleans, and committed the murders as some twisted form of harassment."

A wave of regret washed through me. "So we not only kill a man trapped by an irreversible curse, we throw him under the bus and brand him as a murderer in the process."

Festus put a paw on my arm. "I know, kid, but the humans will buy the story, especially now that John's in on the whole thing."

Ruining Andre Melancon's memory wasn't the only thing on my mind in that moment. In order to distract Jean-Baptiste and buy Bertille and the others the time they needed, we had to use a different, and much dearer form of bait—my best friend.

Chapter Thirty-Seven

John Johnson took two actions designed to get the townsfolk more upset with him than with the monster loose in the community. By the time I opened the store, the local radio station KBHL had already made the announcement of a stay-at-home order, and a weapons ban starting at 6 p.m.

Anyone found outside their home would be fined. If they had a gun on them, they'd be arrested. You would't think the chess players who spend their days with us would be the type to get up in arms about that kind of thing, but you'd be wrong.

Throughout the day I heard one outraged screed after another, but as the 5 o'clock hour approached, even the malcontents headed home along with everyone else on the square. There's no rule against being mouthy while you're also obeying the law.

Dad left for the pond with Chase and Festus around 5:30, which gave him enough time to get back to the fairy mound before the community-wide curfew began.

As Chase was climbing the stairs, Willow shot across the open space from the guest rooms, ran up his pants leg, and wrapped herself around her father's neck. Gently disentangling the kitten, Chase said, "Hey, Baby Girl. What's this?"

"My real Dad left to do his job and didn't come home. I want you to come back."

The words came out in a plaintive rush that made my heart hurt.

Chase sat down on the step with the kitten in his hands. Scratching behind her ear, he said, "Do you know what my job is?"

Willow looked up at him. "Festus said you're tanner of Clan McGregor."

"Tanist," he corrected. "That means that I'm his second-in-command, but I'm also the War Chief of our clan."

Willow's eyes got big. "*Our* clan? You mean I'm part of the clan, too?"

"You're a McGregor now," Chase said. "Some day you'll run in the woods with me and your grandpa, and help us take care of Jinx and the others."

From the horrified expression on Glory's face, I knew Chase hadn't run *that* idea by her yet.

He went on. "But right now, I need you to stay here and take care of your mother. Your grandfather and I will be fine, and we'll come home—both of us. Okay?"

Ducking her head, Willow said, "Okay, Dad. Go kick ass."

Chase handed Willow off to Glory, kissing his wife good-bye before she launched into a mostly fruitless lecture about language with their daughter. I followed Chase and Festus up to the first floor. "Tanist, huh? When did this happen?"

"Last night," Chase said. "I told the old man I didn't appreciate being sidelined all the time, and that I wanted to go back to work."

Festus flicked his tail. "I was gonna do it anyway. About time you pulled your weight around here."

"Really, Dad?" Chase said. "You *fired* me."

"Yeah, well now I've hired you. Come on. Daylight's wasting."

Chase turned to me. "If anything... "

"Don't," I said. "Do what your daughter told you to do. Go kick ass."

He grinned. "Yes, ma'am. You're the boss."

Rolling my eyes, I said, "It would be nice if more people remembered that."

After I watched them drive off, I went down to the lair to get Tori to initiate the next phase of the operation—the one that had me as scared as little Willow.

For the first time since the encounter with Dampierre, Tori would come up to the first floor and open her mind to the vampire, which would give Greer the chance to hijack the signal and communicate with her old acquaintance.

At the base of the stairs, Gemma put her hands on Tori's shoulders. "I don't like this."

"That makes two of us," Tori answered, "but Greer will be with me."

Gemma looked at the baobhan sith. "You let anything happen to my daughter, and a stake in the chest will be the least of your worries."

The Scotswoman nodded her head in acquiescence even though a sharp pointy stick wouldn't do anything but annoy her. While Gemma and Tori spoke in quiet tones, I asked Greer how she intended to keep the vampire occupied.

"I will spare you the intimate details," she replied, "but suffice it to say I will appeal to shared memories. When I give you the sign, bring Tori back into the shelter of the fairy mound. No matter what, do not allow her to leave the store."

"Understood." Then, looking to my friend, I said, "It's time."

Disentangling herself from Gemma's tight embrace, Tori started up the stairs after Greer. I took a few steps and looked back. Mom was standing with her arm around Gemma. She caught my eye and nodded. I got the silent message. *"I'll take care of her, you take care of Tori."*

Outside the door to the first floor, I pulled my friend in for a quick, almost desperate hug. "I'll be fine, Jinksy," she whispered. "Greer knows what she's doing."

I prayed Tori was right.

~

Tori reached for the door knob with a trembling hand. Greer's fingers covered hers. "You feel him already, don't you?"

Swallowing hard, Tori nodded. "He's waiting at the edge of my mind."

"Listen to me. No matter what you believe you see, Jean-Baptiste does not stand within the walls of this structure. You will face nothing but a projection of his powers. He cannot control you unless you go to him. Resist."

"That's what Myrtle told me to do, but it didn't stop him."

The baobhan sith's eyes glowed in the dim light. "No, but remember we seek only to distract and delay. If you fall under his sway, as I predict you will, forgive us all now for any means by which we may have to restrain you."

Answering with a jerky nod, Tori said, "Got it. We need to do this before I chicken out."

Greer's gaze softened. "You are not a coward. Of that I am certain."

They turned the door knob together, but Tori stepped into the store alone. Before she had taken half a dozen steps, Dampierre appeared to her, leaning casually against the newel post.

"There you are, Victoria. I knew you could not hide forever. Have you decided to accept my offer?"

Tori froze in mid-stride. Her eyes glazed over. "You want me to come to you."

"Indeed I do, Victoria. You have but to walk through that door and into the alleyway. I would escort you myself, but that tiresome Brenna Sinclair has blocked my access to the building."

When Tori made a move, Greer heaved a sigh and blocked her way. "Do you not tire of this nonsense, Jean-Baptiste? Bending weak minds to your will? I would think you would began to seek more challenging prey."

The shade of the vampire offered her a broad smile. "Greer MacVicar. Morgan told me you threw your lot in with the Witch of the Oak."

The baobhan sith sniffed. "For the time being. Jinx Hamilton amuses me, as does my work with the DGI, but I am no more wedded to a single lifestyle now than I was when we first met."

Dampierre clapped his hands. "I told Morgan you could not have gone over to the side of so-called virtue. What a delightful turn of events! Shall we dine on this human together?"

Greer circled Tori, examining her as if for the first time. "I do not find this one unattractive. Mentally weak, but comely enough on the whole."

"Morgan wishes her to be kept alive, but we both know how long a mortal being can be made to teeter on the edge of death."

"We do," Greer agreed. "We most certainly do. You recall the monks?"

The vampire threw his head back and laughed. "With their pathetic prayers pleading for salvation? That was good sport."

"As it happens, Jean-Baptiste, I fed only yesterday. My hunger comes more episodically than yours. I would prefer you and I enjoy an intimate reunion in private so that we might catch up on the centuries."

Hope and something more feral lighted Dampierre's gaze. "Would you?"

The fire of the baobhan sith rose in Greer's eyes. "I would. We can acquire this one at any time of our choosing. Let us occupy ourselves tonight with more adult pastimes."

The vampire frowned. "What is that sound?"

Greer shrugged, "I hear nothing but the frightened bird heart of this mortal."

"You lie!" Dampierre spat. "There is a plot afoot to deprive me of Andre's faithful service. I must attend to my pet, baobhan sith, but we are not done."

As he faded away, Tori cried out and reached for him. "No, master, take me with you. *Please!* Take me with you."

When Greer moved to restrain her, Tori beat at her friend with closed fists. "*No!* Turn me loose! Let me go to him! He will take me to my father. *Let me go!*"

"That I cannot do," Greer said, encircling the struggling woman with strong arms and moving toward the basement door.

Jinx appeared at the entrance. As she watched Tori fighting Greer, she couldn't stop the tears that ran down her cheeks. "Tell me we didn't do this to her for nothing. Did you buy Bertille enough time?"

"We will know before this night comes to an end," Greer said, moving across the threshold and lifting Tori in her arms before she could fall to the floor. "For now, I fear we must face a more immediate danger—Gemma's wrath."

Tori's eyes fluttered open. "Just so you know," she mumbled, "I'm totally blaming this on the two of you."

Chapter Thirty-Eight

Bertille waited at the edge of the forest. She'd turned down the offer of a ride from Jeff Hamilton knowing she'd need time to prepare herself for what she had to do.

For the hundredth time Bertille fingered the outline of the whistle in the pocket of her jeans. Brenna had assured her Andre would respond to the call even from miles away.

An unbidden memory rose in Bertille's consciousness— Andre as he'd been the first night she saw him over the rim of her champagne glass, a handsome, well-dressed man haloed in a cloud of sparkling bubbles.

He'd been the lord and master of all he surveyed that night in the gallery, exuding a faux confidence that betrayed none of the fragile ego that in the end imploded their relationship.

The foolishness of the terminal incident would haunt Bertille for the rest of her life. How much a person's future could turn on nothing more consequential than cocktail banter gone sour!

Andre had cited the wrong time period for the Impressionists. Bertille corrected him, only realizing her mistake when he downed his wine, excused himself, and stalked away.

An hour passed before Bertille realized he'd left the gathering without her. Assuming he'd cool off by morning, she called a cab, went home, and did nothing. By the third silent day, however, she called and sent text messages. Andre ignored them all.

At first, his childish behavior infuriated Bertille, but as the days passed she realized she missed him. That was when she decided to go to his apartment and apologize in person, only to find the place trashed, and Andre gone.

So many questions would never be answered. How Andre came to be cursed as the rougarou. Why he killed the owner of the magic shop who most likely cast the spell. At what point Jean-Baptiste Dampierre entered the picture.

Bertille had no choice but to end both Andre's killing spree and his cursed existence. In his current state, he amounted to nothing but a tortured plaything in the vampire's manipulative grasp. She couldn't leave the man she'd known and loved to that fate.

What would happen afterwards hinged on a risky supposition on Festus McGregor's part. When a shifter suffers an injury, the wound disappears once they change form again. The werecat counted on the same being true for the rougarou.

Lucas's agents did their job well in New Orleans, even getting their hands on Andre's medical records. He'd been born with a heart defect that, although it had caused him no problems in his adult life, could be used as a convenient cause of death since—if Festus's theory proved to be true—there would be no marks of a violent death on the body.

An hour earlier when Jeff dropped Chase and Festus off in the parking lot, Bertille had resisted the urge to step back as the two mountain lions approached her.

"Hey," Chase said in a deep, rumbling voice, "we're the good guys, remember?"

"Sorry," Bertille said, recovering her composure. "I didn't expect you to be so big."

Festus flicked his tail. "You left out handsome and impressive."

"That, too," she said, laughing in spite of the seriousness of the situation. "Where will you be while we wait for Andre?"

Sniffing the air, Chase said, "Behind you in the woods. The wind's in our favor. We'll shadow you while you ride to the waterfall."

Jeff lifted a mountain bike from the bed of his truck and wheeled it over. "Maybe you should take a practice lap around the parking lot," he suggested. "Going over the handlebars on the trail wouldn't be a good idea."

"I used the ride share bikes in New Orleans all the time," she assured him. "You said it's about 20 minutes to the waterfall, right?"

"Yes," Chase said. "The path gets enough regular use that you'll have smooth going. Stick to the middle and set a steady pace. The bike has a light if you want to use it."

With that, Jeff excused himself and drove off. Chase and Festus disappeared into the undergrowth. Even though she couldn't see them, Bertille felt the weight of their combined gaze on her back.

Unable to put off the inevitable any longer, she drew the silver whistle out of her pocket and blew into the mouthpiece, repeating the long, inaudible blasts until the brush on the far side of the parking area rustled and Andre stepped onto the pavement.

Lowering the whistle from her lips, Bertille whispered, "Oh, Andre. How did you let this happen?"

The rougarou whimpered and advanced with halting steps,

his hands pawing at the air as he drew nearer. The movement snapped Bertille out of her reverie. She climbed on the bike, turned toward the path, and pushed off.

Her heart pounding from fear and the sudden exertion, Bertille risked glancing over her shoulder. In the fading light she saw Andre loping behind keeping a distance of about 20 yards between them.

Directing her eyes forward, Bertille concentrated on the steady up and down rhythm of the pedals until she heard the waterfall in the distance. Braking to a halt at the bridge, she dismounted, leaned the bike against the railing, and threaded her way down the slope to the clearing by the water.

Andre came after her, the leather soles of his dress shoes slipping on the rocks. He rolled the last few feet, landing hard and ripping the knees of his dress pants.

Even as the rougarou the vanity that plagued him in life surfaced. He stopped to run a hand over the torn material, growling in displeasure. Chase and Festus used that distracted moment to enter the clearing.

When Andre saw the mountain lions, his guttural vocalizations became threatening. He moved to get between the big cats and Bertille. In a flash, she realized he meant to protect her.

"Stop, Andre!" she said. "They are my friends. I am in no danger."

The rougarou froze, confused in the moment, but then an intelligent light filled his eyes.

"You understand, don't you?" Bertille said. "You know what we have to do. We can't make you as you once were, and we can't leave you to be Dampierre's pawn."

At the mention of the vampire's name, Andre threw his head back and howled. With the last eerie note still echoing in the night, he dropped his hands, went down on his knees, and lowered his head.

"Damnation," Festus snarled. "I didn't see that coming. He's not going to fight us."

Keeping one eye on Andre, Chase moved beside his father, "I can't commit cold-blooded murder, Dad."

"Nobody's asking you to," Festus said, "but what the hell are we supposed to do with this guy now?"

The surface of the water rippled under the force of a cold wind. The forest sounds died as a figure of an elderly woman in a gingham dress glided through the waterfall and across the surface of the pond.

When she stepped ashore, Chase and Festus moved into deep feline bows, right paws extended toward the figure. "Mother Knasgowa," Festus said. "You honor us."

"You thought to kill a man in my presence, Chief McGregor?"

Keeping his eyes on the ground, Festus said, "We sought to end a danger to your Daughters, and the town, in a place where we knew we would be protected."

"Look at me," Knasgowa commanded. When both cats raised their heads, she said to Chase, "It is good to see you again, Son of McGregor."

"And you, my lady," he answered.

"You are a husband and father now. The recklessness that plagued your life has disappeared, and you have become a man of purpose. I am proud of you."

"Thank you, my lady."

The old woman approached Andre, who stood, watching her with wary eyes.

"Do not fear me, Andre Melancon," she said. "You suffer under the weight of terrible magic. Nothing but death can free you. Do you understand?"

The rougarou made a nervous sound, cutting his eyes toward Bertille.

"She has long since forgotten your foolishness," Knasgowa said, "and the wrongs you have committed were not of your choosing. I can help you. Will you take my hand and come with me to a place where your pain and suffering will be gone?"

With awkward hesitation, the rougarou clasped her fingers. Together they started for the water, but Bertille rushed forward. She put her hands on Andre's arms, looking into the eyes of a man that stared out at her from the face of a wolf.

"I'm sorry, Andre. I didn't mean to hurt you. I didn't mean for any of this to happen."

The rougarou's mouth opened. With great effort the creature rasped, "*My* fault. Forgive me."

Tears now coursing down her face, Bertille stroked the thick fur along his jaw. "I do, Andre. With all my heart, I do."

Struggling to articulate, the beast said, "Stop him."

"Dampierre?"

The rougarou nodded.

"We will. I promise."

When he tried to speak again, the words twisted into a strangled gasp.

"I don't understand," Bertille said. "What are you trying to tell me?"

Frustrated, Andre tapped the side of his head. "Not gone."

Sympathy flooded Bertille's face. "He'll be gone soon, Andre."

"No! *Not. Gone.*"

Knasgowa interrupted them. "There is no time. Dampierre knows he has been deceived. We must go now. The vampire will not come to this place when he no longer hears the beating of Andre's heart."

"Good-bye," Bertille whispered with a final caress. "You'll be at peace now."

With that, the rougarou walked with Knasgowa to the water's edge where his body fell away. Free of that tortured shell, the soul of Andre Melancon crossed the pond with the old woman and together they disappeared into the waterfall.

Chapter Thirty-Nine

We did our jobs well. The people of Briar Hollow bought the story, acceptance aided by the headline in the delayed edition of the *Banner* that came out on Friday—*New Orleans Man Kills Two, Stalks Bookstore Owner.*

The account was neither true nor sensationalized, but it was plausible. The *Banner* also contained Linda's obituary and the notice of her funeral on Saturday.

Scared people will adopt any explanation that puts an end to their fear. No one asked where Andre had been staying, how he'd pulled off the omni-directional howling, what he'd been doing in the woods that night, or who supposedly tipped off Sheriff Johnson to the location of the body.

"You're not serious?" I asked Johnson as I poured his coffee early Saturday morning. "Not one person noticed the holes in our story big enough to drive a truck through?"

The sheriff bit into a bear claw, chewed, and swallowed. "Not when the sheriff himself writes the report and tips an over-worked medical examiner off to a convenient heart defect.

People in this town aren't dumb, Jinx, they just don't *want* to know the truth."

Attired in his dress uniform in preparation for Linda's public service that afternoon at the Baptist Church, Johnson looked downright handsome. When I told him as much he said with a poker face, "You only think that because I'm on your side now."

When I shrugged and said, "*Welllll...* " we both laughed.

After much discussion, Beau, Mom, Linda, and I had decided on a two-part funeral—a church gathering where anyone was welcome and a private internment at dusk so the cemetery ghosts could be there in support of Beau.

Johnson volunteered to stand guard at the gate so there would be no risk of anyone catching sight of an accidental apparition. The lawman was already proving to be a resilient ally. Not one revelation we'd shared with him, including the existence of the lair and the fairy mound, so much as fazed the guy.

The day after Knasgowa took Andre's spirit into the waterfall, Tori insisted on going up to the store to, as she put it, "see what condition my condition is in."

Nothing happened. We couldn't say if that meant Dampierre's mesmerism had been broken in some way, or if the vampire had simply left Briar Hollow.

Tori promised she'd tell us if she heard so much as a whisper of his voice in her mind again. I trusted her to honor her word since I was not prepared to tell my best buddy she had to live in the basement full time.

Beau delivered the eulogy at Linda's funeral, giving a restrained, but heartfelt account of her service to the community. I admired his composure since the deceased was sitting in the front row listening to him with shining eyes.

The "usual suspects" from the lair gathered at the cemetery a few minutes before sunset. Festus shifted into human form and helped carry the casket along with Dad, Beau, Chase, and Connor.

Normally there are six pallbearers, but Brenna magically lightened the load to accommodate for the lesser number. We'd cited the book club members as honorary pallbearers at the church.

Hiram Folger walked with us to the white obelisk. "Beauregard, the others wanted me to tell you how sorry we are for your loss, and to welcome Miss Albert if she wants to stay with us."

"Thank you, Hiram," Beau said. "So far as I know, Miss Linda has not yet decided what she wishes to do."

To our surprise, the lovestruck librarian said, "Yes, Beau, I have. I can't quite explain it, but I feel like there's a force calling on me to be somewhere else. It's like if I just walked toward it, everything would change for me. Do you think that sounds right?"

The old soldier smiled. "I do, Miss LInda."

A deceased preacher among the resident spirits performed the graveside service. He'd conveniently been buried with a Bible in the pocket of his suit, and was thus able to read far more verses than I thought necessary.

While he droned on using the traditional funerary passages, my eyes roamed around the cemetery. That's when I saw him—a man in a dark suit. At first I assumed he was another of the ghosts who had chosen to watch from a respectful distance, but then his power crawled over my skin.

Greer felt the energy too, moving to stop Tori who rose from her seat and walked a few paces in the man's direction. Before the baobhan sith could reach her, we watched in horror as Tori retraced her steps—backward—before moving forward again.

The sick bastard was playing with her like a human yo-yo.

Without consulting anyone, including my horrified husband, I marched across the graveyard while Greer restrained

Tori. Stopping a few paces from Dampierre, I said, "That's enough. Let her go."

Unlike the description Tori had provided of a man out of time, the vampire now wore modern clothing and had trimmed his hair. He still sported tinted glasses, but in a discreet smokey hue.

Giving me an exaggerated bow, Dampierre said, "I have made my point, and will leave you to bury your dead, but before I go, Morgan has a message for you."

"Which is?"

"Round one goes to the Goddess of the Crows."

Then, drawing on the flair for melodrama I've discovered comes with being a vampire, Dampierre disappeared.

Back at the graveside, Tori looked pale and shaken, but assured us her mind was clear. She apologized to Linda for interrupting the service and asked the preacher to continue.

When I caught Greer's eye and nodded, the baobhan sith sat down beside Tori with Gemma on the other side holding her daughter's hand.

At the conclusion of the service, the men lowered the casket into the ground, rolled up their sleeves, picked up shovels, and began filling the grave. Beau reached under his shirt, removed the Amulet of the Phoenix, and passed the necklace to me for safekeeping.

With that, he offered Linda his arm. Before they walked away to share a private good-bye, Linda said, "Thank you, Jinx, for everything you've done. Wherever I'm going now, it pleases me to know that my physical body will rest in Briar Hollow beside Beau."

Together, she and the colonel walked to the top of the slope under the light of the rising moon. Tori came up and leaned into me. I put an arm around her as we watched the ill-fated couple share their first and only kiss before Linda moved into the night, growing fainter with each step until not a wisp of her spirit remained.

Beau stood alone on the crest of the hill staring at the spot where she vanished.

"You're going to have to take care of him, Jinksy," Tori said.

A tingle went up my spine. "You mean *we're* going to have to take care of him."

"No, honey, not us. *You.*"

We argued in the lair late into the night, but Tori wouldn't budge from her decision. Grim-faced and fighting back tears, Gemma supported her daughter's right to choose.

"I can't stay in Briar Hollow, Jinksy," Tori said. "We could fight about this for another six hours and I still wouldn't change my mind. Dampierre has the power to control me. You saw what he did at the graveyard."

Choking down tears of my own, I said, "Then go to the Valley. Be with Connor. Watch Addie for me."

"No," Tori said, with an enviable level of self-possession. "Under no circumstances will I risk endangering that child. I'm going to Drake Abbey and that's final. Seneca and Edgar will need help at the library, and I'm dying to know what secrets that place holds."

Grasping at straws, I said, "But what will I tell people when you're not in the store?"

"Tell them I've gone off on a barista tour of Europe or something. I think John Johnson has proven the people of this town will buy pretty much any story we toss out rather than deal with reality. You know, like a gang on PCP?"

That was a Buffy reference. Principle Snyder's explanation for every strange thing that happened at Sunnydale High. A gang on PCP. Tori wanted me to laugh, and I did, but the sound came out like a wet gurgle.

"Stop that," she said, hugging me hard. "I'll be one portal

hop away and it's only until we figure out how to get Count Dracula out of my head."

"But you won't be here," I hiccuped. "You've always been here."

I felt a tremor pass through her. "And I always will be, Jinx. But this has to happen and you know it. Now let me go before we both lose it and get the moms started."

"She's right, Norma Jean," Mom said looking at me with red-rimmed eyes. "Let her go."

Playing my last hole card, I appealed to Gemma. "You can't be okay with this?"

"I'm not, honey," Gemma admitted, "but I don't have to be okay with something to know it's what has to be."

How I stood there and watched Tori go around the lair saying her good-byes I'll never know. Rodney was so upset, he burrowed under my collar where his hot tears soaked the fabric of my blouse.

Darby wrapped himself around Tori and cried so hard Glory had to basically peel him free.

Dad gave Tori a gruff cuff on the arm. "You watch yourself with those big lizards," he said. "You need me, you call me. You hear, little girl?"

She answered with a rib-crushing hug. "I will, Jeff. Thank you."

From the corner of Beau's desk, Willow said, "I don't know you very well, Aunt Tori, but I like you, so please come home soon."

"I will, sweetheart," Tori assured the kitten. "I want you to be nice to Miss. Myerscough when she wakes up, okay? And make Festus be nice to her, too."

The werecat lashed his tail. "I make no promises. That Abbey of yours needs a bar. Rube and I will get on that. You know, a classy joint like The Dirty Claw."

The raccoon stood on the back of the sofa. "Damn straight we will, Doll. We can't have you hanging out with Captain Iguana all the time. Me and the boys will be there for poker night regular like."

"I'm holding you to that," Tori said.

Beau, now back in corporeal form, offered his handkerchief to Glory, who sobbed brokenly into Chase's shoulder.

"People, *come on*," Tori said. "I'm not dying."

Instead of helping, the attempted joke only made the waterworks worse.

The rest of us held back as Gemma walked to the portal with Tori. Connor carried her bags. After one last embrace, the matrix flared. My brother went through first. Tori put a foot into the opening, then turned and sought out my eyes.

All our lives we've been able to have complete conversations without saying a word. In that moment, I knew what Morgan meant when she had Dampierre tell me the first round went to the Goddess of the Crows.

The instant my best friend disappeared through that portal, I knew I had lost my greatest strength—the companion who had been with me all my life, buoyed my confidence, restored my good humor, and made me believe anything was possible.

When Lucas put his arms around me, I met my husband's eyes with determination. "That's it. First Addie and now Tori? I've had *enough*. Game on. How do we take this bitch down?"

A Word from Juliette

Thank you for reading *To Twist a Witch*. There are many things I love about being an author, but building a relationship with my readers is far and away the best.

Once a month I send out a newsletter with information on new releases, sneak peeks, and inside articles about books and series currently under development.

You can get all this and more by signing up www.juliette-harper.com.

About the Author

"It's kind of fun to do the impossible." Walt Disney said that, and the two halves of Juliette Harper believe it wholeheartedly. Together, Massachusetts-based Patricia Pauletti, and Texan Rana K. Williamson combine their writing talents as Juliette. "She" loves to create strong female characters and place them in interesting, challenging, painful, and often comical situations. Refusing to be bound by genre, Juliette's primary interest lies in telling good stories. Patti, who fell in love with writing when she won her first 8th grade poetry contest, has a background in music, with a love of art and design. Rana, a former journalist and university history instructor, is happiest with a camera in hand and a cat or two at home.

For more information . . .
www.JulietteHarper.com
admin@julietteharper.com

Made in the USA
Monee, IL
13 May 2021